T0253330

Also by Laura Taylor Namey

A Cuban Girl's Guide to
Tea and Tomorrow

A British Girl's Guide to
Hurricanes and Heartbreak

When We Were Them

WITH Love, ECHO PARK

Laura Taylor Namey

atheneum New York London Toronto Sydney New Delhi

An imprint of Simon & Schuster Children's Publishing Division
1230 Avenue of the Americas, New York, New York 10020

Simon & Schuster: Celebrating 100 Years of Publishing in 2024

For information about special discounts for bulk purchases, please contact Simon & Schuster Special Sales at 1-866-506-1949 or business@simonandschuster.com.

The Simon & Schuster Speakers Bureau can bring authors to your live event. For more information or to book an event, contact the Simon & Schuster Speakers Bureau at 1-866-248-3049 or visit our website at www.simonspeakers.com.

Interior design by Karyn Lee
The text for this book was set in Edita.
The illustrations for this book were rendered digitally.
Manufactured in the United States of America
First Edition
10 9 8 7 6 5 4 3 2 1
Library of Congress Cataloging-in-Publication Data
Names: Namey, Laura Taylor, author.
Title: With love, Echo Park / Laura Taylor Namey.
Description: First edition. | New York : Atheneum Books for Young Readers, [2024] | Audience: Ages 12 and up. | Audience: Grades 7–9. | Summary: Cuban American teenagers Clary, seventeen, and Emilio, eighteen, grew up together in the Echo Park community of Los Angeles clashing over their visions for the future of the neighborhood, but they find there is something stronger than local history tying them together.
Identifiers: LCCN 2023043258 (print) | LCCN 2023043259 (ebook) | ISBN 9781665915366 (hardcover) | ISBN 9781665915380 (ebook)
Subjects: LCSH: Teenage girls—California—Los Angeles—Juvenile fiction. | Cuban American families—California—Los Angeles—Juvenile fiction. | Cuban Americans—California—Los Angeles—Juvenile fiction. | Echo Park (Los Angeles, Calif.)—Juvenile fiction. | LCGFT: Romance fiction.
Classification: LCC PZ7.1.N3555 Wi 2024 (print) | LCC PZ7.1.N3555 (ebook) | DDC 813.6—dc23/eng/20230920
LC record available at https://lccn.loc.gov/2023043258
LC ebook record available at https://lccn.loc.gov/2023043259

For Ohilda Victoria, beloved tía

Dos patrias tengo yo: Cuba y la noche.

I have two homelands: Cuba and the night.

—José Martí, "Dos Patrias"

One

*Clary (**Salvia sclarea**): The clary or clary sage is a flowering plant native to the northern Mediterranean Basin, along with some areas in North Africa and Central Asia. The plant has a long history as a medicinal herb and is now grown all over the world for its essential oil.*

When I tell people I work with dying things, I'm only joking. For a brief stretch of beautiful, though, picked flowers appear deceptively alive. Days for most, weeks for some. I get them during this small pocket. I trim ends and strip thorns, arranging them into the kind of art that only lasts in photos. Or if you have a family like mine—maybe a Cuban abuela like Mamita—you keep them mummified, their afterlives shriveled brown. Throw away your quinceañera bouquet or your homecoming boutonniere before your abuelita or mami enshrines it? Why would you ever want to invite the wrath of an elder Latina?

Day-old tulips are the worst. If not properly prepped, their bulbous heads bend lower and lower until they're kissing tabletops and dropping bits of black pollen. This afternoon, the arrangement on my counter features no tulips. I call this one Sunset Echo, both for the area of central Los Angeles where we live and work, and for the colors: an upward spray of roses imitating a Malibu sky before dusk. As a base, I lined the rim of a canister with a circle of white hydrangeas and a layer of apple-green cymbidium orchids and Hypericum berries.

"Oye, paging Clary Delgado, thief of my favorite denim shirt!" Lourdes calls from the rear loading bay.

My friend appears as I place a coral rose in one of the most expensive arrangements available at La Rosa Blanca, my family's florist shop. "For the millionth time, it wasn't me." I add one last sprig of berries.

"Wow, fancy." Lourdes updates her delivery tablet. "Wait, that's for Jody Ramirez on Russell? I was just there last week. Her dude's totally cheating."

"Lulú!" Her nickname darts off my tongue. *I said what I said* is written plainly across her face. "Yeah, well, this is his third order this month. The word *sorry*'s been on every card."

"Mm-hmm," she says. "And he picked Sunset E? Spendy. He's busted."

Also waiting for lucky recipients are four smaller arrangements. Lourdes carts those out while I pack the container for the short drive from Echo Park to Los Feliz.

When our junior year at Silver Lake Charter School ended three weeks ago, Lourdes joined our delivery team for some summer cash. Four days a week, she drives one of the La Rosa Blanca vans around

Greater LA, transporting standing orders for hotels and restaurants and "I'm sorry for whatever reason this time" arrangements.

I tuck the customer's message into the box. There's something about these little flat cards I've always loved—that it doesn't take an overblown word dump to make a big impact. Our most popular dedication is a simple *Thinking of you*. Perfect.

My friend returns, her lashes fluttering with the promise of a little neighborhood chisme. I keep floral dedications confidential, but this is Lourdes Colón, my trusted ally since fifth grade. "Okay, okay. Today it's 'Sorry, babe. Sunnier days ahead,'" I quote from memory.

Lourdes snorts dramatically. At five-four, she stands two inches shorter than me, but her hair is another something. Waist-long and asphalt black, it acts like our personal life gauge. Feeling flushed, or is it only the weather? Consult Lulú's hair, which swells in high humidity. In SoCal's nonexistent fall season, her locks flat-iron themselves and track the Santa Ana wind as well as any scientific instrument. Sometimes, she'll gather the whole mass forward and hide behind it like a curtain. *Do not disturb*. I respect the hair.

"Me voy," Lourdes says, and grabs the box. "Oh, your abuelo just finished the frame for Señor Montes's funeral cross." Her face dims as she backs away. "It's in the back when you're ready."

My next breath hitches. *Señor Montes*. It's been two weeks since we learned our beloved eighty-nine-year-old community leader checked into the hospital (for what, we still don't know) and never came home. Salvador Montes held me as a baby and watched over so many of us local kids. A fierce Echo Park advocate, he was never too far from his friends, a cafecito, and a Cuban domino set.

I find the huge cross-shaped wreath frame Abu made—ready for my floral design—and can't help the fall into pure memory. At the forefront, there's the jovial Señor Montes stopping by the shop on his afternoon walk after I arrived from school. Every time, I'd take a single scrap bloom and pin it to his lapel. Now, with his memorial two days away, I have to form a hundred flowers into something worthy enough for goodbye. And for the first time since I began working here as a kid, I don't know how to start.

Hissing and crackling sounds from the two-way radio; I leave the cross and my design sketchbook for now.

"Rose Two here," Lourdes announces over the airways. "We have a situation. I repeat, a situation. Over."

Lulú finds too much amusement in the delivery van communication system. She's the one who named the three La Rosa Blanca vehicles in order of size. Rose Two is our midsize cargo van. I grab the radio. "What situation?"

"You didn't say 'over.'"

Way too much amusement. "Just tell me." *Ugh, Lourdes.* "Over."

"I'm stuck. There's a big truck blocking the driveway and tons of bikes in the way. Over."

The culprit's no great mystery. Our historic storefront faces bustling Sunset Boulevard, but our corner property also has a fenced rear lot where we construct floral installations and park the vans. The gated driveway is directly across the street from the side wall of Avalos Bicycle Works. Their shop faces Sunset, too, but they don't have any loading space.

"On it," I announce.

Outside, I hang a right and march around the side street we share with the bike shop. Lourdes waves from the window of Rose Two. Sure enough, the truck is using our property to unload, but no one's around. The driver locked a group of road bikes to our gate with one long tether right in front of the exit. Resourceful.

I wedge the radio into my jeans pocket and send a text to Emilio.

Me: I'm assuming that the truck and bikes outside have something to do with you guys?

Emilio: Racing team dropping them off for maintenance

Me: And blocking our driveway

Emilio: Is this the flower shop owner's version of get off my lawn?

I glare at the phone, wishing that instead of a talking bubble, it was Emilio Avalos's tanned, angular face. I need him to see my glare.

Since we were kids with neighboring everything, there's been an ongoing bout of strategic play between us, like a living version of the domino game Señor Montes played daily. It varies, but just as in dominoes, winning between Emilio and me usually amounts to who can outsmart the other. Or out-annoy. After years of practice, we've gotten good at doling out comeback quips like those little ivory tiles with black dots. We know when to play them.

Get off my lawn? Cute. Like Abu has ever yelled that from our kitchen window.

Me: We can provide you with some excellent landscape maintenance references. Meanwhile, Lourdes has DELIVERIES

Emilio: My lawn is perfectly trimmed, thank you

Emilio: Yeah, yeah we're coming

Moments later, Emilio strides out of Avalos Bicycle Works, followed by his dad and a couple workers from their repair department. The driver jogs up to the cab and proceeds to move forward, and the guys unlock the chained-up bikes.

Emilio's expecting annoyance, so I unclench my jaw and try to appear extra calm. Underneath, there's a brisk pull of adrenaline. "Feel free to move the truck back after Lourdes leaves," I offer with great diplomacy.

"Cool. But why didn't she just call me or Papi?" Emilio asks. "Lourdes needs you out here playing traffic guard, Thorn?"

He's called me this for years, maintaining that a girl who spends half her day stripping roses of their one painful flaw, and the other half aggravating him, deserves such a moniker. If I'm being honest, I've never minded the Thorn nickname. But I'll never let him know that.

Dropping my own nickname for Emilio now would seem too predictable. "You'd rather deal with a ragey Puerto Rican than me?"

Rage might be stretching things. One glance pegs Lulú as way too entertained watching my exchange with Emilio, chin perched on folded arms over her rolled-down window.

"It's funny you think you're the safer bet." Emilio grins infuriatingly.

The horn beeps twice; with her path finally cleared, Lourdes rolls away with a cheerful wave.

"A-ny-way," Emilio says. "The driver came in asking for help unloading, but he saw this new mountain bike, and Papi and I got carried away with the specs for a minute. Sweet ride."

"If you say so."

His eyes twitch with perplexity—the kind where he has to rewind what I've said to see whether or not he should be offended. Half a second later, he pivots toward Sunset Boulevard. "Wait, Varadero Travel closed?"

I nod, wincing at the darkened windows and boarded entrance. "As of today." Another founding piece of Cuban Echo Park is gone, just like that.

Emilio crosses his arms loosely; they're carrying twice as many grease stains as his gray T-shirt. "Hopefully she'll find some cheaper digs off Sunset."

"Why should she have to, though? Ana's parents started that agency. Right there."

"It's sad, but what can we do? Times change. What if we're supposed to let the neighborhood move the way it moves?"

Move? How fitting. But this issue is about more than Emilio's habit of sitting near doorways and hovering under exit signs. "Our businesses started at the same time as Varadero. You're okay with more Cubans losing a big part of who we are?" I press. "Do you think Señor Montes would've been down with that take after he devoted his life to Echo Park?"

Emilio lets out a thick exhale. "Listen, you know I loved that guy. And our history is a great thing." He motions to the fence where the bikes were chained. "But our past isn't made of links that lock for good. I don't understand why we have to be so massively tethered to it."

My mouth drops. "Tethered? Try grounded to everything we came from." I motion across the street to the former travel agency. Its side wall mural with two macaws flanking a slice of Cuba's Varadero Beach adds big Latino vibes to that corner. But now . . . "I can't believe the building sold to Hole Punch Donuts."

Emilio studies the pavement. Twists his jaw.

"What? What do you know?"

"That they make ridiculously good donuts."

Nice try, Avalos. I cough, sharpening my stare.

"Okay, okay," he says. "I knew Hole Punch was gonna open somewhere on Sunset. About a year ago, they posted for people to suggest new locations, and I said that Echo Park needed a shop. Then there were a couple DMs. The CEO saw that my family owns a business around here, and he reached out."

"Oh my God, this is your doing?" I jab a finger, narrowly missing his chest.

"Seriously?" Emilio pantomimes devil horns on his head. "You think I got up one day jonesing for a donut and thought, 'Hey, what sweet, respected Cuban and their business can I personally boot off Sunset today?'"

I square my stance. "I didn't say that. I said you had a part in the sale."

"Not like you mean! I made a general suggestion. How could I possibly know they'd buy Ana's whole building? All I wanted was a double cream glazed."

"But you just said they—" Oh, he totally *said*, but my head is now a trash bin of confusion and runaround. "All *I'm* saying is you seem to care more about your sugar fix and something shiny going in than the cost. Or Ana. Or Echo Park history and . . ." I rattle my head back and forth.

"*And* we're back to the start," he says. "Surprise, surprise."

"Hey, pequeño, phone call!" Dominic waves from the bike shop entrance. At six-one, there's nothing pint-size about Emilio. But Dominic Trujillo's rank as Emilio's bestie and repair department whiz lets him get away with tons.

"So, that's me," Emilio says.

"Yup."

But he doesn't turn. We're just standing here.

A few seconds pass before he powers back on with a twitch and struts away. The atmosphere feels lighter with him gone—even though this is hardly the first time I've argued with Emilio or challenged him about giving up on our shared heritage and our place here. Today, the threat is too close—only a few strides across Sunset. And coming right off Señor Montes's death, it feels too personal.

Air leaks from my mouth; I haven't been outside the shop for hours because of two bridal consultations and a busy delivery day. Bypassing the front door, I rest my eyes along Sunset, letting my blood cool.

With a bird as your Echo Park tour guide, you'd see Dodger Stadium looking east. Due west, Sunset Boulevard forks, leading toward Santa Monica and the beach in one direction, or on to Hollywood Boulevard in the other. The small notch on Sunset where La Rosa Blanca stands holds unique history within its two square miles. As I so pointedly reminded Emilio, my family was a part of that history. Same for the Avaloses and their bike shop.

Lately, though, Sunset Boulevard looks less cohesive than ever.

There's the odd indie store. A Starbucks across the street from an old special-occasion dress shop. Our beloved muraled walls host trash at their feet. Shiny, well-kept places gleam next to forgotten ruins.

Rusted iron bars cage in too many windows from a time, well after my bisabuelos and abuelos arrived from Cuba, when crime and rising rents forced so many out. A few have stayed. Pride that my family and our business have remained branches through my chest. If Echo Park still has one thing not rusted and boarded up, it's legacy. Isn't that worth more than big-business donuts?

"¡Clarita, ven!"

Abu's voice carries through brick and glass. When I return to La Rosa Blanca, I find him in the showroom, where Vivaldi pours from the speakers and we serve bubbly drinks to clients. *It makes it more bougie, no?* Mamita remarked once. My abuelo rarely sits in this room. Now he perches on the edge of the settee as if he doesn't completely trust the workings of the plush jade velvet. It's mid-June, so his tan is in stage one.

"What's up?" I ask, dropping into the space beside him.

He motions toward the picture windows flanking our front and side walls. "I should be asking you the same thing."

My next breath sticks. Abu is a living floral message card. Pages of commentary and concern dropped into a single line. Apparently, he witnessed most of what went down between Emilio and me.

"Everything hit me at once," I admit, making a detour around anything Avalos. "I got your cross frame, and the funeral became super real. And no design I've come up with seems good enough for el señor."

"But you will figure it out. You have the talent and creativity. And remember, when the estate manager sent the order, Salvador specifically left a note that he wanted *you* to make his cross." My abuelo pats my knee. "Use what you know and loved about him, and what you love about Echo Park, too. Because he sure loved this place."

My eyes glaze with moisture. "So much, which is part of the problem. Just now, I went outside and saw that Ana moved out for good."

"Claro." Abu makes it more breath than word.

"After everything Señor Montes did for Echo Park, he couldn't save Varadero." He'd tried, though. Organizing fundraisers and contacting local media outlets. But it wasn't enough. "Those boards and nails are all wrong." Along with Hole Punch Donuts and Emilio's questionable involvement in their Sunset takeover.

Abu hinges forward, resting chapped elbows on his thighs. His short-sleeved button-down shows off the forearm rose tattoo Mamita side-eyed for months when I was nine. "Between internet travel sites and her new lease terms, Ana couldn't make it work anymore."

A moment of fear grips my chest. "What about our place? Are we doing okay?"

"It's not your job to worry—"

"It *is* my job." I feel my cheeks flush with heat. "La Rosa Blanca will be mine one day, and now you're saying that—"

"No, nena." Abu cups my shoulder. "I am not saying *that* yet. We are okay for today."

Relief comes, but only by half. "But you're not sure about tomorrow."

"We're getting by," he stresses. "All you need to worry about is enjoying your beautiful work here and your education."

Something coloring Abu's tone and worming through his body language makes me fear he's leaving out key details. Either way, he's wrong. We might be okay this second—but the future belongs to Papi and me, so I need to keep it safe. And what Abu doesn't want to say, but what I know simply by being a part of this community, is that it's not enough to rely on your past alone. To keep it alive, you have to be more creative than what's new. A step ahead, an inch smarter.

But with me, there's even more. Bigger than keeping on the lights and placing bouquets into hands. My past makes me long to do more than simply live—I want to thrive. My birth mother abandoned me and my dad ten days after I was born. All she left me was my name. I want it to mean something. It's important for me to leave this world with something that lasts. *Clary Delgado was here, and it mattered.*

I just don't know what that something looks like yet, which is annoying for someone who generally likes to know things.

On this summer day, staring out the window at Sunset Boulevard, I know one thing for sure. I promise La Rosa Blanca, and my family, and myself that our entrance will never be boarded up against our wishes. Delgados will decide when it's time for our white rose to die.

Two

There's a flicker of movement across the aisle. It's him. Emilio is actually on time for Señor Montes's memorial. I've always believed he's the sort of guy who'd roll in late for his *own* funeral. But king of wonders, Emilio is fifteen minutes early.

Per el Señor Montes's request, Saint Athanasius Episcopal is a color wheel of cheery, summer-weight fabrics. I pull aimlessly at a loose thread from my turquoise minidress as another disturbance arises from the area where Emilio has just settled. Most everyone's staring in that direction now. I note his royal blue polo and . . . *chinos*? Is he trying to tilt planets? His usually unkempt hair, the color of Malibu sand, rolls back into a neat ponytail nub.

This time, though, Emilio is not the biggest calamity. It's his abuela Ynez, who has risen, strutting toward the altar.

"Ay." The word curls around Mamita's breath. "What is she up to?"

Señora Avalos makes a grand show of surveying the memorial setup. The deceased's remains fill a brass urn on the altar. Blessedly, she leaves that alone. But she makes needless adjustments to the oversized photograph of Salvador Ángel Montes—silver-haired and Santa Claus–cheeked, his linen suit glowing white from the frame.

After a satisfied nod, she retreats and smiles gracefully at our side of the church.

That does it. I fear what's coming. "Mamita," I warn.

"Elena." Abu drops a steadying hand over his wife's arm.

But it's no use. Mamita's already beelining toward the altar in her pink shift dress. Sighs echo. The only missing commentary is my papi's *Ay, Mami, por Dios.* Only because he's running late after dealing with a mishap at another floral job.

Meanwhile, I'm trapped under the cloud of secondhand embarrassment wafting across Saint Athanasius. Mamita approaches the mass of floral arrangements my family crafted, straightening containers, plumping lilies. Emilio's abuela is seething behind a frosted smile.

"Was that really necessary?" I ask when Mamita returns.

Her face reaches Level *Wounded.* "It is my job to see to these things."

Right, her job. Which is half the problem. Mamita and Ynez have cochaired the Saint A's social committee for fifteen years. They've mixed gallons of punch, stepped in as wedding or quinceañera hostesses, and overseen the details for every funeral since I was little.

Except this one.

Señor Montes curiously denied these two grandmothers the planning (read: bragging) rights of organizing his memorial. Not that they wouldn't have clashed. Even the Echo Park grass is aware of the years-old rivalry between these two neighborhood mainstays, who'd be the first to tell you that they certainly don't hate each other. No, Mami Elena and Mami Ynez—so addressed with venerable respect by locals—are simply longtime competitors with differing views on style and aesthetic.

There's another rustle. Mami Ynez is up again. This time she straightens the stacked music books near the organ.

"Anyone can see why Ynez is doing this. We got to do the memorial flowers and she wasn't allowed to . . ." Mamita trails off with an absent gesture.

"To what? Choose napkins, or order fancy cupcakes so that *she* could look good and important in the community?" I ask.

Mamita makes a Cuban noise of irritation and leans in. "Promise me, Clarita. If Dios calls me home before Ynez, do not let her plan my memorial."

I thrust both my hands up. Apparently, their pseudofeud began long ago over one bridal shower where Mamita and Ynez both broke protocol and secretly did their own thing. Decorations and party-ware showed up in two distinct themes. The bride was miffed, and the abuelas blamed each other. Ever since, they reluctantly consult, but rarely agree.

My phone vibrates.

Emilio: Papi and I are taking bets on how long Mami Elena will last before she gets up again and starts polishing the organ keys

I do not turn.

Me: I wouldn't wager any fancy road bikes if I were you

Emilio: I know when something's worth losing my shirt over

Sometimes he makes it too easy.

Me: TMI

Emilio: Wow, Thorn. Gutter dragging in the house of God?

Now I turn. And so has he. We volley a brief, appraising look between us.

Me: Speaking of thorns, I left a couple in the arrangements just for you

Emilio: Figures. You made the cross, right? Looks like your work

I flinch. Sometimes he'll do this. Twist a compliment just to knock me off our teeter-totter for a bit.

Still, not even Emilio can muddy the view of the tall floral cross standing next to the altar. Yesterday, I ripped up three designs before the idea came—from el señor himself—in what felt like his final piece of advice. It came from my own history too. I used a domino set.

The game of dominoes is more than a Cuban hobby; it's practically a religion. The fichas—tiles—carry symbols within their black dots. The prized double-nine tile is nicknamed la caja de muertos. The coffin. A bittersweet image for a life gone to rest. The two tile—my favorite—is known as la mariposa. The butterfly. Abu used to jiggle the double-two ficha like a butterfly and land it on my shoulder. There are more nicknames in this cherished pastime among friends. And once I started, it was easy to translate this language into flowers.

For the final product, I made a patchwork of white roses and mini pom-pom mums for the base layer. And in tribute to la caja de muertos, I strung a double helix swag of nine pink star lilies and nine orange tiger lilies from top to bottom. At the center, I placed twin miniature coral calla lilies tied to look like butterfly wings. Las mariposas.

Mamita, Abu, and Papi did their own beautiful work. The entire church front is a floral tribute to the bright shades of Señor Montes's birthplace. Opposite the cross stands a Cuban flag made from white gerbera daisies, blue mums, and tomato-red roses.

Pastor Duncan breezes in before I can send any more texts. The organist follows and begins a peaceful underscoring melody.

"Welcome, dear friends," Pastor Duncan starts. "We gather here today to celebrate the life of one of our most beloved members—"

Rustling to my right takes the form of my dad sneaking into the seat Abu saved for him. Papi's face droops in apology. I see him and Abu every day, but they look eerily alike today, both in navy trousers and pale blue dress shirts. Abu likes to smooth his graying dark hair with heaps of product. Papi's is looser, and he wears a bit of scruff like Emilio.

I relax into my seat as Pastor Duncan gestures at the large photo. "Salvador Montes took part in the unique history of our neighborhood, emigrating from Cuba in 1962 along with so many."

Along with Abu and Mamita as children, with both sets of my bisabuelos. Fidel Castro had assumed power, and Cubans were suffering under oppression and political unrest.

"Immigrants like Salvador were given plane tickets out of Miami by our government; there was work and opportunity here. If you were him, you walked along Sunset in the sixties and seventies to a throng of Cuban entrepreneurship and industry. Bodegas and shops and cafés.

"Regretfully, our barrio is not the same as it was forty years ago. Crime, gentrification, and skyrocketing rents have forced many

Cuban settlers and their storefronts away. Many, but not all," he says, and looks at Abu. "Salvador had one mission—to protect and remember what was his and theirs, the Cuban history and spirit of a bygone era."

At his cue, the organist stops midsong, causing a stir across the congregation. Pastor Duncan steps away from the pulpit. "If you knew Salvador personally, my next words in this service will be of no surprise. There will be no service at all."

I sit inside a sea of gasps.

The pastor says, "Instead of a funeral, he wanted a fiesta, and one is being set up in the park right now. His wish is that you do not sit inside and mourn, but rather eat, laugh, and dance." He holds his arms out toward the double doors. "In his words, 'Go, and know that I celebrate with you.'"

"Can you believe all this? Balloon arches? A petting zoo?" Papi says, sidling up next to me. We're standing in the stretch of the Echo Park recreation area directly across the street from Saint A's, in what might be a living demo of the term *total wonder*. Part of Echo Park Lake is a nature preserve and home to Canada geese, mallard ducks, and even a few turtles. But today, plenty of non-native creatures are here. Just ahead, a farm is setting up a corral with bunnies, goats, and baby chicks. If Lourdes hadn't already committed to a college tour weekend at Davis, she'd be first in line at the face-painting booth.

I throw on a pair of shades. "It's so like him to order all those church flowers just to punk us all."

Papi snorts. "That Salvador. At least everyone got to enjoy them for a bit, and it boosted our month." He darts his gaze upward; when it falls, his face wrinkles thoughtfully, making him appear older than thirty-eight. "But I like his style—always did. 'La Vida Es Un Carnaval,' for real."

The legendary Celia Cruz anthem pops into my head. Maybe not all of life itself, but today is a carnival. Echo Park looks like a miniature version of our annual spring Cuban Festival. Dozens of rental tables and chairs cover the lawn bordering the lake, and a platform is already set with instruments and AV gear. Delivery trucks from Porto's—one of the best Cuban bakeries in the country—line the street. Servers unload trays to a large formation of banquet tables.

"But how did he pay for all this?" I ask. Señor Montes always wore the same few outfits, lived in a tiny studio, and hadn't owned a car for more than twenty years.

"You know, I always thought he was too predictable," Papi says. "Same routine, same getup since *I* was a kid. Apparently, he'd been stashing some coin." He tilts his head upward. "Óyeme, Salvador, you got any more secrets?"

My stomach rumbles, competing with the nasally squawk of birds. "Come on. They opened the food line."

Papi follows, but we split up at the buffet. One side is overflowing with Cuban appetizers. Papas rellenas, ham croquetas, and pastelitos de carne steam from tureens. I'm all about the other side, though, with trays offering three varieties of Cuban sandwiches.

And so is Emilio. I step in line behind him without saying anything. Greetings are reserved for friends; we rarely bother, so why start now? Plus, he's on a call.

"No clue," he says into the phone. "Wait." He flags my attention and pulls the device away. "Dominic's in Los Feliz on a boba tea run. You been to either Boba Freeze or Feliz Tea?"

"Aren't you Echo Park's resident foodie?" His food obsession goes miles further than designer donuts. Last year I found out Emilio has a bucket-list goal of consuming the official food from every state. There's even a map with pictures.

"Foodie or not," he says, "I can't stand boba."

"Your loss. And I like Boba Freeze," I tell him.

An actual demon crosses Emilio's face, and I know exactly what's coming when he raises the phone and tells his buddy, "Do the Feliz Tea place, bro."

Hilarity. He pulls this sort of move when trying to equalize our standing. I wasn't aware he was feeling bested.

As we reach the table, he pockets his cell and hands me a paper plate.

"Thanks." I'm after a medianoche—griddled egg bread filled with pork, ham, pickles, and Swiss cheese. Twelve times out of ten, Emilio will pick a Milanese pork cutlet sandwich instead, and they're here. "Still can't believe all this," I say, shifting for him to grab a Milanese (as predicted) as I take the tiny plastic container of whipped garlic dipping sauce he's simultaneously nudged my way. He hates it, but it's my favorite.

"Yeah, Montes has officially raised the bar on funerals—if there's a bar, because that's messed up." Emilio steps away from the tray of mariquitas—these particular fried plantain chips are of the gods—so I can swipe a handful, while he grabs the adjacent chili sauce that he'd drink if possible. "Either way, he was a class act."

"Mamita and your abuela are forever going to wonder why el señor didn't ask them to help with all this." Our hands cross over plastic cutlery like dueling swords. He shifts just as I reach for a wad of napkins. "Damn, talk about zero non-spill trust in yourself," Emilio says. "That's *not* why I hoard napkins." I am not a slob. But I spare him the real reason because there's no point. Meanwhile, the crowd has quadrupled. We tote our plates to a less populated zone by the bird sanctuary at the north end of the lake, eating in a rare moment of companionable silence.

"Pretty sure I know why Montes left out our abuelas," he says before his next bite.

Emilio recognizes Mamita as my mother—the only one I've ever known. The one who picked me up at ten days old and barely set me down. Yet, since she's the schoolmate rival of his abuelita Ynez, sometimes the notion of abuela is just easier.

"Let's hear it, then."

"So this . . ." His free hand flails. "This quién carajo sabe situation between those two." He rips off another hunk of sandwich; smashed avocado plops onto his plate, leaving a stain on his wrist.

I hand over two of my prized napkins, with not a little satisfaction. "I'm aware."

"No, I mean—look, I'm *trying* to say that Montes always pushed to get them to dial down the drama and talk it out."

"Mamita would rather jump off a moving train."

"Same with my abuelita."

On that truth, I savor one last bite. "So instead of Montes simply wanting to give them the weekend off, leaving them out of his non-funeral party was more of a chancla smack for their stubbornness?"

"Hmm. A from-the-grave chancletazo. Just as painful," Emilio says over a laugh. Like he knows from experience. "The power of a five-dollar rubber sandal."

With that, I'm struck by a memory I've never shared. "You're lucky Señor Montes kept your little second grade Sunday school escape a secret. If *I* had told on you all those years ago," I start, pointing over to the concrete steps leading up to Saint Athanasius, "you would've encountered a chancla or two. I cannot believe you gave him the excuse that the classroom door was open."

His face quirks, half with annoyance, half with something that could be admiration. But Emilio clearly remembers the day when he ditched our class somewhere between "Our Father, who art in Heaven" and pretzels. Señor Montes happened to find him on the landing, grooving to some street performers below. And *I* had a first-hand view coming back from the bathroom.

"The door *was* open," he says. "But now you're graciously reminding me that your silence literally saved my ass?"

"Is that what it sounds like to you?" I crunch a couple of plantain chips. It typically irks him when I answer a question with another question.

But Emilio doesn't appear irked just now, eating a good sandwich, the midday sunlight ringing his head with an undeserved halo. "Sounds like you were storing that secret for leverage. Thing is, I'm an adult now, so your time of using it for some nefarious purpose has passed."

"Sometimes knowing is enough, Wheels."

He tries to grimace but ends up trapping an unwanted chuckle in his chest. Whether my nickname for him annoys, he's never said; plus, he started it by calling me Thorn first. His move, my counter-move. I'm the sharp-edged part of his day, and he's a force rigged for motion.

Emilio owns three bikes and rarely drives. While I grew up staying in place—faithfully at my family's side learning floral artistry—Emilio rode free. Away from his house. Away from school and work, taunting boundaries. Since he was little, there's not an inch of Echo Park where he hasn't left tire rubber.

He hikes our trash into the bin with a three-point toss. "Sue me for taking a few liberties with *wheels*. Or feet," he says, and points to my sandals. "Better than standing in one spot so long you could grow bark and sprout leaves."

A match strikes inside my belly. Is this what he really thinks of me? That I'm stagnant and going nowhere? I open my mouth, trusting something brilliant will fall out, but live music erupts across the park. Emilio's already turned toward the makeshift stage, and the moment vanishes.

Puro Sabor has stepped up for a concert. They're local, with a signature sound blending indie funk and Afro-Cuban jazz. All the band members are prime, but they blur into the background when Ivonne Dominguez steps up. The talented front person was more than Señor Montes's favorite musician; he rented her tiny backyard casita for years.

This crowd cheers as the Afro-Cubana wraps around her stand-up double bass. Tall and brown-skinned, her pouf of sepia hair rises from a headscarf. She wears an ivory sleeveless dress, highlighting the play of her limbs and fingers along the strings.

I search for Papi. He's with high school friends, but his eyes are full of Ivonne. It's not the first time. A couple years back I started to notice the way my father would fragment himself into a string of ums and aahs around her. The one time I mentioned it, he said I was totally "off base." I've stopped bringing her up, but it doesn't mean I've stopped noticing. Now, even the birds notice.

Ivonne amps up the bassline and raps deftly into the mic as the song builds. Then she sings. The music is so vibrant and powerful, I've almost forgotten Emilio's still next to me. Instead of shuffling off to his next *whatever*, he's present, lost inside the beat. We manage to occupy the same space of Echo Park without incident because of one reason: we're not talking.

Sometime later, I lose Emilio on a band break. Easily. The neighborhood has caught on: free food and games are open to all. But there's no line in front of the drink coolers.

"Clary!"

I turn, popping the top of a soda, and find Miranda, newest member of the Saint A's social committee. "Oh hey! Have you seen my dad or grandparents?"

"Not since the service." The petite redhead steps closer. "Can you believe this crowd? Anyway, a few minutes ago a woman was asking about you."

I take a quick sip. "Asking about me, how?"

"This is where it gets strange. She asked me to point you out, and

I told her you were wearing a turquoise dress. But then she used the words . . . las fichas?"

My knees go entirely slack.

Miranda's brows curve in. "Right. And I was supposed to say some-one unexpected was looking for you, and I should include the 'las fichas' bit, and you would get it."

More than just the Spanish word for domino tiles, *las fichas* was the neighborhood safe word Señor Montes came up with years ago. Echo Park immigrants knew this word. So did the reliable commu-nity members who maintained a network of caring adults watching out for local kids. If an adult approached a child and used the code, it meant you could trust them.

"You okay?"

"Sorry. The woman. What did she look like?" I ask, caught under a wave of apprehension. A week-old tulip wilting under too many unknowns.

Miranda cocks her head. "Hmm, wavy blond hair. Perfect tan—" Her gaze shifts over my shoulder. "Oh, there she is."

I consider not turning and walking straight out of the park, but I won't. Even though I don't want to know who's behind me, I *have* to know.

"Clary?"

It's a voice I've never heard. My feet are faster than my head when I pivot. Wavy blond hair. The notable tan, too. And the first thing I take in all the way, exhaling it across the globe, is this woman is too young to be Vanessa Holt. This person, wearing a stack of gold bangles and a paisley slip dress, isn't the birth mother who abandoned me seventeen years ago. But why does she look like she jumped right out of my dad's old photo album?

The stranger wobbles her mouth into a smile. She stops a respectable distance away, hands pressed together like a praying goddess. "I'm sorry. For all this. I didn't know how, and I think I did it all wrong."

"Who are you?"

"I'm Jada. I'm your sister."

Three

*W*hen I was young, my house felt like a massive space despite the actual square footage, boundless in the magic only children believe in. Santa Claus and tooth fairies, monsters under beds. The carpet under my toes rolled across state lines, and the roof hung a thousand miles high.

As I grew, my home stayed the same, but I began to feel the press of the walls and the narrowness of the hallway. Still, I've never wanted a huge house. I want ours—tan with a poppy-red door, and no good flowers out front even though blooms pay all the bills here.

For seventeen years, I've been the daughter and granddaughter who sleeps in the cozy third bedroom. An only child, a teen florist who does all right in school. I've got one best friend and a handful of good ones. Top it off with a miniature schnauzer named Rocco, and one aunt—Papi's older sister, Roxanne, who lives in Brooklyn with her girlfriend.

Now barely two hours after the memorial party, I learn that a totally different life has been running parallel to the only one I've ever known. And the blonde sitting in Mamita's living room club chair is my twenty-two-year-old half sister.

"All these years," Abu says, "you did not know Clary existed?"

Jada's barely explained anything so far, but any forthcoming details don't matter because she cannot stay. I decided that on the way home from the park. Rocco (gullible traitor) curls into a letter C around Jada's feet, one paw slung over her gold sandal, which will soon be an issue. Because Jada will have to leave so my world can tilt back the way it was.

She faces me. "Our mother and—"

"You mean Vanessa," I clarify. "*Your* mother." Because the only person I know as mother is the dark-haired woman on the couch who always has a puzzle going and endearingly defies the stereotype that all Cubans are fabulous cooks.

"Right," Jada says, abashed. "Vanessa got pregnant with me at sixteen. Her mom was dead, and her dad got really pissed." She pauses to see how that lands—ten points to her for not using the word *grandfather*. "He threw Vanessa out, and she became emancipated and moved in with my father. He was older. Had his own place in Atlanta."

Papi's head shakes in disbelief, and in the kind of numbing shock that says all these details are new to him. So far, he's been the quietest since we left the park. But he's likely studied every inch of Jada by now, this half mirage of the girl who broke his heart and abandoned him and their newborn daughter.

"So, yeah, I didn't know about any of you until recently. See, Vanessa left for California three months after I was born. Stuff was horrible between her and my father. He gave her some money and a one-way ticket out of Atlanta, motherhood, responsibility—everything. And she took it. He married a year later." Jada's eyes compress, darkening. "When I was three, he started drinking. Using. He turned into a monster—the definition of bad energy. Never cared to change until it was too late. He died last year."

Sympathy. That's what sneaks in unexpectedly. Jada can explain the rest, and then she can go back to wherever she came from. But I have feelings around this dad-shaped vacancy for her right now. I've grown up with the best father anyone could ask for. Never perfect, just mine.

"Where are you living now, Jada?" Mamita asks, her accent bumping slightly over the name. *Jeh-tha.*

"I guess you could say I live everywhere and nowhere. I'm a modern nomad," she says, fiddling with the oversize leather hobo bag on her lap. "Although I've never liked that term. I prefer *traveler.*"

"You mean, this is your choice?" I ask.

Jada nods. "The best one I've ever made. After I left Van—" She cringes. "Sorry. I'm getting ahead of myself."

Mamita rises into the cloud of blank stares hazing our living room. "I will make us some tea." Translated from Mamita-speak: por Dios, this is going to take a while.

Although she starts her day with pan tostado and café con leche, Mamita is obsessed with tea and even orders it from England. Because Maxwell's tea is just better, she claims. And Jada Morrison and her Mediterranean tan and nomadic secret-sister existence mean emergency teatime.

"Something herbal, please?" Jada requests.

After a nod, Mamita slips into the kitchen. "Keep going! I can hear you!"

"Right. Okay. When I was six, my home got so bad that my step-mom finally left my dad. She said she'd come back for me, but she wasn't the one who did." Jada pauses, face levered downward, as if she's figuring out how to say what I already know is coming. Or maybe she's just giving me time to open up a place to receive it—like she assumes I have one set up.

But here's the thing: that place doesn't exist. It never has. And so, I'm—yes, *I'm*—the one who says, "Vanessa came back for you."

(But not for me. Not once, not ever.)

I don't voice this part. I barely finish processing it. What's the use? I've never wanted my life to look any other way. But now it seems that even ghostly notions can rattle the walls in homes like mine, and I tuck my hands under my thighs to keep them from shaking.

"Bingo," Jada mumbles. "She took me away to Europe. It's a long story, but the gist is that I grew up with her, traveling with her and her band. Staying for one or two years in different regions. For, what, eleven years?"

"Eleven? You said you're twenty-two," Papi notes.

"At seventeen, I had a huge falling-out with Vanessa. I took off on my own this time, moving around, making a new life in a hundred cities. That freedom grabbed on and stuck, so I never stopped." Her eyes brighten, and for the first time I notice the dimples under her cheekbones, identical twins to mine. "I love it."

The room quiets for an unknown span of time until Mamita enters with a tray. Her pink-tinted lips are pressed into an impenetrable vise.

And if I know her, she's stored up a hundred words with a set of exclamation points and question marks to dress them up, like the bows she used to clip into my hair.

For now, Mamita settles on passing out tea. She's probably fixed turmeric-ginger for herself and Abu because it's good for aching joints. Papi gets a Dodgers mug filled with the only tea he likes, Maxwell's Earl Grey. Mint for me, and it's likely what our visitor gets too.

Jada tests the heat level. "Last month, Vanessa tracked me down." A wry smile breaks across her face. But it, too, runs off, leaving everything pensive behind. "She said she wanted to make amends, so she invited me to Barcelona. Her band was holed up in a rental for a solid year. I had just finished securing a renter for my dad's old Atlanta house—now mine. So I set off for Spain."

With that, my resolve falters. I sink into the couch, fighting the urge to actually cover my ears. So far, all her revelations were going down okay when they were slotted into past tense. But a month ago? That's too close. And I simply don't want to hear about what Vanessa is like now. Spare me any tidbits about what hand cream she likes or what she eats for breakfast.

"Clary," Jada says quietly, "I know. I get it. She left me, too. Twice."

I nod, even though Jada has misunderstood my reaction. It's not sadness, it's absolute fullness. I have no more room for Vanessa Holt—happily. I'm tapped. She merely spans the ten months I shared her body and ten days after, seventeen years ago. Barcelona-Vanessa doesn't fit into anything I am inside.

"What do you mean Vanessa left twice?" Papi asks.

"For a few weeks it was really nice," Jada explains. "She did everything she could to repair the rift between us. I moved into the house and played percussion in her band. We cooked and talked on the veranda and just ate up the city. Eventually, she told me about Clary and all of you."

Jada lowers her head. "Obviously, the news was, well, a *lot*. I took a train to Bilbao, just to clear my head. When I came back to the villa earlier than planned, she and her band were packing up. Basically, it was time for her group to move on, and she was happy we'd reconnected, and the place was paid through the month. If I hadn't come back early, all I would've found was a note. That was three weeks ago."

Papi leans forward. "I wish I could say I'm surprised."

Jada rests her mug on an end table. After a quick scratch behind Rocco's ear, she pulls an envelope from her bag. "Before she left, Vanessa asked me to take care of something. It has to do with Salvador Montes."

"Wait, what?" I blurt. While I'd known el señor and Vanessa had crossed paths during her time in LA, I'd assumed that connection had vanished right along with her.

Jada faces me. "She kept in touch with him sporadically. For years."

My throat goes dry. Señor Montes would never have hurt me in any way. Yet he was communicating with the one person who'd harmed my entire family?

Papi rises, and his movements toward the hall are slow and defeated. But he halts at the threshold, one hand on the frame. "Okay . . . God. Okay, that's it," he says, and volleys a strained look between his parents. "Right? We agree?"

Mamita tries to hide a rush of tears with her teacup. "Sólo dile," she says, and Abu nods along, the pallor of his skin speckled with red.

"Tell me what?" I ask, a rush of heat raging through my body.

My dad strides over and crouches low. "What we're about to say is going to sound really confusing and harsh. But please. Please, mija," he says, his voice breaking. "We were only thinking of your well-being."

I swallow hard, a sheen of sweat lacing the back of my neck. The opposite of *well*.

"Señor Montes told us years ago that Vanessa had been conversing with him about you," Mamita says softly. "One time, he heard Jada call Vanessa 'Mom' in the background. This is when he came to us with her confession. He thought we should know."

"This whole time? Years?" I point to Jada, who actually seems as broadsided about this revelation as I am. "You've all known about her?"

Papi grabs my hand. "We found out about ten years ago, but only of her existence, not even her name. And I swear to you, I had no idea Vanessa had another child the whole time we were together. She hid her past from all of us when she moved to Echo Park."

"But then *you* kept hiding it from me. You hid Jada!"

Papi braces my arms. "We thought we were protecting you. We did this out of love and care."

I pinch my eyes shut, my face tensing over so much truth spinning around the greatest lie I've ever known. My family loves me impenetrably and fiercely. Being theirs is like existing on the safest, most secure rock. It's my favorite part of us. But the fact that they knew about Jada and kept silent feels like acres of quicksand pouring in, and I can't stop it. "What else? If you kept this from me, what else don't I know?"

"Ay, mi vida, no," Mamita says. "We were going to tell you when you turned eighteen."

I search Papi and Abu, find them nodding in agreement.

"So, Jada ratted you out ten months early?" I exhale a windstorm. "God. Wow."

My dad sits beside me now, cinching his arm around my shoulders. "I'm sorry, Clary. I mean it."

"I know," I say, because I do. But the hurt? The confusion? I have a feeling those will outlive all the flowers at La Rosa Blanca. Still, I sink into my father's hold, testing the space for the first time in my life. Secrets and lies poke through like briars.

He pegs Jada with a look. "Now that you've seen us at our worst— sorry for that, by the way—can you tell us the rest?"

Jada's holding Rocco on her lap, which strikes me right between my ribs. So many times, he's been my emotional support schnauzer. "Vanessa said Señor Montes was her only link to Clary and Echo Park. Back then, he seemed to be everywhere in the neighborhood. She liked him, and it was mutual."

"Salvador always believed in her as an artist and encouraged her," Papi says. "One of his greatest traits was his biggest fault. He was too trusting."

Jada shakes her head. "It's more than that. He knew of her past—all except for me at that point—and he wanted to sponsor her way into art school. Late into her pregnancy, he offered a ten-thousand-dollar loan so she could enroll the next year."

Too much becomes entirely too clear and all at once. I finally know how Vanessa was able to leave my dad and me the way she did. "She used the money to escape. She stole it."

"Ay, Dios mío," Mamita says. All the turmeric-ginger tea in her kitchen can't ease the ache marring her features.

"Vanessa worked for years to save enough to pay Salvador back. But he refused to accept it. And he wouldn't report any news beyond the basics, like you were safe, healthy, and loved. Any more, she'd have to learn on her own."

Which would happen the day after never.

Jada holds up the envelope. "This money."

Abu gapes. "You are sitting here with ten thousand dollars?"

"Almost. This is a statement from her account. Vanessa never understood why Montes wouldn't take back the cash. The longer she kept it, the more it began to eat away at her." Jada waves her hand aimlessly. "I'd call it guilt, but it seemed like something bigger was at work. She said she was experiencing a personal black hole. She tried everything—saging, meditation. She consulted a spiritual advisor who claimed she was holding a ring of darkness around her soul. While I was there, I sensed it myself. I knew it was the money."

Abu glares, pointing his finger. "And this paper, you thought it was okay to bring even a part of this mal de brujería into our home?"

Jada holds out both hands. "No. No—first of all, Vanessa thought I could get through to Señor Montes, and he might accept the funds from me."

"To rid herself of all the bad juju? To ease her so-called guilt?" Mamita says.

"I tried to reach Señor Montes, and that's when I learned he'd passed. I told my mother before I left for Bilbao," Jada adds, facing me again. "With her link to information gone, so is her peace of mind. Clary, she wants you to have the ten thousand. Doing one right thing for you will shine some light into the darkness she created. She'd like to give it to you herself, and she hopes it can be a point of closure for both of you."

It takes me a few moments to realize this isn't a joke. Closure? For Vanessa, maybe. But I am already whole and closed. "Not gonna happen," I say.

Mamita's eyes spit fire. "After all this time, she would even think to ask our Clarita to face her?"

"She feels it could maybe help Clary, too."

I let out a caustic laugh.

Abu's drawn silent, but his frame remains upright and solid as he crosses the room to sit by my side. During stressful times, Mamita is the voice. And he is the rock.

"Forgive me if I get real basic now," Papi says. "Vanessa has a ten-thousand-dollar check ready to make out to my daughter. In exchange for a meeting?"

Jada holds her arms up. "*Exchange* is a sticky word. She wants it to be a gift. And Clary doesn't have to actually see her. It can be a phone call."

Papi's eyes narrow. "It sounds like a transaction. But since this scheme has *Vanessa Holt* written all over it, I actually believe you're not making it up."

"I promise that's not what's going on here. This money wants to be good and true," Jada says. "I feel it—the pull of its energy. When I agreed to help put this plan into the world, my entire being loosened, and so did Vanessa's. I found the courage to reach out and meet my sister and her family. The money will never make up for what Vanessa did to all of you. But it could help?"

"You mean help *her*, right?" I note. "To get rid of this so-called ring of darkness." It feels weird even voicing this stuff. While I know there's more to this world than what we see right in front of us, I'm not down with using random metaphysical excuses to explain away bad behavior. Maybe Jada got into all these beliefs and practices because of Vanessa. Fine for them. But it's feeling a little too convenient for *me*.

"She wants to leave you with one good thing," Jada says. "It's a lot of money! You could use it for something awesome. A trip, or your education, or to save for—"

"No." Sometimes I make a bridal bouquet with a single type of flower. A spray of calla lilies. Or peachy-pink La Perla roses that spread like cotton candy in the hand, without any fillers or greenery. *No.* This single word is all I need, too.

I turn to Papi, and we talk in a silent way. *I know this money could help with bills and college and life. But it is from Vanessa, and I don't want anything from her.*

My father nods in contemplation but keeps his face blank. He rakes a hand into the cowlick bending through his hair. "Look, it's been a *day* for a million reasons."

"I'm one of them—I know," Jada says.

"Claro que sí, chica," Mamita says, and casts a glance to the heavens. "Where are you staying now?"

"I've been at Orange Drive Hostel for a few days. It's cute, and I've met some really great people. It's one of my favorite things about moving around. New friends." Jada wrings her hands tightly. "I was originally planning on just the week, but now that I'm here, I'm feeling led to make Los Angeles my next home base."

Chills skitter along my spine. Staying? This newly unearthed sister with her wild ideas and messages, in Echo Park?

"I swear I didn't know this when I set out—thought I'd move on to Vancouver," she continues. "An LA summer—who knew?" she muses. "And I do love surprises."

I nearly spit out my next sip of tea. "*Surprise*, but I hate them. And you chose to drop the biggest one I've ever had by showing up at the park with no phone call or warning?"

Jada hinges forward. "Sorry for that. I didn't know how to start. I don't have any other siblings or much of any kind of family. All I'm asking for is a chance. I clearly don't know how to do any of this."

"Cool. That makes two of us." For the first time in my life, my home feels too small. Ivory walls packed with family pictures close inward with unwelcome fragments—the stolen escape money. The bruising secrets my family kept from me. And now news that this person who shares blood with my birth mother wants to stay?

I can't stay. "I need a minute."

"Clary, wait," Papi says, but it's Mamita who strides into my path.

"Querida, I know this is so confusing, and you are upset over what we kept from you. But, please," she says, "let's work out these matters as a family, and we can all decide—"

"No," I repeat to the only mother my heart understands. "I need to be alone."

I catch a flicker of Papi's nod as I unloop my purse and key ring from the coatrack. I have *way* too many keys, but I refuse to separate them. Lourdes calls it my janitor kit.

I scramble out onto the porch, dropping the clangy bundle into my bag as I scan the block. I don't have my own car. I really don't need one yet with Blue Ivy—Lourdes's ancient navy Subaru Outback—plus access to Papi's SUV and the Prius Mamita and Abu share.

But right now the SUV is down the block because of roadwork, and the Prius is garaged for the night. And time matters. I need to bolt before one of the overly concerned Cubans in my world changes their mind and reels me back inside. So I choose the closest mode of transportation, currently parked on our sloped driveway. And will myself not to crash it.

Four

*R*ose Three is a beast. We barely get along, this full-size cargo van and I, but it's the quickest way out of the scene unfolding inside my house. The van's here because we used it to haul the memorial flowers to Saint Athanasius, and then ourselves home with a surprise sister in the back.

Rose Three wakes grumpily, mimicking one Lourdes Evangelina Maria Colón before school. I cut off Abu's Radio Salsa LA station, needing *less*. I'm already tapped with shock. With a sense of betrayal I want to shake, but can't. And with Jada Morrison and the look on Papi's face when I told my family that ten thousand bucks could rot in hell.

Now the sky plays dusk, but there's enough light left in Echo Park to illuminate what my choice means to roads like these. To families like mine. One side of the street says: *You don't spit upon the kind of money that could fund a year of college. Or pad a bank account, or even pay a lease on a historic Sunset business.*

Two days ago another one of those businesses closed right in front of me.

But as I inch around a corner, an opposing view argues back like the second of two feuding abuelas. This side reminds me that Cuban Echo Park was not built from tainted handouts. We were made from the clean blood of hope and resolve, not crime. And gifts don't feel like this.

Bien hecho. You chose rightly, hija, the proud side says into this quiet van. Two voices, two points of conscience. But which one might have to tell an insta-sister, a half hermana, that she can't stay because she comes from the wrong part of my past and a deceitful secret?

That's another choice to make as I cover roads that barely hold this van. In a white metal marshmallow, I'm more hazard than vehicle as I maneuver Echo Park's twisted hills and terraced blocks. *Don't die don't die don't die.*

Halting fully at a stop sign like a dutiful driver, I see it from across the street. A bright blue polo shirt beams, as much out of place against the white wall of the Spanish-style apartment building as it is on Emilio's back. And that's no door he's exiting, but a third-story window. He shimmies down the fire escape with admirable skill, and I'm still locked (stunned?) as his body communicates better than any phrase he's ever said out loud. He's in trouble.

Clary, he's in trouble!

We're both in motion now, and Emilio has never looked at me with such relief. Amusement, irritation, paper-thin tolerance—normal. This is different. This is him bolting toward the corner and waving me forward. I skid up to the curb and unlock the passenger door. "Come on!" I yell through the glass.

In a whoosh of mussed hair and commotion and *boy*, he's in.

"Thank God," Emilio says. The door slams shut, and I ease away.

"Can't this thing move any faster?" he says to the window, craning his neck, then checking the rearview mirror.

I grumble audibly because no, this is Rose Three. "People who flee apartment buildings like cat burglars can't be choosers."

"Hmmph."

"And you still haven't put on your seatbelt," I note.

"My what? Of all the—"

I hit the brakes. "It's the law. Do it, Wheels, or I swear I'll dump you out on this block."

"Coño," he mutters, flubbing around for the harness. He makes a big show of clicking it in. "There. Now can we get the hell out of here?"

My tongue clucks with disapproval. "Why were you running?"

"Why are you driving around in this rig? Also, thanks, you know, for the save." He checks the rearview again.

"Oh no you don't. Talk, Emilio. Should I be concerned that we might be tailed by a pack of mafia hit men? Loan sharks?" I face him briefly. "Drug dealers?"

"That's what you think of me?" Before I can even start another glare, he dashes out his hand. "Okay, okay, but it's worse. Ten times worse. Try a living room full of viejitas."

I gasp at the thought of a horde of meddling abuelas or tías, then finally let out a grin. "So, it was about a girl."

"No—dude, watch it!"

I swerve *just* in time to miss an abandoned scooter. After a half block, my heart rate drops.

Emilio helps himself to a black hair elastic in the cup holder. Mine or Lulú's. He must've lost his on the fire escape. "Okay, it was not *not* about a girl."

Aha!

"After the memorial party, I biked over to Abuela's to assemble her new dining room sideboard thingy."

His abuelo passed three years ago after a grueling battle with multiple sclerosis. The way Emilio tends to Mami Ynez isn't the worst thing about this runaway boy in my flower van.

"And because she is always on the phone," he stresses, "her friend heard I was there with tools. Twenty minutes later I find myself at Mami Isabella's apartment, crashing some Mexi-Cubana-Boricua domino tournament, to which my abuela slides right in. And waiting for me is a slice of flan and an entire unassembled bedroom set."

I cringe. "There's a spare saint medal in the glove box."

"And the thorn goes right for the tease."

"Um, that wasn't teasing?" After ten-plus years, doesn't he know the difference between commiseration and poking fun?

"Two hours, three pieces of cherrywood veneer." He uses his fingers to punctuate. "It was painful, Clary."

Emilio rarely calls me by my given name. I almost crash into a second *something* on this road. I don't even know where I'm going. I'm just circling Rose Three through Echo Park, eating up fuel. And I'm still not sure his whole escape-evasion story hour isn't leading me into some kind of trap. I guard every word. "I believe you."

"Okay, yeah, so I make it to the final piece. And right as I'm screwing in the dresser knobs, all living-room chatter turns to me and my personal business, and they forget my naturally good hearing."

"Canine level," I mutter.

"First cat burglars, now dogs? Cute."

"It's a compliment, okay?" Why did I bother?

"*An-y-way*, they drop the news that Mami Isabella has a granddaughter from Miami going to USC in the fall. And how she's convinced this Lizbeth girl is my perfect match. So she needs my number so this nieta and I can chat before we meet, but it will all work out because I'm single and obviously looking."

"Are you?"

"Am I what?" he says cheekily, with too much anticipation trailing his ask.

It *is* a trap. "Huh? Nothing. Go on."

His chin crumples before he blinks like he's clearing more than vision. "Er, so I realize I've had enough of shit like this. And I'm going to literally leave it this time. Ever since Silver Lake Charter used my face as the welcome brochure cover photo, I've had a casamentera homing device on my forehead."

I'm driving around a matchmaker's dream target. "Okay, fine. But this is when you decide, 'Hey, I'll just fire-escape myself down a perfectly sound building instead of dealing with a bunch of elder Latinas'?"

"I texted Abuela. Plus, the window was open."

My head jiggles back and forth over that recurring Sunday school escape memory. *The door was open.* "So you vanish? They gave you flan. You should have faced them like . . ."

"Like a man?" he spits out. "Don't pull your punches, Thorn."

My punches would not be so sexist. "Like a human being."

He rips the band from his hair. Sandy waves flop around his face, and he rakes through, over and over, as if nothing's really smoothing out. "You can rejoice in karma getting me good, then. I left my tools in Mami Isabella's bedroom. I'll never see them again. And my road bike is still in Abuela's yard from earlier. I don't want to grab it now and risk her seeing me. I need a solid twenty-four hours between us."

"Have you forgotten we're Cuban?" Our people recognize no statute of limitations on guilt extraction or expressing big feelings over offense.

Emilio's mouth purses but stays shut, and I click into our surroundings. I've driven us south toward Sunset and the Echo Park commercial district. Rose Three, with all its sluggish, oversize faults, knows where to take me. We're about four blocks from Avalos Bicycle Works and La Rosa Blanca. Another café has just hoisted an *Opening Soon* sign.

"New Hampshire. What's its signature dish from your map?" With food on the brain, I choose a random state.

"Boiled dinner." When my nose wrinkles in confusion, he adds, "Corned beef. And the sides like potatoes, carrots, turnips."

"Interesting." I ease up on the gas and notice a parking spot in front of the muraled side wall of an insurance office. I've always loved the murals and street art of central LA—so much that I did a freshman-year research project on their history and significance. But this one has always been my favorite. I park the van parallel to the walled masterpiece, simply needing something that's trusted and literally rock solid right now.

"Something up with the engine?" Emilio asks, but he's gazing out the passenger-side window, too, even though he's likely seen this gigantic mural a thousand times.

"Nope, I just wanted to visit her for a minute." Her, because the artwork depicts a brunette, light brown woman in a white gown. One hand holds a goblet. Her feet rise up from a verdant field. Ruby lips, piercing eyes, an acid-green snake coiled around her neck like a choker. Her left hand holds a bouquet of purple Roman hyacinths. Sin Nombre—nameless. That's what locals call her. The Cuban muralist who created her died without ever hinting at her identity or story.

She still has a story, Clarita, Mamita said when I was little. For years before my research project, we'd pass the white-dress woman, walking from La Rosa Blanca on a break. Strolling to the bodega for an orange soda.

I always asked to stop, and my imagination made stories about Sin Nombre.

She's angry, Mamita. Her eyes look like she's mad because of bad people.
She wants to dance.
She's scared.
She has enough juice for everyone in her cup.
She wants to be important.

Mamita said yes to all my guesses, even when they'd contradict one another. Now, at seventeen, I know that all of them could be true at once.

"I haven't forgotten," Emilio says, whisking me back to the present. "That we're Cuban. I haven't forgotten that."

"Right. Okay," I say, like Mamita did back then, to a child with contradicting words. I start up the van, pull us away toward Emilio's house on the other side of Sunset from mine.

"You never did answer my question. About why my ride—let's call it Chisme Rescue Services—showed up in the form of a gigantic white van."

"Maybe you're not the only one who felt like leaving fast," I admit, and bite the inside of my cheek to keep the rest in. I am not telling Emilio about Jada, or the money, because it would be like talking into a vortex that spits everything out again, but backward. And upside down. So I am *not*.

"Gotcha."

He rarely gets me. It's polite enough, so I nod. But after I drop him off, an ironic truth slides into the space he just left. Emilio ended up rescuing me back, mainly through his fire-escape actions. Because he reminded me that Clary Delgado is not like Emilio Avalos. I don't run through open windows from discomfort. I don't deflect and text excuses later. And even if it's hard, I face the people and the prickly bits that want to disrupt the way my world turns.

It's time to confront Jada Morrison. I know what I need to tell her.

The sky is all the way dark when I steer Rose Three into the drive-way. A lone figure sits on our porch, keeping watch, and it breaks my heart. Abu lifts his head, and his arms fall open as he rises. I exit the van and burrow in close, unshed tears burning through my sinuses.

"I am sorry, too, Clarita."

I nod into his shoulder. My abuelo smells like Tide detergent and the Valentino cologne he saves for special times. *It's okay. I forgive you.* I trap these phrases on the edge of my tongue, like I'm a kid again and about to jump into the deep end. So many times, I didn't jump. I ran back to Mamita and a warm towel. Tonight, I keep my words just as close.

"Mamita is walking Rocco," Abu says. "Your papi went out, and Jada is in the kitchen eating frijoles." He pulls back and thumbs my cheeks. "No matter what, in this family we do not turn people away."

"Yo sé." *I know, I know,* because this statement comes from a root I understand. The soil I grew up on didn't turn his parents and him away, either, fifty years ago.

"Pero, we told Jada she had to wait for you to come back. That you will decide how it will be while she is in Los Angeles." He lobs a knowing look. "That you will decide about *everything.*"

"I'll talk to her." I kiss his ruddy cheek and step onto the porch. The door is unlocked; I don't need my janitor keys.

I find Jada where Abu said she was, occupying a portion of the kitchen floor where he often dances with Mamita while they're drying dishes. Maybe in my abuelo's eyes, our snack-size kitchen is a grand ballroom and our house, for just a minute, is infinitely bigger for him, too.

Now the person taking up space here feels so imposing between these ivy-papered walls, and the ones hedged around my head. Oddly, she's leaning into a seventy-five-degree angle against the counter, eating a bowl of beans and rice.

Jada turns; a nervous smile flutters across her face. "I've eaten the world's version of beans in twenty cities. But these are probably the best I've ever tasted. She's a wonderful cook, your . . ."

"Mamita." I put weight behind the name. "And no, she's not the best cook. But she can make a mean congrí." I pause for two beats. "So, yeah, about summer, you can stay."

Jada rests the bowl. "Honestly, I wasn't sure after your reaction."

"Same." My palm juts out. "There are rules, though."

"I figured."

"First, you can't stay in this house. Whatever you've heard about Cubans and Echo Park, and us taking in as many people as possible until they get on their feet, that can't happen here."

"Assumed. I have perfectly good feet. Plus, your—your mamita has already been so hospitable, and given me some leads." Her features shrink. "Just in case."

Just in *Cuban*. "Right. So, the next rule is about Vanessa." I dislike the shape of the word on my tongue. "You brought your message. Beyond that, I don't need to know about her. Believe me when I say I am not at all curious. If we're just going along and you think of some story from your childhood, or how I'm just like her in some way, please save it."

"I understand."

Does she? "I mean it. If I need to know something, I'll ask first."

"That's fair." Jada runs her teeth in a swift line along her bottom lip. "I don't blame you."

Solidarity. The friend or family kind. Maybe even the sisterly kind, if I had any clue about sisters beyond Lourdes and her sister, Sofia, or movies and TV. Still, I sense it in the short span of kitchen tiles between our feet. And I *note* it, but not with any trust. Not even close.

"Cool," I say. "And I'm not trying to be rude, but I only agreed to this summer because it's the right thing to do. It's not like I blame you for anything. I just like to be clued in about where I'm headed. Loose variables and unknowns don't get along with me."

She ventures forward a half step; gold bangles clang as her arms gesture in and out. "Maybe I can help with that. Part of my lifestyle, well, I know how to manage expectations. Let's just start with I'm Jada and you're Clary, and we have this summer. Three known variables. We'll talk about the money and the, um, request after I get settled."

No. Wasn't I clear enough earlier? I'm too beat to argue my point anymore. But there's one more rule I have to get out. "Last thing, no more shady surprises like your little park pop-up. No more 'cosmic brujería crystal power' awakening points or visions leading us wherever. It's fine if you're into that stuff, but I'm not. So just be plain and up front with me."

"I promise."

I wonder about promises from Jada. How, or even if, they work. Our shared past is the opposite of promising.

But she is not HER, one side of my brain says. This person is Jada Morrison, not Vanessa Holt. An innocent half sister, not an absent birth mother. Tonight, that's all I know.

I hear the stirrings of Rocco and Mamita out front. I'm not sure what Abu is still doing out there. I motion toward the dining room. "We have perfectly good chairs and tables."

Jada smiles, shrugging before picking up her bowl. "Nah, I'm fine. I usually eat standing up."

Maybe she finds standing more natural because it's one step closer to movement and traveling. To *that next thing,* wherever it lives. Tonight, I've never been less sure of what's coming next for me.

Five

Papi: You awake? Breakfast?

The text from my dad trails the final topcoat on my manicure, the last item on the series of tasks I crammed into Sunday morning. I've been awake for two hours, starting before the sun on laundry and bedroom organization, breaking only to feed Rocco and send Mamita and Abu off to Saint Athanasius. I barely slept. After the whirlwind of Jada, and Emilio, and Jada again, I woke with restless fingers. My family's deception—the bloodred stain of it—lingers like a leftover party foul.

But . . . Papi. Even though his text was only three words, I sense a million more spinning around his brain. He's worried and torn. That makes two of us. Awake for too long, I write back.

Papi: Jumping in shower. Come up for bfast? I went to the store last night 🥖 🥣

My heart snags and my mouth jerks wide for a beat. These emojis form our secret code. Because Mamita would ream us if she knew what Papi and I are about to eat.

Me: Be right there

I toss a gray cardigan over my pj's and slide into flip-flops. Papi lives with us, but also alone—both of these facts are true. He'd gotten an apartment just before his engagement to Vanessa. But after she left, my twenty-one-year-old dad moved back home so Mamita and Abu could help raise me. Abu and some friends renovated the casita over the detached garage so Papi could be with me, but also have his own space. Tía Roxanne's old bedroom became my nursery.

I ease through the dining-room slider with Rocco trailing behind. I've been making this short trek since I took my first steps. Sometimes with my chunky toddler legs slung around Papi's shoulders as he'd carry me up the stairs leading to his studio.

The wooden staircase is solid but taunts climbers with moans and creaks. Inside, the shower's running. Papi left his door cracked open with Brownstone (he lives for nineties R & B) harmonizing from his speakers. The space, consisting of a studio and bath, is church-mouse small. Rocco trots to the double bed in the corner, burrowing his salt-and-pepper fur into the pillows.

Opposite the bed, a love seat faces an entertainment console. Since Papi eats with us at the house, there's only a kitchenette here. But the two-burner stove holds a griddle for our weekly pancake dinners. The junior-size microwave heats popcorn just right when we watch eighties rom-coms. And the square table has always been big enough for our frozen pizza and hot chocolate feasts before video games. Basically, we are both children.

Childish is the theme of the breakfast Papi hinted at. He went all out this time. Never did Mamita ever allow him or Roxanne sugary cereals growing up. Tía never cared, but a box of Cocoa Puffs was one of the things my dad bought—and hid unsuccessfully from Mamita's illegal-azúcar radar—with his first allowance coins.

About the time I reached kindergarten, we invented rainbow bowl, which morphed into *Rainbowl*. It's simple. We pile tons of different kid cereals together. Fruity types plus chocolate and cinnamon varieties? Sure. The more disgustingly mismatched, the better.

"Build mine for me!" my dad calls from beyond the pocket door when the water stops.

I open the new cardboard boxes. Transform into an aisle-five mixologist.

We don't eat Rainbowl all that often, but it's there when we need it. Papi swears the concoction once cured a bachelor-party hangover. We had it when we found out Señor Montes died. And after yesterday's appearance of his ex-fiancée's secret daughter, I'm not surprised Papi took off last night and fortified our stash.

I set our bowls on the table; there's barely any room left with my dad's laptop and a manila file folder spilling out a wad of papers. I'm no snoop, but random words cut into plain view. Sunset. Historical Preservation. Echo Park. Salvador . . . ?

I jerk away as Papi appears with a miniature schnauzer trailing behind him. Damp hair, old jeans, and a Dodgers T-shirt comprise his fit. He eyes my creation approvingly and tosses a few Froot Loops to Rocco, which he's never done.

I pass him the milk. "That can't be good for him."

"Like it's even remotely good for us?"

Our laughs falter as we dig in, another kind of mix crowding the table. *Pero ten thousand dollars, Clary.* Remorse from last night clouds Papi's eyes, shading the candy colors and whimsical shapes in our bowls. He's waiting for me to bring *everything* up. And I'm too shaken to know how to start.

"What's up with that folder?" I deflect, gesturing with my spoon.

"Before he passed, Señor Montes was trying to apply for historical distinction for part of Echo Park," Papi says. "The lake and some other structures nearby already have this designation. But this would be for our Sunset business district, to preserve the area and honor its role in fostering Cuban culture on the west coast."

Preserve. Honor. Cuban culture. Oh, I'm listening, and my head feels clearer than it's been in hours. "How could it help the neighborhood?"

Tiny etched lines around Papi's eyes soften. "More funds to maintain our murals, and restrictions to keep the architectural integrity of some of the buildings. Tax incentives and rent protections, too."

"Could that have saved Varadero Travel?" I ask as another question lurks behind. *Could it protect La Rosa Blanca?*

"The situation with Ana and Varadero was what made Salvador investigate this option months ago," Papi notes. "He was putting together this packet."

I let out an undignified snort. "The guy who didn't even own a computer."

"He used the library. And Abu and I helped. We were reviewing this file when Salvador went to the hospital." Papi opens the folder, leafing through the papers. "Abu and I found out something at the memorial that made us want to complete his work and honor his wishes."

"What something?" Didn't we find out more than enough at that memorial already?

Papi takes a bite. Swallows. "We knew Hole Punch Donuts bought the building Ana was renting, but yesterday we learned the company is planning an expansion into the side lot. Hole Punch could work with the existing structure and save the beach mural, but they're choosing to destroy it. Salvador appealed to the CEO with our history here to save the artwork." Papi shakes his head. "Probably one of the last things he did *before*. But they dismissed it. So, the mural goes."

The birds, the Latino artistry, the beachy Cuban landscape. "Can they do that? I thought street art was protected."

"Yeah, but other variables factor in. The artist is gone with no one to claim the copyright, and it's up to the new building owner to preserve the art and incorporate it into their design. Without the added layer of protection from any existing historical designations, they have more freedom. Apparently, the mural doesn't fit their branding."

In this case, Hole Punch branding means vintage schoolhouse furniture, and striped "lined paper" exterior walls covered with fake tardy slips with outrageous excuses for being late for class. I face my dad, realizing I've clenched my hand into a fist. "The building fits the *neighborhood*. It fits into our history."

As an unwelcome add-on, Emilio's face pops into my head. Damn his foodie meddling and DMs to corporate.

"I love that mural," I say, tightening the sweater around my chest. "It's outlasted so many businesses around here."

And if the Varadero beachscape can be so carelessly destroyed, what about my favorite Sin Nombre mural? From my project research, I learned there's no one around to claim that copyright, either. If the insurance firm sells and new owners decide to follow in Hole Punch's bulldozing ways, the haunting mujer in white could be more than nameless. She could be faceless.

Our Cuban heritage and people are already fading from Echo Park. We can't lose any more of our artwork, too. "Show me how the historical preservation works."

The tour my dad gives me through the papers and the pertinent government webpages seems straightforward enough. We click through links, scoping out comparable districts that were success-fully awarded honorable distinction. According to the comps, Echo Park qualifies. With its commercial pocket that employed thousands of immigrants and hosted documented anti-Castro campaigns, plus the legendary social clubs and colorful murals, our neighborhood is more than worthy of historical protection. The governing board only has to agree.

While Papi's stuck in a research rabbit hole on his phone, I plug in a flash drive that was taped inside the file folder. The drive contains the recent neighborhood photos the application checklist requires. I find our part of Sunset Boulevard and the area el señor felt was wor-thy of distinction. But as I scroll through, the photo file stops short. Again, I cross-reference Señor Montes's folder with the require-ments. One major component is missing, and I know exactly what to do. What I *have* to do.

"Let me take over this project," I say.

Papi eyes me warily as we return to our soggy breakfasts. (Somehow it adds to the charm.) "It's your big 'rising senior' summer with Lourdes. And you're already at the shop so much. Why add more?"

Why? Because you and Abu and Mamita already work more hours than anyone should to keep us going. Because Echo Park has enough legacy for me to fight for until I can find a way to leave my own.

There's one last reason, too, the only one I voice. "I need this, Papi."

After last night, I need something to focus on that I *know*. And I know about the remnants of our Cuban heritage in this neighborhood, so well I barely flinch when Señor Montes's safe word drifts into my mind. *Las fichas.* There's no secret history Echo Park has kept from me.

"Okay, I get it," my dad says. "It's all yours. But now we—"

"The file," I rush out. "Some items in there aren't complete." And I can't face our unsaid matters yet.

"Fine." Papi thumbs the scruff along his jaw. "What items?"

"Señor Montes was missing historic pictures with captions. He's got everything covered for current documentation, but the board wants to see old photos that back up any personal accounts."

"Right. Weird they're not in there."

After Papi's earlier cereal tease, Rocco comes back in full annoyance mode, pawing at my shin. I bend around and grab his box of jerky treats and toss one across the room. A few minutes of peace.

"You could check with Ivonne?" Papi says. "In fact, she called last night. She's been clearing Salvador's belongings from the casita. She found Abu's drill."

I hide any signs of delight behind my spoon. "Ivonne called *you*? About *Abu's* stuff? Don't you know what flirting looks like?"

He scoffs. "And you do?"

My eye roll comes out easily and feels like simpler times. My dad is fully aware I've dated a few guys. Okay, more like two. And the fact that neither stuck around very long isn't because I can't read signals. I have my own reasons for being currently unattached. I simply want the high-school version of the easy, dependable steadiness that my abuelos share. Apparently, that's too much to ask for.

"The phone call means Ivonne has Abu's drill, and that's all," Papi says.

"Sure. I'll take care of it. I'd better not wait too long, or it might be gone before I have the chance to *claim* it." Ivonne's been divorced for two years. It's time.

But Papi does this thing where he'll counteract my annoying call-outs by instigating a staring match. I lift up and join in. Who will break first? The wall clock ticks loudly behind us.

"We need to talk about your new sister," he says midstare, which knocks my game off-center so fast, I feel my entire body break away.

I turn to Rocco and his blissful chewing in the corner. Sunlight cracks into the picture window between the love seat and the bed. "So, it's weird. I look just like you, but Jada looks totally like *her*." My voice comes out small. "It must've been a shock."

Papi's hand settles over mine, and I can't look away anymore. "That's not where I wanted your thoughts to go, cariño. I felt my pain, hard and long, but that was years ago. Jada has *your* blood, not mine, and her appearance in LA is about you alone. Tell me how to support you through this."

Instinctively, I shake my head. He's wrong. Our situation is not about me needing the kind of support he thinks I do. My heart, my planet—it's always been *him*. It's my tía in Brooklyn, and Abu and Mamita. It's Lourdes and all the friends and neighbors who walk these streets by my side. But now my family's deceit has shaken that planet to its core. My whole life I thought it was made of unbreakable stuff.

I thought *we* were.

But still, Jada came to LA dragging a bigger situation along with her bags. Oh, she brought a *whole lot* more. So, yes, there's one way my dad can support me. "You can trust how I feel about the money."

"I heard you last night, amor. And my heart broke for you," he says, his voice chipped and cracked. "Having to hear those words. But when I slept on it—or tried to, at least—I saw some parts differently."

My stomach churns, Rainbowl turning stormy inside my gut. "What parts?"

He presses back against the seat. "Vanessa owes you, Clary. She *owes* you. She wronged you and our entire family. And you can fight that. She wants you to pick up the phone for a couple of minutes, let her give you this gift, and she can get her closure. No, you *take* the money, in your full power. And I'd be right there with you."

My lip trembles even picturing this scene. I whisk it away when the colors and shapes saturate too deeply. The ghost I come from may sing for a living, but she has no voice inside of me. "That's my whole point. You've always been there. You've already given me everything I need."

"No." Papi's eyes well. "Not everything. Not a way back to the faith you've lost in your family."

My face closes up, cheeks sucked in. "Just because you acted out of love doesn't make everything automatically okay." I find his entire body strung tightly with regret. "That's gonna take a minute."

My dad tips his chin, conceding. "There's something else I can't give you, and it kills me. Today, I can't write you a check for ten thousand dollars for college. Or pay down accounts if we have a bad month. But she can."

I breathe around a strong pull of emotion. "I know, okay? I just can't separate the money from her betrayal. It doesn't feel like a gift or closure. It feels wrong. I need time to figure that out, too."

He picks up his spoon and eats two last mouthfuls before he answers. "Jada is here now, and that's more than enough adjustment for you on its own. We'll revisit everything before senior year." One shoulder jerks up. "I slept on it for one night and saw another side. Remember *Sleeping Beauty*? How you'd beg me to play the DVD over and over?" When I nod, he says, "Rest on it for the summer, bella."

Six

*T*oday's bride-to-be is crying. The culprit of these happy tears: a white star-shaped blossom, roughly the size of a quarter, called stephanotis. It's a common bridal bouquet add-in, but this bride's mother revealed she's been secretly growing a stephanotis vine in her backyard. And could I use some for her daughter's bouquet? Yes, yes, I can.

Instead of using them as an accent, I love grouping tons of stephanotis and placing a pearl pin into the center of each bloom. I show the ladies my sketch of a tight bouquet of the white flowers bunched together, with whimsical blossom-strung streamers that trail down to midthigh. What I keep to myself is the fact that my bisabuela Margarita grew these flowers in her garden in Cuba. These, and the white roses our shop was named after, were her favorites.

And it's over. My bride has reached full-blown wreckage. They make better mascara than this girl is using.

Over the duo's shoulders, I catch Lourdes back from a delivery run.

She takes three steps into the showroom, mouths PERO WOOOW, and spins back around, arms in goalpost formation.

Fifteen minutes later, after the mother-daughter duo approves the floral plan, the shop is empty again. I check my phone to see if my dad replied to an hours-old text about the build restrictions for the venue of an upcoming banquet, and nada. *I need to prepare, Papi!* Lourdes strides into the showroom, interrupting my frustrated grumble and the drone of a true-crime podcast from Abu's office.

Unlike Papi, Lourdes has been reachable, even during her UC Davis tour. As her mom drove them back home, I spent the better part of yesterday filling my friend in on a weekend where me rescuing Emilio from a room of matchmaking viejitas *wasn't* the most dramatic highlight.

"Hey, the dog groomer just called on the shop line," Lourdes says. "Rocco's all done."

"Good timing. Come get him with me. Plus, we need to stop by Ivonne's to pick up some stuff, and I might need a hand."

"Aye, aye, carnation chief." She actually salutes me, deftly evading my elbow as we head out onto Sunset. I cringe whenever customers insist on basic carnations in their arrangements, and Lourdes loves to poke at my flower snobbery. We reach Avalos Bicycle Works, and I will not peer inside for a glimpse at Emilio.

I do, in fact, peer.

"See anyone interesting?" Lourdes trills.

"No idea what you're talking about." Plus, there was window glare. I quicken my pace.

"Well, here's what didn't come up yesterday that clearly should have. Why didn't you take Emilio straight home? Why the random detour?"

"I . . ." My tongue freezes because she's right. Why didn't I? "I guess we were talking, and I lost track of . . ." *Time? Sanity? The current phase of the moon?*

"Mm-hmm. I was just wondering because you said you two had a conversation."

"Yeah, and?"

She looks both ways before we cross another intersection, and her eyes bug out. "You. Emilio. Conversation. Three words that do not ever go together."

Lourdes would know. Too often during our stint together at Silver Lake Charter, teachers paired Emilio with me for group projects. He was a year ahead of Lulú and me, but the three of us shared a photography elective. A chemistry class. And a drama class my sophomore year, where I swear fellow students began to look forward to the Avalos-Delgado showdown that always erupted during improv hour. Namely, the bickering. Our existence *was* the drama.

Then for academic pairings, instead of showing up to meetings for projects, Emilio would simply populate our Google Docs with his portion of the work. When presentation days came, he'd wow teachers with his smooth delivery.

"What does it matter, Thorn?" he'd say anytime I'd confront him about his flightiness and lack of collaboration. "We aced it. Who cares if I dialed it in from the park?"

Or the beach, or the repair bay at Avalos Bicycle works. Or

anywhere . . . else. That was forever my point. Which he never got, and always argued right back about—typically on our Sunset Boulevard cross street.

"You're assuming I didn't end up with a headache," I tell Lourdes, feeling my temples throb simply from reliving my Silver Lake Charter days with Emilio. "You had to be there."

She lets out a bright cackle. "Would've been worth my entire college fund."

College, another school-adjacent thought that pinches especially hard right now. The only thing that helps with knowing STEM-whiz Lourdes will move away next year, pursuing her dream biochemistry degree, is that I've known this for years. I've had time to accept that I'm staying in LA for school, and she's headed for dorm life. Many high school friends drift apart after graduation, and we've already vowed to crush those odds. We have to. I'll be devastated if the opposite happens.

This time I try to will the future away, letting it drift off into the streets of my barrio. Lourdes is here now, ribbing me about carnations and unreliable Cubans. "Everything *Jada* made me go all haywire," I tell her. "I needed to drive around to think, and there he was. Emilio may have provided enough distraction to snap my brain into gear to make a hard choice."

"Like those old electric shock treatments," Lourdes says before she stops, dead center, in front of a pharmacy. "Hear me out. I could play you on the phone."

My face scrunches until I catch up. *Oh friend.* I told her about the money, and the request for closure, but we haven't had time to really hash it out, just the two of us. "I love you for this, but—"

"No—listen. Vanessa's never heard your voice. I'll play the part and let her say her business, and then, boom." Lourdes makes an explosion with her hands. "Ten grand, and you don't even have to be there. Like I couldn't pull it off?"

I breathe around the rash idea, letting the air leak out slowly. "Of course you could. But I can't even go there yet."

"Fine. But my offer doesn't expire." Lourdes links her arm into mine, and we set off again. "Hey, so when do I get to meet this Jada? If she makes you sad and treats you weird, she's going to become my problem real fast."

For today's look, my friend gathered her hair to the side, then wove it into a long tail so hefty and thick, it's more weapon than braid.

"Ready-to-strike Lulú is my favorite Lulú."

"Better than Clary-impersonator Lulú?"

"Only slightly. And soon, okay?" I add about Jada. "First, *I* need to figure out la hermana nueva."

Five minutes later Lourdes and I are in possession of a Rocco with a shiny salt-and-pepper coat. While I part with fifty bucks at the reception desk, Lourdes studies the wall of flyers tacked to a corkboard.

One blue lined leaflet stands out; I'd know that branding anywhere. "God, it's like Hole Punch is stalking my every move," I grumble, and tug at Rocco's leash.

"I know, I know. And their demo plan is so gross," Lourdes says. "Why does their double custard glazed have to be so magically delicious? It's not fair."

She gets a *look*. "You trying to cochair Emilio's spot on my gentrification shit list?"

We maneuver ourselves and Rocco out the door. "My girl, I hate what's happening to Echo Park every bit as much as you do. And I'm with you on this preservation thing." Lourdes bumps my side. "Weird Hole Punch is waiting more than ten months to move in, though." When my brows narrow, she says, "Yeah, that's what the flyer said. Coming . . . er, not all that soon. I know they're remodeling, but still."

But still indeed. My ears perk up, not unlike the ones on my sweet-smelling pup. I need to research, but I'm wondering if a new, even sweeter-smelling Historical Landmark plaque could do more than just save future at-risk murals and structures. Maybe it could land in time to save the Varadero Beach mural, too. I'm certain Hole Punch would sell just as many donuts with a side wall that fits the neighborhood. And we'd preserve something historic, something Cuban from our Echo Park golden age.

The sweetest thing of all.

A few minutes later we're heading up the hill to Ivonne's street. We love visiting her place—a two-on-one property with her larger cottage in front and a backyard casita where Señor Montes lived out his last years. Ivonne's a good fifteen years older than us but has always treated Lulú and me like family. Sipping homemade kombucha while watching her play, bingeing old eps of *America's Next Top Model*, or ogling her incredible wardrobe—that's what we do.

Our trio scoots around the final bend. When my awareness catches up to my feet, it's all wrong. Ivonne says something to a woman on her porch before going inside—a tall woman with wavy blond hair and an airy blouse that knots right above her stomach. *It can't be. . . .* And the man I've been trying all day to reach is just a few yards away. Papi's here, his SUV parked in Ivonne's driveway, hauling two suitcases out of the back and up the front steps.

"Yo, Clary!" Jada calls, waving. A huge straw bag sags over her shoulder. "Here I was just thinking about you. I mean, actively focusing, and boom—you appear!"

Absolutely not. No one manifested me. I came here for Abu's drill and hopefully some old photos, on my own. My head spins and I ground myself into blooms. Sweet peas gasp their last breath of the season. Morning glory purple and strong pinks and yellows sing from Ivonne's thriving flower beds.

Before I can answer, Jada gives a *be right back* signal.

"Wow," Lourdes says. She's instinctively drawn closer, and she has my dog. I don't even remember handing her Rocco's leash.

Coming here and finding this scene, Emilio would somehow vanish into the smog-filled air. Emilio would find a way to disguise himself between the jasmine vines. This thought alone gives me enough nerve to face yet another new reality. I take a fortifying breath. "Remember how you wanted to meet my sister? Go on, 'cause that was her."

"I got that part," Lourdes says as Rocco pulls her toward Ivonne's bushes. Lourdes tends to him as Papi shuffles down from the porch.

"This is where you've been all day? I texted you a bunch of times."

My dad motions me toward the curb and shuts the liftgate of his SUV. "No, I—we just got here. My phone was dying, but I messaged you."

Dubious, I reach into my bag. I'd missed my text notification with the dog-bark chorus at the groomer's. Inbox: one. Sorry been tied up but all good, talk venue stuff in a few

"See, I didn't—"

"Papi!" I more than whisper. "'Sorry, all good' is, like, one millionth of an explanation for what's going on here."

He makes a noise between a sigh and a grumble. "Which is why I was working up to it." He nods toward the porch. "To her and *this*."

This being the suitcases, and the fact that my family is the only common denominator between Jada and Ivonne. I work out everything myself: Señor Montes's old cottage is my sister's new home for the summer.

"Clary! There's eats in here!" Lourdes calls from inside. Leave it to her and Rocco to ditch me for food.

"Go on in," Papi says. He kisses my forehead and slides into the driver's seat. "I'll be home for dinner. And everything here is gonna be fine."

I try my best to believe him.

"Rob, wait. Since you're here." Ivonne appears with a black-and-yellow case marked *DEWALT*. She hands Abu's drill into the SUV. For way longer than necessary, the air between them charges with muffled words and spurts of laughter.

Finally, Ivonne shuts his door and turns, a flush pooling her light brown skin, matching her cherry-red sundress. She slings an arm around my shoulder. "Sorry, I know you came for your abuelo's contraption, and I forgot to save you the trip with the rush of getting the casita ready. Plus, your dad dropping off Jada. All that."

I shoot her an eye roll. "I have a feeling 'all that' just travels along with her."

Ivonne laughs, then softens another shade. "We didn't have a chance to speak about her renting the place, and I don't love that for us. I'm sorry, amor." She leads me toward the porch. "I fixed drinks and other snacky things. *Maybe* Lourdes left us some. Come on, I got you."

Ivonne gets me in more ways than one.

Seven

*I*f **"music-ish"** were a design style, Ivonne Dominguez has mastered it. Her living room walls morph between minty green and arctic blue depending on the time of day. Restored pale wood floors span the perfect backdrop for a flea-market leather love seat and travel-trunk coffee table, with all the dents and dings of a worn-out favorite song.

A stone fireplace wall is literally filled with music. Vintage guitars and smaller stringed instruments are mounted, waiting for musical friends to grab picks and keep the neighbors up all night. In the opposite corner, her massive double bass slants on a stand.

The kitchen is a stretch for two cooks but gleams with white marble and seafoam cookware. Right there, in the lemongrass fog from an essential-oil diffuser, Jada and Lourdes are leaning over the counter, laughing. Rocco happily snacks on baby carrots at their feet.

"Lulú was just telling me about biochem and UC Davis," Jada says. She's got a tiny glass plate filled with fat green olives and cheese.

Already down to nicknames? How cozy. I give the whole room a smile, but it's forced. I need to shake this funk, but a lot of new information all at once tends to do this to me. Without a little warning, I default to ice mode.

Ivonne saves me by pouring us glasses of the chilled agua de jamaica she brews herself from her hibiscus plants and fresh mint.

"I once hung out with a biologist in Cape Town," Jada says, but her body—the hint of smirk, the flighty gesture from fingers piled with golden stack rings—adds another layer to "hung out." She sips, then goes on. "Brilliant, too. Environmental research or something. A brain I'll never forget even though it was only a couple weeks."

"Hopefully his outside was good, too," Lourdes says. She tosses Rocco another carrot.

"Hers." Jada strikes a grin so drunk with memory, it almost staggers off her face. "And better than good."

Ivonne bursts into a throaty cackle and picks up the snack tray. "Let's get you settled?"

We step through the potted garden courtyard, with a trickling fountain Ivonne installed to mask the never-ending buzz of kids and traffic and *city*. Advantage: Echo Park. It's still an oasis out here and one of my favorite spots.

The casita is a cropped version of Ivonne's place. When I don't follow Lourdes all the way in, she turns. "You okay?"

Am I? One realization eclipses everything that's changed in my life; it's the first time Lulú and I have been here since Señor Montes's death. "It's eerie," I say, searching for any trace of him still inhabiting the air. Today I can't feel anything but a memory.

"A person never really leaves a place completely," Lourdes says.

"You just come up with that?"

"More like leftovers from the *Sandra Colón Reglas de* . . . de shit to tell her daughters to sound wise."

The laugh that sneaks in has never felt better. "Gotta love your mom."

"I'll remind you of that Friday when we have Sofia's floral consultation. And she changes everything last minute."

What is time? Lourdes's younger sister is having her quinceañera ball in, as I've just been reminded, only a few weeks. Of course, I'm doing the flowers and coordinating everything. Like the historical designation project, Sofia's party is something to look forward to that actually makes sense. A date Sharpied on a calendar, known and expected. Unlike the blonde in the corner, scrawling her name over Ivonne's rental docs.

Lourdes grabs Rocco from his post guarding the snack tray in the kitchenette. "Let me walk this boy back and actually do some of the work your family pays me for."

Panic skitters down my back. "Why do you have to be responsible Lourdes right now?"

"She's your third-favorite Lourdes." Lulú air-kisses both my cheeks like always and stays hush-close. "You're fine. She's really nice."

"Yeah, but she's also . . ."

"I know. You can do *also*." And with a wave, my emotional support pieces—my best friend and my dog—are gone.

Ivonne is the next to excuse herself after promising to leave the snacks for unpacking fuel. It's not until Jada immerses herself in the straw tote big enough for two schnauzers that I remember the other reason I "manifested" myself here today. This time I flash Jada a *be right back* signal and dart into Ivonne's cottage.

I find her packing her bass into its massive carrying case. "Sorry, I know you have practice. But I need your help."

Ivonne rises, waving me off. "We start when I get there."

I still make it quick: Señor Montes. Belongings. Photos for a community project.

Ivonne leads me to her spare room. "Salvador didn't have a lot, but it's taken some time for the executor to get everything to the right people." A card table is set up near her guest bed. Ivonne reaches for a small wooden box and hands it over. "In fact, he just secured this from Salvador's friend. It's willed to your family. I was gonna wait until I had the rest sorted, but you're here."

Oh. I recognize the item instantly as the domino set Señor Montes brought from Cuba, his most prized possession. "Seriously?"

"I know, Clary." Ivonne rustles my shoulder. "He left it to his favorite."

Emotion stings the back of my throat.

Ivonne pulls another medium-size lidded box, dusty with peeling edges. "But you said photos. It's all fair game at this point as a notice went out two weeks ago to claim stuff. This is what's left." She removes the lid, revealing a small bunch of photographs and some faded newsprint pages. "I kind of shuffled through. I've only been in Echo Park for ten years, so this was like a history lesson. And I didn't want to throw them out, but you can't keep everything, you know?"

"I'll take care of them."

"He'd appreciate that. He loved your family." We share a smile, and she checks her watch and kisses me goodbye on the forehead.

When I return to the casita, I find the statue version of Jada Morrison mounted in the center of the room, head tilted back. I set the photo box and dominoes on a table, and the noise eases through her as if she's waking from a long nap.

"I do this every time I come to a new place," she says.

"Do what?"

"Listen, mostly." Jada's already opened her two suitcases. She returns to dresses, loungewear, and flowy tops, arranging them inside the wardrobe. "I try to feel the energy of a room to see if we'll get along." She pulls a pair of tan suede ankle boots. "All things possess an inner network of memory and motion. So, my little ritual is just about trying to sense, acknowledge, and flow along with it."

Motion. Flow. My mind instantly snaps to Emilio. Open doors, wheels, and even a third-story window. "What did it *tell* you?" I can't help the sarcastic bend of my words. "This place? You found it so fast."

"It found me. And we'll get along just fine."

My skin prickles. But there's more, like I've been opened up and studied against my will. I instinctively step back, because now I'm not sure if the energy she was poking into wasn't my own. Not a new place, a new sister.

It's too much. Then there's her fixation with readings and signs and wonders. Maybe *she's* too much.

Can I do the entire summer I promised? I hastily reach for the old domino set I will cherish forever. And protect, too, as well as the man who owned it protected me. *Las fichas.* I clutch the frail balsa wood box, willing it to be true that safe words don't stop working when children turn eighteen. That they change instead.

Jada pauses her wardrobe organization, eyeing the dominoes. She gives a flat smile before pulling a cloth sack from her second bag. "I travel light. But I always throw in a few things to make a rental feel like mine." A navy love seat and a double bed. An IKEA end table and matching tiny dining table—that's what comes in Ivonne's furnished casita. It's purposely bland and functional. But I watch Jada unwrap golden votives and a crystal picture frame. She holds each item briefly before deciding on a place.

"Why not just have an actual house?" I ask. "Don't you miss having somewhere dependable, where you don't have to set up objects each time to make it feel like home?"

A shadow passes over her face. "No house has ever meant dependability for me. The first time I felt real safety was the day I left . . . well, you know. And then I just kept going." Jada reaches for one last item, a glass sparrow. "My friend owns a ranch in Arizona. She lets me use a renovated art studio on the property for storage and a physical address. It's where I land between longer trips. But not for more than a few weeks, just to take care of any business or medical appointments. I don't *live* there. My passport is my real home."

We stand across from each other, conflicting ideals and mismatched birth certificates, even entire worlds turning between us. But we're both holding on to objects so tightly, our fingers clamped over the raw materials. Into the energy, if I believed the way she does. Mine—the domino set—grounds me into my safest place. Hers has wings and feathers, fitting perfectly into what I know for sure now. She'll fly away in August.

Jada's stomach growls. "I skipped lunch. Ivonne confirmed with Elena about the vacancy this morning. Then I was packing up, and they sent your dad to get me from the hostel." She rests the sparrow figurine on the dining table and helps herself to Ivonne's snack tray.

I pick up the bird, admiring the swirl of color inside the round belly.

"That's Murano glass. From Venice a couple years ago."

"All you'll get in LA is Venice *Beach*."

"On my list." She piles fruit, meats, and cheese, then takes a cocktail knife and spreads the dip Ivonne made onto a cracker. "What's in this concoction?"

I join her and fix a cracker and spread for myself. "It's guava jelly mixed with cream cheese. Popular Cuban appetizer. Puerto Rican, too. Lourdes and I grew up on it." I taste the simple comfort food and note, again, that Jada is leaning against the counter to eat even though there's a table right here. "Something even Mamita can make."

"It's so good. Watch me eat the whole bowl." Jada rests the plate and wipes her hands on a blue dish towel. "Look," she says, "I need to come clean about something. I know you said not to speak of *her*. But I left out some details Saturday because my arrival was already so—"

"Just say it. I'm officially asking you to."

Seconds pass before Jada faces me. "Vanessa's ask for closure, and to reach out to give you the money, wasn't exactly her idea at first. I may have . . ." She shakes her head over a grimace. "No, I *did* influence her."

"What do you mean?" The wooden floor planks lose their form. I yank out the chair and sit. "It's your fault she wants me to call her? That she's holding out this money like a carrot?"

Jada moves to the other side of the table, grasping the top of the empty chair. "After her confession about you, I was the one who brought up the word *closure*. My father had recently died. Just before, he called me to the hospital. I only went out of curiosity. I was healthy and whole, and he was dying of liver cancer, so I felt powerful around him for the first time. But I got something different. I told you I like surprises? Well, surprise, Jada, here's some genuine remorse from that bed. And *wow*."

She ducks her head a little.

"He apologized for the home I'd had, for being a terrible father. Gave me his house, too. I accepted that and said goodbye without ever excusing his actions. It was more about releasing us both from the space we were in."

"Vanessa isn't dying," I say.

"That was my point in Barcelona. I challenged her to not wait until she was. And to release enough light into the darkness."

"No, I get it. Without me giving her closure and accepting her gift, you're afraid whatever bad luck happened in Spain is gonna start up again. What's next, breaking out in hives or your stuff going missing? A blizzard in LA?"

Jada visually shudders. "I wasn't exaggerating, Clary. Or joking. The feeling of dread was overwhelming."

"Sure, okay," I say over an eye roll. "Listen. It's not like *you* shouldn't believe in whatever's leading you or spooking you and Vanessa. But you're using it to try to influence me. To fix *your* problems!"

She steps forward. "I promise I'm not trying to manipulate you or play you. I mean, you haven't asked if I thought about keeping the money for myself and telling Vanessa I was going to donate it or something. I know you're thinking it."

My eyes pinch tight, and I don't know what irks me more. That she's right, or that she keeps anticipating my feelings. "Did you, then?" I say with some hardness.

"Fuck yes, for about five minutes." Jada barks a laugh. "Who wouldn't?"

I have to respect the blatant honesty—*this* I'm down with. I'm still reeling from the harsh lack of it in my own home. "What happened on minute six?"

One corner of her mouth jerks upward. "I saw the big picture. The money wants to be good, and the energy of it centered me real fast. This money is not my good thing, Clary. It's yours. Señor Montes gave it out of genuine care, and it *wants* to go to you. After I put this idea out there, Vanessa and I both felt a positive shift. I believe it led me here. I don't for a second think that I found you, or got this place today, just because of luck."

Once again, this is beyond me. Miles away into a cosmic realm I can't even imagine. "Okay, let's pretend this is all true. Shouldn't these signs match up with how I feel?"

"And how is that? Put the words out there clearly."

For the second time today, I'm not manifesting anything. I am simply answering a question. "My family has done perfectly well on our own. Nothing changes now because of some closure and misguided money."

"Um, no." She traces the empty far wall before settling on me. "It's very much guided. I'm simply declaring how I feel, too."

"Whatever. I asked my dad for some time, and I'll take it." I jab out a finger. "You can tell Vanessa that word for word. And she better not show up anywhere near LA to see *you*, when she . . ." I trail off, unable to complete the thought out loud. But it's still here, pressing against my lungs.

"She came back for me, and not you," Jada says. "We should probably hash that out."

I go into snarls. "No, we shouldn't! How many times do I have to say that I never wanted her life? See, it fits with me not wanting her check. And I'm sorry that means that I didn't want the only childhood you had. But I can't even process that because I didn't know about you."

"I didn't know about you, either," Jada counters. "And I'm glad for what I saw in your living room Saturday. Your home is the absolute real deal." She leans in. "You never wanted her to come back—that's cool. But it's still okay to admit that you wanted *her* to want to."

The thoughts that connect all those dots in my head are everything but okay. "I can't. We literally just met. You haven't earned that conversation. *We* haven't."

"Fine. But I'm on the same side of surprise sisterhood as you, so we're even. Maybe think of it this way. Vanessa probably thought there was no way she was getting past the Wall of Delgado. My walls could've killed me, Clary." Her eyes flare, tearing up at the corners. "That was, like, the lowest of the bars for her to rise to."

"You have to resent me for that," I whisper.

"Oh totally," Jada starts, and right when I spring up from the table, she gives an odd, chaotic laugh that stops my feet. "Ten years ago," she stresses, "I would've despised your guts."

"And now?" I force out, my jaw set like stone.

"Now I know my life unfolded exactly the way it was supposed to."
She throws both her arms out wide. "I'm a traveler—destined to be. I
believe that as much as I believe in the way I was led here. And you
were destined to land in the best home ever. The best family."

"Who kept the truth about you away from me." I grip the edge of
the table. "My walls aren't feeling so strong lately," I say, even though
Jada Morrison hasn't earned that admission, either. Stronger walls
might've kept my words in better.

"Families lying? That's another thing we share."

The words land like an elbow to the gut. Too real, too close, and
my head is already blazing. "I don't . . . I can't talk about this anymore
today."

"Understood."

My phone rings inside my bag. It's Lourdes, also known as
good-timing Lulú.

"Clary," my friend begins, but her words tumble out in fragments.

"Hey, breathe. You're in Rose Two and what?" All my heartbeat
knows is something is wrong.

"Ambulance," Lourdes chokes out. "There's an ambulance parked
between LRB and the bike shop. Mami Elena had me gas up Rose Two.
I just pulled up and . . . ay, a fire truck is coming."

A siren wails in the background. "Who?" Mamita? Abu?
"Lourdes!"

"Sorry," she says. "I'm all shaky and no one in your family answered
the shop phone or their cells. I need to park. I'll find out what happened and call right back. Just come quick."

Jada steps up. "I heard everything. Should I get you an Uber?"

I grab the domino set and place it into Señor Montes's photo box. "Faster to walk. It's not that far."

She nods, arms crossed over her chest. "Go. And keep me posted."

I take off with the box through Ivonne's side gate. For the few moments that are mine alone before Lourdes calls, a frantic prayer lives on repeat in my head.

Dios, not them. Not one of my people. Please.

And when I reach Sunset and run-walk east, random thoughts come together. How I wish I could move as fast as Emilio. And how convenient it would be to have a bike right now. And how I wish I even knew how to ride one—something I've never told him, or anyone.

Finally, Lourdes rings back. I hit the green button, rushed by a sense of apprehension bigger than this whole metropolis. "Tell me."

Eight

*F*ernando Avalos. Not my abuelo, or my dad, but Emilio's father. This is all Lourdes was able to find out by the time I'd made it halfway to the shop. When I reach our corner, the ambulance and fire truck are gone, and Mamita and Abu huddle by our front entrance.

"What happened?" I yell as I cross. Onlookers trickle back into cafés and stores.

Mamita reaches me first. "Fernando fell off a ladder. He broke his ankle and wrist."

"Since when do you call an ambulance for a broken ankle?"

"No, mija." She tightens the strings of her green canvas apron. "He had numbing and tingling on one side of his body and lost his balance. That's why he fell. He hit his head también and blacked out for a few moments. Dominic said Fernando probably has a concussion."

Señor Avalos is the injured one. But my mind only whisks around the image of our fellow business owner. I can't help but picture another face and how terrified he must be. *Emilio?*

"He rode with su papá in the ambulance," Abu says.

My head jerks up. *I said that out loud?* "Um, right. Okay."

My abuelos lead me inside the shop. "We saw him when they were wheeling Fernando into the back, and he was crying," Abu adds. "Pobrecito."

Many times, I have seen Emilio cheer and swear and grumble. I've seen him laugh with his head levered back toward the heavens. I've seen the exact moment when my words or my very existence tips him into total frustration. But I have never seen him cry.

"Flowers . . . I mean, I should bring an arrangement to the hospital from all of us." It's what we do.

"Wonderful." Mamita gestures toward the bike shop. "Go ask Dominic where they are taking Fernando. I don't want to bother Wendy now."

I feel a stab of sympathy for Emilio's mother, who also teaches at the same elementary school as Lourdes's mom. They're friends. Even in vast LA, I really do live in such a small world. "What about Mami Ynez?"

Mamita's mouth slips into a thin line. "I should wait. I'm not sure if hearing from me now will make anything better for Ynez."

"But that's her son!" And *this* is not the woman I know—the one who gathered me close at ten days old without a second thought. Mamita didn't wait. I trap her gaze; I'm the one who won't let go this time.

Finally, she huffs. "Sí, I will call. Maybe I'll get voicemail."

I thrust up my hands, then use them to make something beautiful.

Hours later I'm at Los Angeles General Medical Center with a vague idea of where I'm going. Conversing with Emilio-cohort Dominic was a feat in decoding grunts and murmurs while he tackled a frame repair on rush order. Best I got, the broken ankle and wrist have been set, but Señor Avalos has a severe headache. Doctors are still trying to pinpoint the cause of the other symptoms and assess the head injury.

The fifth-floor clerk looks up from her computer. "I'm sorry, dear. Only family is permitted to visit at this time."

Dom left out this detail. I rest my Desert Dawn arrangement on the reception counter. The soothing blend of pale peach roses, lilies, silvery dusty miller, and succulents is secured inside a bamboo cube. "What about this?"

"We'll make sure it gets to his room," the clerk says, and fingers a white lily. "This is much more unique and detailed than the arrangements from our gift shop." She scrawls the room number on a sticky note and flags an orderly to deliver Desert Dawn.

"Thank you. I made it at my family's florist shop." I reach for one of our business cards and slide it forward.

A text from Dominic buzzes before I can call the elevator.

Dom: Hey, you still at the hospital? Any word? Don't want to bug E right now

Me: Still here and none. Only my flowers got past security

Dom: In that case, you do know about the secret cafeteria cinnamon rolls, right?

Me: What? Here?

Dom: No time to explain. Run! They only make a limited batch. Legendary

This is all I need to sign off and beg the elevator to hurry.

Ten minutes and five dollars later, I'm holding a Styrofoam plate with a cinnamon roll that might be bigger than my head, and I owe Dominic Trujillo some kind of reward. A stealth finger swipe at the register confirmed perfectly sweetened icing. The couple behind me actually gasped when I took the last one on the tray.

They were also out of boxes, which means I'm eating a cinnamon roll for dinner at a hospital cafeteria table, and I'm only moderately fazed. After last weekend and my earlier showdown with Jada, my "shock-o-meter" has a new redline level. But I take one forkful of the warm, yeasty dough, swirled with cinnamon and a perfectly executed roll-to-icing ratio, and wish life held more of these kinds of surprises. *Hospital cafeteria cinnamon rolls. Who knew?*

"I knew."

The familiar voice slips over my shoulder. His uncanny hearing aside, I really, *really* need to quit letting my thoughts escape out loud.

Emilio steps into my view and tips his chin. "Hey."

Emotional strain and stress do different things to a body than overwork. His posture slumps, and he's half lost inside gray jeans and an oversize black sweatshirt. The usual golden, earthy shades of him are off. Faded and creased. "Um, hey."

What am I supposed to say? We've been known to spar over Spotify stations and how much taco filling inside a shell is acceptable. This night is not that. "Your papi?" is the only way I know to start.

"Resting and waiting for another doctor. It wasn't a stroke or his heart, which were the first concerns. No tumors, either."

I exhale in relief.

He acknowledges it with a grunt as his hand flicks out. "Hope you're enjoying that."

My gaze ping-pongs. The roll. His face. (I'd totally misread his eyes. That's longing and regret swimming in all that grassy green, not worry.) The empty tray by the register—oh. *Oh!* "You came down here for a cinnamon roll, and they're . . ."

"Sold out, yeah." He gives a wry laugh. "You win, Thorn."

I *win*? He thinks I'm relishing some score? "How could I have known you wanted a cinnamon roll? I came to bring flowers for your dad."

"I know. They're nice, and they made my mom smile. Anyway." He salutes, pivoting away.

"Wait."

Emilio halts.

"This thing is easily the size of two normal cinnamon rolls. We can share." I rise, urging him into the other chair. "Do not bail," I add, because you never know with him.

I run to a service cart and set Emilio up with a plate and utensils, plus a cup of water from the dispenser.

"Hydration is key, Wheels."

"'Kay." He points to my own ample napkin stack, then to the double-tall supply I brought for his side of the table. "Really?"

What? I sit, feigning innocence, and push my plate toward him. "You do the splitting honors."

"Thanks. It does look good." He slices through and takes his share.

"Can confirm," I say. "Wait, you took the half I already ate from." Didn't he notice the finger-shaped trench in the icing?

He shrugs, digs in, and barely swallows before saying, "I'm fine with living dangerously."

Sometimes I set my own traps. I ignore the outcome of this one with commendable grace and cut into my portion. "Did Dominic tip you off about these, too? God, they really are the best ever."

"Dom? Nah." He downs half the liquid from his cup. "They're all over this foodie site I lurk on. The USC med students are prime consumers, but most people don't want to deal with the whole hospital situation to get one. Plus, the vibe can be tough." He lifts up, eyes hooded. "Can confirm."

"They still don't know what caused the numbness and loss of balance?"

"Short answer, Papi has a bad migraine, but he's not in any immediate danger," Emilio says after a pause so long, I wasn't sure he was going to answer at all. "Look, there's more, but I think I just need a minute for it to gel."

"You don't have to say anything else." Like I'm one of his trusted confidants anyway? It's more that I'm here. Clary-convenient. Just like Saturday night when I was *there* inside a huge white van with bad driving and good timing. Sharing my cinnamon roll is simply another way I can help this horrible situation besides arranging blooms. If I flashed him a mirror, even he'd acknowledge that a little bit of sugary dough has nudged some color back into his cheeks.

"So, about the foodie following," I say. "Your state food map doesn't name a hospital cinnamon roll as its California pick, right?"

He snorts. "Not even. The map is way less niche. Opinions are split, but California's is noted as either avocado toast, which is down-right grievous. Or fish tacos, which is correct."

I concede with a wave, unable to disagree. Which kicks my mind sideways. "Especially the ones from Señor Fish."

"From Ricky's," he counters.

And there it is. I was getting worried.

Emilio's abandoned his fork in favor of attacking his pastry with his fingers. He's also gone through at least three napkins and has a nice little pile in the works. "What?" he says to my self-satisfaction. "They're thin. Like ghost napkins."

"Mm-hmm." And then I say, "Food map. Montana."

"Huckleberry pie."

"Sounds yummy. Illinois."

"So easy, Thorn. Deep-dish pizza."

I wrinkle my nose. "Naples-style thin crust is so much better. But you do you, Illinois."

He recoils. "I'll pretend I didn't hear that. Like, I'm ready to pick up my chair and move to that table over there and finish this fine cinnamon roll without your culinary bullying."

"Our seats are literally bolted to the floor." They do swivel, though. I swing myself back and forth a couple times. "But I'm sure you'd find a way to escape with one."

I brace myself for his comeback. I get down two more bites and a couple sips of water, and he's never this slow.

He's staring at the table as if the turquoise Formica's keeping deep secrets. Lips curl under; he's stopped eating. He pushes his plate sideways with two bites still left. Now I'm really concerned.

"Are you okay?" I ask. "I mean, besides the obvious?"

He fiddles with the (only two) remaining clean napkins. "I mentioned the flowers but didn't thank you. So, thanks for making the arrangement and bringing it all the way down here. And mostly for just thinking of my family."

Twenty seconds ago I probably said something off, but I don't know what, and now he's thanking me. I'm never quite sure where I'm going to end up in an Avalos-Delgado conversation. Apparently, we're back to flowers, which is fine because I do all right in that zone. "You're welcome."

He lets out a one-note laugh. "Knew it was La Rosa Blanca material even without a card."

"Huh? I put in a card."

"Maybe it fell off on the way over," he says.

Yes, but that's not what sends a stir through my stomach. "You still knew I made it?"

"No carnations, for one."

The stir grows into a whirlwind. "I . . ."

"You hate them."

Has he been mentally cataloging my arrangements over the years? What kind of guy does that? I'm certain I've never told him. We never make it to the carnation realm during our talks, if you could call them that.

"It fits with other stuff you've done, too. Like, the aesthetic. It's good work."

Now I'm scared. I shouldn't be. With his father upstairs and injured, Emilio's not trying to outwit or trap me. So, what is this?

"You mean good, even though you still think flowers are best when they're left in their natural habitat? What do you call it—valleys over vases?"

"Even though," he stresses. "But you left out the disclaimer. That my valley-over-vase notion is subjective and not some knock against your business or skill level."

I break out a little smile, but it fades when Emilio's roving glance lands on me and stays. His face changes, dimming then darkening. Mist gathers over his long eyelashes. And this little table with its bolted-down chairs and mostly eaten cinnamon rolls has no more room for one-up digs. Whatever's swirling inside his mind, we're both going to think it's terrible.

"MS," he says.

"What?"

"That's the something more I was talking about. Papi might have multiple sclerosis."

Nine

The hospital clerk waves at me from her information counter, and I return it. I'm back on the fifth floor, banished to the same receiving area after Emilio's mom called him up. Before her text, before we scrambled out of our chairs and tossed sticky plates and napkins, he'd only gotten through a few of the harsh details. So far, I've learned that Fernando Avalos has recently been experiencing too many possible MS symptoms for doctors to rule it out. He'd felt slight numbing and tingling on one side of his body earlier that morning but brushed it off and got distracted with work. Later, the fall happened after he'd felt more numbness, tingling, and weakness, which caused him to lose his footing on the ladder. More frightening, an MRI showed a small brain lesion—MS's most glaring marker. But even that's not definitive because Señor Avalos also has high blood pressure and a history of occasional migraines, which can cause similar lesions in scans.

After I hit *send* on updates to Lourdes and Dom, Emilio strolls out from the hallway.

"Hey. Turns out Mami just wanted me there when the financial rep came up," he says, and zips up his sweatshirt. "They're keeping Papi overnight for observation, and I'm going to hang a little longer, but I need some air. The nurse said there's a garden." He presses the down button on the elevator. "I'll fill you in more and make sure you get to your car."

"That's okay. I walked through that courtyard when I went the wrong way out of the parking garage. It's totally on the other side of the hospital. I'll go myself."

The doors open; we step inside. "This neighborhood can be sketch," he says. "Plus, it's dark out."

"But well lit. With alarm station things posted everywhere."

We sink lower and lower, silent for the rest of the ride. It isn't until we reach the lobby that Emilio steps out wide in front of me, halting. "Humor me, por Dios. You're good at that. My mom knows you're here, and she'd ream me if I didn't play Avalos Escort Services." He snorts. "And no, not *that* kind of escort."

"Clearly. But is that an offshoot of Chisme Rescue Services?"

"Not even close."

Still, he brought out the Cuban Mami factor, which grinds my argument to a halt. "Fine. Watch her ask for photo proof of the two of us by Mamita's Prius."

"Would be funny if it weren't true."

The exit doors swing open to a Los Angeles June night doing its best at being predictable. Cool and balmy. I'm glad I changed from a tank to a stretchy long-sleeved top with gray and white stripes. And Emilio was right about the mood. Visitors come and go, their faces painted with countless emotions. A lone woman weeps against the wall, and I gaze heavenward, mouthing *gracias* for Abu and Mamita at home reading and doing puzzles.

"So, about your dad? You did say MS isn't hereditary, right?" I'll never forget Emilio's abuelo, suffering for years with the type of severe MS that took mobility, and speech, and then . . . everything.

"It's not necessarily hereditary, like some cancers, but Abuelo's health history does factor in." We reach a walkway bordered by hot-pink azalea shrubs and lit with lanterns. "It's hard because there's not one test they can do. Mostly, diagnosis starts with ruling out the other conditions MS can mimic, one by one. That could take weeks, if not longer. They're gathering baseline data of his brain imaging and vitals. And he has to start a daily symptom log for doctors to monitor him and note any changes."

For me, it would be next to unthinkable to walk out with discharge papers and not know what I was facing for sure. I stride next to Emilio with a gash across my heart. "I'm sorry," I say.

"Thanks. Me too."

"Not exactly the post-grad summer you were expecting before college."

"You have . . . ," he says over a choked laugh. "You *really* have no idea."

"About unplanned, unexpected summers? Try me." This slips out unconsciously with too much Jada and complicated money invading my thoughts. I do a quick check to see if Emilio's even noticed.

His mouth parts, one brow dipping as if he's looking for words. Or maybe he has them but remembers how we usually end up.

The four-story garage hails around the next curve. "I'm good from here," I tell him, pointing. "Blue Prius, straight ahead."

"Yup." He pulls his cell to mock-snap a picture for his mami, and the playful gesture almost makes me trip over my white Chucks.

I'm no snoop; I'm standing close enough to tell he's missed a voice-mail.

He presses *play*, drawing the phone up to his ear.

"Greetings, this is the British Airways callback center. We're sorry we've missed you at your designated call time," croons an operator with a deep English accent.

British Airways?

Emilio jerks the phone away, his face instantly flooded red. He'd pressed the speaker button by accident. "Shit," he mutters as the screen shifts. But it's too late.

"Please call again to reschedule your upcoming flight or utilize our online interface," the operator continues. "Good day and we hope—"

Emilio finally manages to cut the replay, swearing again under his breath.

I'm slack-jawed, trying to catch up. His flight? And why didn't he want me to hear? "Your family was going somewhere? I mean, before tonight?" His papi's fall and injuries are the kind that wreck vacation plans.

Emilio's head hangs low.

I back up two steps. "You don't have to say any—"

"Not my family." He looks up. "Just me. Solo."

British Airways isn't an airline you take to Chicago for their deep-dish pizza, or to Montana for huckleberry pie. "What, like a graduation present? To . . ."

"To London, for a start. And yeah, sort of." He drops onto a bench a few steps away.

Am I supposed to follow? Leave him here by the parking garage?

"I might as well tell you everything now." He hooks one hand onto his face, dragging downward. "Can you swear to keep this to yourself? I mean not one word to Lourdes. And for the love of God, not to anyone with the last name Avalos. Especially my abuela—or yours. Porque qué pena if Mami Elena finds out. She'll use this somehow—you know those two." Mid-ramble, his blush fades to blankness, leaving him the kind of pale best reserved for bridal gowns and snowstorms. Not faces.

I march over. "What did you do?"

"Swear it, Thorn."

I flop onto the bench and raise my right hand. "I will not tell a soul, on my hatred of carnations. And on my love of the Cubano sandwich, which is, in fact, better than the Milanese."

"Wrong, but I'll take it." He opens his photo app and scrolls to a picture of a huge travel backpack and a smaller day pack. "I've been hiding these in my closet for a month. And saving up for two years. The trip was a graduation present to myself."

"Oh, you were going backpacking in the UK for the summer."

"And all over Europe. Anywhere I wanted."

I instantly think of Jada, but for only a flicker. "Why are you hiding everything?"

"Because no one in my family knows about the trip." He sighs. "I was going to tell them this week and leave next Saturday. Dominic knows, and the other guys from the shop. They were gonna cover for me. But now I need to cancel the flight and try to use my dad's

emergency to not lose a shit ton of money—hence the airline call."
His hands wring together. "And it wasn't just for the summer. I'm not
going to school in the fall. I canceled my enrollment at City College. I
was planning on being gone for almost a year."

My insides flare, and I can't help but spring up, physically turning
away. I don't know where to put the revelation. This is not a summer
escape; it's an exodus from his entire life.

"Well?" he asks. It comes out gravelly and low.

I shake my head. Refuse to turn.

"I bet I can guess what you're thinking right now."

"Oh, you can?" I all but spit toward the garage. "I don't even *know*
what to think."

"Nah, you do. You're thinking I'm an ungrateful, irresponsible dick
of a son. To leave my family like this. To wait until the last moment—
playing their frugality—so nothing, not even their guilt trip, could
make me change the flight. And how could I leave the bike shop to
Dom and the crew? Drop out of college and abandon that business
degree I'm supposed to get so I can take over the shop?"

I pivot, but only halfway, glaring. "You forgot the part about Echo
Park."

"What part?"

I finish the turn. "You forgot how our history works. Your family came over right after mine. They escaped terror and left Miami
for Echo Park full of hope and unknowns, with nothing. *Nothing*,
Emilio." Emotion beads between my lashes—not for him, but for all
we have here as Cubans, and for the small bits of us we lose every
day. "But you? You wanted to lie and ditch a place of opportunity that

others have built for you like it doesn't even matter. Your family set you up with *everything*!"

"I know, Clary. I've *known* that, just like you said. Through every paycheck I stashed. Every secret." His chin wobbles. "And if that makes me a villain, then add it to your shit list. I'll risk it from you, or anyone."

I dash my hand out. "Why?"

"Because I have no clue who I really am. Which doesn't mean everyone else around here hasn't tried to decide for me, with all their labels. Let's start with dutiful Cuban hijo and nieto. There's high school poster model and homecoming king. Heartbreaker." He rattles his head. "They call me golden boy in two languages, and most eligible, and *most likely to* . . . Take your pick. That's on me, wherever I go. No matter how fast I am on two wheels."

He paces along the short space.

"Next we got bike shop pro. Business heir." He halts on his blue Vans, spinning. "And now that I graduated, I wanted to go off on my own. Go off all these fucking grids and see who I am, not as the Cuban guy who works on bikes on Sunset Boulevard. But simply as myself."

"Okay, but now that Varadero Travel is gone, there are only two original Sunset Cuban businesses left. Your bike shop and my flower shop," I point out. His older sister, Esmé, lives in Florida with her husband. She worked for her family in high school, but that was it. Emilio is the last option to carry the place forward. And now if he doesn't, the business and building might remain, but its ties to our Cuban history here would sever. "You would actually sell your shop? Just let it go?"

"I dunno, maybe? You really believe that just because I'm good at fixing bikes and helping Papi create his custom rigs, that automatically means it's my lot for life? What if it's not?"

A future for him without bikes is almost impossible for me to imagine. There's rarely a time this boy isn't attached to two wheels and a triangle seat.

"Lately I've been feeling I'm not ready to commit to taking over ABW. But here's the thing—I am not saying I'm *not*, either. I just want to be sure, without my family reminding me every day about expectation and duty. I want to see the world and let it show me if that place is really my future. What if there's a better one I can't see for all the smog in this city?"

"Oh . . . wait." I shake my head, a light flicking on in the middle of my skull. "This is why you climbed out of Mami Isabella's window instead of dealing with her scheme. You weren't even going to be around for the aftermath."

"That was part of it. And you've been right across the street since we were kids. Can't you see, even a little bit, why I need a break?"

I stack my spine. "What I see is that going on your secret gap year was apparently worth hurting your family. You could've talked to them."

His eyes darken. "It's cute you think they would've heard me. Anytime I even hint at other options, or taking some time to travel, or maybe exploring other majors in school, I'm reminded of where I come from and what puts food on our table. And how I am tied to that and expected—heralded—to do my part. They don't jibe with any *gaps*, Clary." He rakes a hand through his hair. "For a few months, I wanted to know what it's like to visit a place and not leave more than foot-prints. I wanted to come and go and feel like an anonymous no-name for a while."

Anonymous. Nameless. Sin nombre. "I want every opposite of that," I tell him. "I want my name to mean something and last. But I don't have to leave our neighborhood to do that. It makes me want to press in more, to do more here."

"Yeah, well, the same place that holds you close traps me, Thorn."

This whole time, I've been trying to figure out why his stance is so hard for me to ingest. Talk about knowing things, knowing what to expect—I have known this Emilio since childhood. The one fleeing churches and windows and sticky situations. If he's only trying to be a more extreme version of the person he always was, why do I care?

And why does *he*, about making me see his side? As if he's balanc-ing on my words. As if my opinion matters. "We can't agree on a sand-wich, Wheels. Why tell *me* and trust me to keep your secret when—"

"Will you? Keep it?"

"Every word," I blurt. It's another thing I do. I stick. I keep my promises.

"Good." He shrugs; our bodies make distorted shadows along the paved walkway. "And about trusting you. Well, I . . ." He trails off.

"Now?" The noise I make is almost a gasp. "I stump you *now*? You're finally admitting defeat?"

"Let's not go that far." Emilio lets out a rough breath. "It's more, I can finally unload some of this guilt to someone who's used to being irritated by me. Same as it was, you know?" His eyes flash clean and green in the lamplight.

"Yeah," I tell him. But the flicker of sympathy that sneaks in, for him, for this, is anything but familiar. "Just don't think I approve of what you were going to do. Or that I can't picture Mami Ynez and your parents if you would've gone through with it."

"I don't."

"I do get why you wanted to go now. And I am sorry you're stuck in a place you don't want to be."

"And terrified." This is so soft, I almost miss it. But the words come up clearer than anything ever has between us.

Ten

*T*he next Friday afternoon finds me cross-legged on my bedroom floor with Lourdes, sipping the milk tea with boba Emilio hates. With the last four days since the hospital packed with corporate event arrangements, a much-needed beach day, and polishing up Señor Montes's other work on the historical preservation application, it's time to sift through his old photos to finish the last piece.

Fifteen minutes of recon around my neighborhood and online confirmed what Lulú and I found out at the dog groomer. Hole Punch Donuts is coming, but they're opening a Buena Park location first, which means there's still time to save the beach mural. Even if we can't influence Hole Punch legally, the Echo Park optics would totally shift if they're planning to demo native Latino artwork in a district with a brand-new Historical Landmark plaque. Optics are everything in business, and I'd bet a thousand roses that Hole Punch won't want a social media storm calling out their blatant disregard for culture and history. Or a red *CANCELED* notice stamped over their kitschy lined paper branding. I need to submit this application as soon as possible.

The earliest pictures laid out in front of us are faded black-and-white squares. Later shots, from around the time my family arrived from Cuba, preserve time and people in muted color and matte texture.

On the registration form, Señor Montes signifies our barrio as the Little Havana of California. Echo Park became the smaller west coast bookend to the Florida landing spot of so many Freedom Flight airplanes, full of exiled Cubans. Our people trickled in when they could and found one another as we commonly do. We learned, worked, and thrived in the commercial district with Sunset Boulevard cutting through like a pathway to economic promise.

The Sunset district was small in area, but great in spirit and influence, he writes in the section reserved for historical narrative. *It launched enterprises that went on to prosper elsewhere in the city, and beyond. It kept the secrets of a displaced people, plotting and fundraising for counterrevolutionary measures at the Echo Park Lions Club. It housed the rally cries and demonstrations of the anti-Castro community. "We were here,"* *this street says. Our legacy marks sidewalks and storefronts; it is already preserved.*

These were the words my dad helped polish—ones I've typed and added to the application. Lulú and I choose three of his photos to scan and annotate, hoping the images illuminate the sentiments Señor Montes so lovingly penned.

Circa 1963: Six Cubans huddle in front of the old
Saint Athanasius church site where they met for
English classes in loose suiting and A-line dresses.

Circa 1969: A young Salvador poses with his friends inside their newly established travel agency, a poster held proudly in his hands.

Circa 1976: A ceremony that packed the park. A bronze bust of Cuban revolutionary and poet José Martí is unveiled in Plaza José Martí, steps from Echo Park Lake.

Before leaving for work, Abu contributed a color photo of the day his in-laws moved into La Rosa Blanca, well before Papi and Tía Roxanne came along, and years before they expanded into the neighboring storefront to create the larger space we inhabit today.

"I can't believe she started your business in their garage. Your bisabuela," Lourdes notes, squinting into the photo.

Back in Cienfuegos, Bisabuela Margarita and Bisabuelo Jorge had a small flower shop. When they arrived, Jorge worked for Gaviña Coffee, where he met Señor Montes. And Margarita began selling her creations on their street. As Cubans began hosting gatherings and parties, they wanted to keep their business in the neighborhood. My bisabuela took over the one-car garage and got another secondhand fridge. Mamita helped with arrangements after school.

I take the photo. "From street stand to Sunset."

Lourdes sips her tea. Chews on the sweet and squishy boba. "Because centerpieces. There was a *need*."

I laugh. Don't even bother throwing a true Cuban fiesta without at least one centerpiece. "That rule keeps the lights on at our place." I hold on to the thought even after it leaves my tongue. "You know, they got shit for our business name. It was fine for the Cuban community—naming your shop after a famous Martí poem. But the old landlord feared it would deter a wider range of customers."

"Tell that to Lana Candela and the gown that could've housed a small country underneath," Lourdes says over a chuckle.

As you enter our shop office, a signed photograph hangs of the eighties Hollywood starlet. Her voluminous wedding gown is accented with the white rose, ivy, and orchid cascade bouquet Mamita designed for her. Lana kept asking for *grander* and *bigger* and *más* each time Mamita showed her mock-ups. The final version clocked in at ten pounds and probably caused an elbow injury for her maid of honor, who had to hold it during the full-length mass.

But La Rosa Blanca won out. Lana wanted to honor her Argentinian roots by choosing a Latino-owned florist for her superstar wedding. We got the gig, and the press. The wedding made the pages of *People* magazine and every bridal publication. Even a one-line mention of us as one of the vendors helped secure new hotel contracts and countless events. Musicians and local politicians became regular clients.

"All we need is another famous bride or two to level us up again," I say, with my future lingering in the aftertaste. Lourdes stays quiet, and I whip around.

She's studying a withered copy of *20 de Mayo*, the newspaper that served Los Angeles Latino communities from 1969 to 2013. La Rosa Blanca and Avalos Bicycle Works were featured many times until printing shut down. Lulú and I found this copy in the box, but only briefly glanced at the little caption noting Señor Montes as the employee of the year at Gaviña Coffee.

"Three more pictures were stuck inside." She stacks two on the carpet. "Those are just more of the lake." She smiles and places the third color photo into my hands. "But look at this one. Your fave."

It's Sin Nombre, shot as close as Señor Montes could manage while fitting the entire mural into the frame. Even time and old tech can't dull the power and pulse of the anonymous woman dressed in white. The purple hyacinths in her hand, the green snake and goblet. "I should include this one in the submission. Even Mamita and Abu don't have a picture of her this early."

Lourdes scooches over and nods. "I looked, but the artist isn't written on the back or anything."

"We know him. When I did that project, I found out Juan Rosario was one of the Freedom Flight Cubans. The Lions Club commissioned this mural, but he died, like, twenty years ago."

I decide to scan the photo and frame this copy for my desk, next to Señor Montes's old domino set. But as for the other pictures fanned out across my carpet . . . "It feels wrong putting these back in that box. I wish I could do something more with them."

"Keep them safe for now," Lourdes says. "Like you do my heart and soul."

"Weirdo."

My phone rings; I drag it over and see Mamita's name on the screen. "Hey," I say, and before I can tell her she's on speaker, she goes forth, full speed.

"Bueno, Clarita, Sandra and Sofia are here for the quinces final consultation. Where are you?"

"Um, at home working on the community project, not being late for the meeting?" I rise, gathering the photos into a pile.

"It's me, Mami Elena," Lourdes says. "Wasn't our appointment in twenty minutes?"

"Ahh." One, two, three seconds of silence. "Sí, pero they are here now. Sofia is playing with Rocco in the office. And your mother has champagne and she's catching me up on *Pasión de Gavilanes*." One, two seconds of silence. "Because I am not watching it that much anymore. Anyway, just come down."

After Mamita cuts the call, there is a flicker of time in which Lulú and I feed each other twin looks of bewilderment. It snaps, we grab our stuff, and we talk as we walk.

I start with "She's early? *Your* mom?"

And then Lourdes says, "She has maybe one drink every month, and Mamita has her on that velvet couch hitting the bubbles. In the afternoon. Discussing shirtless dudes bent on avenging . . . something evil."

I secure the house and stow my janitor keys, and we scurry over to Blue Ivy in the driveway. The blue Subaru has a few years on it, hence no power locks. "Mamita's idea of not watching *Pasíon* that much is bingeing it while doing her puzzles."

Lulú ushers me into my shotgun throne and runs around to click in. "My mom watches it when she cooks." The engine revs. "It's a joy."

I barely hear her. Lourdes's car carries something savory in the air. One more sniff, and I've caught her. "Oh my God, you had Señor Cluck's. You said you were cutting out fried foods for a month to see if it would help your skin."

She glares.

"You *said* you've been sticking to it—mentirosa!"

"I had a coupon."

In our world, that explains enough.

Lourdes steers us down the hill toward La Rosa Blanca. "Besides. Sometimes people lie."

Only for the Colón family would I give up part of my day off to accommodate their schedule and help with Sofia's quinces ball flowers. We also agreed to handle all the decor and theming to save the family money in hiring an event planner.

Only because I know the Colóns nearly as well as my own family am I not surprised when Sofia decides to change the entire theme *seconds* before it's time to place vendor orders. Lourdes is perched across the fabric-swatch-and-scrapbook-covered coffee table as "Autumn" from Vivaldi's *The Four Seasons* plays on. An *I told you so* look twists up her features.

"I don't want to make stuff hard for everyone," Sofia says. "But I don't want to be a mermaid anymore."

Props to Sofia Colón. She knows who she is and who she isn't. And Fia is not a mermaid. The fourteen-year-old *is* a mini Lourdes but keeps her dark, center-parted hair trimmed right beneath her shoulders. Both share a love for vintage denim, which causes many thrift-store battles.

"Fia, you have to tell Mami Elena and Clary what you actually do want," Lourdes says.

"Let's start with the most important part. Did you order a new gown?" Mamita asks.

Sandra snorts. "Not even. The dress stays. It's gorgeous and it should arrive any day now." She rummages through the scrapbook and shows Sofia's cornflower-blue chiffon gown with a beaded illusion neckline that would've suited the mermaid theme perfectly.

"It's like all my friends are suddenly doing ocean or beach themes," the birthday girl says. "I want my quinces to feel unique and special. But now I don't know how."

I take a second to mourn the beautiful mood board I'd dreamed up for mermaid Sofia. Tables with shells, coins, and faux jewels spilling from treasure chests. A twisted vine-and-shell arch for pictures. Strobe lighting for an underwater feel.

I scoot forward and catch Mamita topping off Sandra's champagne flute. The mujeres shrug gleefully. I need to work fast. "We can do this. When brides come in with no idea what they want, we have them make a list with two columns to get a feel for their taste." I bend around and grab a yellow legal pad. "On the left, list random things you hate. Think of songs, colors, fabrics, movies. Stuff like that."

I glance up absently; my view through the side picture window leads right to the entrance of Avalos Bicycle Works. And right there, under the striped awning, is Jada. I told her I needed a few days to let my new reality settle a bit more. She'd actually listened and hasn't even texted. But what is she up to now? I regroup, puffing out a single breath. "Um, right. For the other column, try to come up with something you like for each hate you listed."

The trio gets to work, but my attention falters again as Dominic strolls up to Jada, chatting. He's always rocking squarish glasses and nut-brown hair, but today's blue collared shirt really sells his Mexican Clark Kent vibes.

I lean into Mamita, whispering, "What's going on across the street?"

Mamita sticks her neck forward just as Jada follows Dom inside the shop. "Huh. She came by to see our place and mentioned renting a bike for the summer, but that was this morning."

And now *anything* could be happening. Jada went from hostel to prime casita in two days. I purposely block her out and focus on my work.

Soon after Mamita and I clear the Colón job file of anything mermaid, Sofia hands over her list. I start with the hates, noting her dislike for wearing pink, snow or cold places, catty girls, sports, horror movies, and most bugs.

I flip to likes, an idea budding inside my head. Sofia wrote: castles, books, going on trips, her best friends, old Disney movies, thrifting, the color blue. At once, I see it all—grand and detailed—as if I'm in the center of a decked-out ballroom gazing over the finished product. "A library," I say.

Sandra stares at me over her bubbly crystal flute, and the room arrows onto me, perplexed.

"Tons of girls have done *Beauty and the Beast*-themed quinces balls."

"It's my favorite Disney movie," Sofia says.

I grin. I do not suck at this. "Yeah, and you love reading. It's totally you. But instead of the yellow ball gown and red roses most girls pick, we can make yours unique. What if we do Sofia's Library, based on the one from the movie? Your gown is already blue, like Belle's market dress with the white apron."

Sandra leans forward, intrigued.

Mamita claps her hands. "Ay, this is so cute."

On my iPad, I show the group pictures of book-themed center-pieces. "You can order vintage books by the foot." I face her mother, the writer of checks. "Already I can tell it's more reasonable than most decor options. I can order lots of old books and combine stacks with French country wildflower arrangements for the tables. I promise to stick within the original mermaid budget you already set."

Sofia's eyes are moon-wide. "I love it."

Lourdes slow-claps with arms raised high.

With the new theme settled, Lourdes has to drive her sister and champagne-buzzed mother home in Blue Ivy. The Colóns let me have free rein on the Belle's library concept, which is more than I would've given any vendor for my own event. I'd insist on photos and a mood board and samples. Overwhelm me with every detail, please. The fact that they've left Mamita and me with their full trust means we need to get it right.

We divide up tasks, and Mamita moves to the office to work up a new job form. But I stay on the velvet settee and let my imagination out. At once a single starting image blooms into two ideas, then four, until an entire aesthetic comes. Jotting and sketching, I trap the details before they vanish. In countless events I've worked, brides and party-goers say the same thing when the big day comes: it went by so fast.

Mamita says this, too, about me. She'd swear it was only fifteen minutes ago that she picked up my little baby arms and legs as her daughter. Five minutes ago that she dressed me in frills and curled my hair into bouncy spirals.

Clarita de mi corazón, she'd sing as she worked with sections of deep brown. *Bella Clarita, Clarita. Clarita de mi corazón. My heart, my heart, my heart. The beautiful girl of my heart.*

Seventeen years whizzing by in a blink.

But here, another task floats over my work and into my head—unwelcome. A FaceTime or phone call with a stranger that could literally take five minutes but feels fairy-tale cursed to last a thousand years.

Eleven

An hour later, with my La Biblioteca de Sofia plan fully detailed, I have every intention of hitting my first stop for cool library materials. My feet have other plans. The *What is Jada up to?* kind.

I move the opposite way along Sunset, right into Avalos Bicycle Works. The bell dings as the shop greets me with the pungent scent of grease and tire rubber. No customers are here now, but my arrival brings Mami Ynez out from the back.

"Hola, chica," she says. "Emilio is not here."

What? "I . . . Okay, thanks." Despite the fissure between her and Mamita, Mami Ynez has always been kind to me. Still, Ynez loves to "remember" key details regarding my personal business to "mention" later with Mamita. Today her work here is clearer than her assumptions. She's toting a covered casserole dish. Emilio's mom often cooks lunch for the crew during her summers off from teaching. Her mother-in-law pitching in today makes perfect sense.

I march up to the counter. "I'm sorry about Señor Avalos," I say, deflecting away from her *other* family member.

"Gracias." Her mouth shifts into a bland smile. "He is resting at home and hating every second of not being around his bikes. The flowers you brought were very beautiful."

Bikes. Flowers–Sunset. I'm reminded about a key item missing from my preservation packet. "Doña Avalos, do you have a photo of this shop from around the time your husband's family started it? I'm working on a historic district project." Her brows dip, and I add, "I only need to scan it. I'll give it back."

She rests the dish and smooths back her chin-length hair, tinted a light golden brown on clockwork rotation with Mamita's darker shade. "Ay, Elena did not tell me of any projects. And we are involved? She can be so busy with her secret workings, no?"

I speak Ynez-Elena well enough by now. She thinks Mamita is trying to one-up her again. "This was an idea Señor Montes had before he passed. I'm just taking it over for him."

Her face thaws a few degrees. "Ahh, I see. For el señor–okay. I will be seeing Elena tonight for the social committee meeting, and I will find a photo to give her."

This should be fun, I'm thinking as she exits with a curt farewell.

Dominic appears and fiddles with the computer, squinting even with his thick frames. "Oh hey. Emilio already left."

Okay, that's it. Did Emilio say something about me? I'm quite sure *Seeking Emilio Avalos* is not printed anywhere on my forehead. Even though girls from school might be in the habit of dropping by for "bike shopping" while secretly trying to catch the attention of the lead maintenance guy around here, I'm definitely not one of them.

"Not Emilio," I stress. "I'm looking for Jada. My sister." The word still sounds weird. "I saw her come in earlier."

"Yeah, sure. Jada!" he yells through the archway. "She's filling out some forms in the office."

"Hold up!"

The voice fits, but nothing else makes sense. Is this my new lot? To live in a constant state of confusion? I spin around, weaving through the rows of display bikes in all colors, sizes, and prices. Half the world thought I needed to know that Emilio isn't here. But it's hard to separate him from this place and all these wheels.

Jada materializes in a white cropped tank and wide-leg jeans that are one wash away from disintegration. Lourdes will covet them. "Clary! I was wondering when I might see you next," she says, with no trace of tension left over from our last conversation.

I give a throwaway wave. "Mamita said you came in here for a bike. This morning?"

Dom snorts as he disappears into the back. I plunk my elbow on the glass counter, feeling the patience seep out from my skull.

"Technically true. I caught a nasty stomach bug a couple days ago. All good now, and I wanted to get out and visit your flower shop," Jada says, brightening. "Of all the trades I've picked up, flower arranging isn't one of them. Maybe you can teach me—"

"Why are you standing behind the counter like you work here?"

"Because I do. Starting Monday." When she sees my face redden from a lack of information, not oxygen, she barrels on. "Right. So I came to see if this place does summer rentals, and Dominic said they don't. But he mentioned his uncle owns a used car lot in Culver City. And after a quick call, Emilio drops me off at the lot, and I leave with the *sweetest* 1998 VW Rabbit Cabriolet." She pulls out her phone and shows me a picture of the bright red car with a white top. "One of the band members from when I was little had one, and I loved it. After all these years it came back to me." She stows the phone. "I got a rental deal in my budget. Just for the summer, of course."

Of course.

"On the way there, Emilio and I got to talking about Fernando's injury, and that they might need some temporary help with the front counter."

"Which is perfect because you're only temporarily here, too." It comes out harsher than I mean it to.

Jada jerks away slightly, her gaze landing over my shoulder. "I see it more as two needs finding each other. The car was a cool surprise."

Because surprises are stellar when you're talking about red convertibles. Not so much when they're unwanted parts of your past, or tightly kept secrets. Or if you're Emilio and your escape flight is grounded into a time of extreme worry and uncertainty.

"Want to see the VW? I had to park about two blocks east."

"Sure." It's the way I'm going anyway.

What starts as a walk to Jada's rental car, which is admittedly awesome, becomes a mini tour of this part of the Sunset commercial district. Strolling with Jada, I begin to see how she gets things for herself. Needing to work on el señor's project and Sofia's quinces, I probably would've said I was too busy to agree to a full walking tour. But my sister operates need by need, little by little, getting a win and building on it. This method has gotten her a network and a casita, a car and a summer job. And now, a native tour guide who is full of facts:

La Economica shop was here. Mamita and Abu came with their parents when they were younger.

El Carmelo restaurant had the best Cuban food.

This was a bank . . . a toy store . . . a jewelry store.

When we reach Sin Nombre, I share the mural's history. Jada approaches the painted concrete, her head level with the subject's knees. She hovers a palm over the brightly painted surface without touching it.

I remember her thoughts on energy. "Is she telling you secrets?" I ask, half joking. "I made up a bunch of stories for her as a kid. I wonder if I was right about any of them."

Jada jerks backward, and I gear up for all things supernatural. I still don't buy into my sister's mystical ways, but I'd be lying if I said I wasn't a tiny bit curious.

"She's your favorite," she says.

Chills erupt along my arms.

"She didn't tell me that," Jada adds. "You did. The way you were talking about her."

Oh. My pulse stills. I nod.

"The application you're working on—I get it. I would want to save her, too, and that beach-and-bird mural. And everything around here."

We edge back onto Sunset from the cross street. "But you'd still move on," I note. "You wouldn't stay, even if a place meant as much to you as Echo Park does to me."

There's a quiet pause. "That's how I've always saved myself."

The words don't even fully land before Jada halts.

"A thrift store? It's so close to the flower shop, I'd come all the time."

We've made it to Marlow, home of secondhand bargains and vintage treasures. "I do. This is the place I was heading to earlier." Or trying to.

Owner, Neil, changes the window display as finds come and go. Today a cozy reading nook is set up the Marlow way. A turquoise trunk coffee table holds old magazines and a blue-and-white tea set. A tall, baby-pink shaded floor lamp flanks the corner. But the object at the end of Jada's dreamy expression is the piece of furniture next to the trunk: a club chair in peacock-blue velvet, trimmed with brass rivets.

"That," she starts, "is perfection in a chair. Look at those claw-feet."

She's right. It's in great condition, too. "Why don't you get it for the casita? It would fit in the corner."

Jada purses her lips. "I couldn't bear to leave it behind when I go."

No way of life is perfect. But the regretful shadow crossing her face over one blue chair marks a definite con to her traveler ways. Jada tears away and follows me inside the shop that greets us with a dozen scents. Lourdes once said it wouldn't feel right if the place smelled like Nordstrom. Marlow casts a disorganized cloud of musty wool, tarnished silver, and vinyl. Lavender, and lemon wood polish, and sun-bleached cotton.

"Miss Clary Delgado!" Neil calls from a stepladder, waving with his duster. "No Lulú today?"

"She's banned, remember?" By me. For being annoying in here. And spending five hours trying on every single pair of jeans.

The owner snorts. "Then I won't mention that new Levi's batch."

He covertly gestures with his head to an antique dresser, drawers hitched open to house neatly folded stock.

"I see nothing," I quip, pivoting to introduce my new companion. I've already lost her in the vast hoard of curiosities. "That *was* Jada. My, um, sister."

"I'm back here! Nice to meet you, Neil." Her voice sounds from the clothing section. Jada pokes around a carved partition, waving a corduroy vest on a hanger. "I found my happy place."

Neil hops down and folds the ladder. "That's more like it."

Now it's time for business. "Do you have some old, cheap paperbacks I could cut up for a craft?"

Neil taps the blond stubble ghosting over his chin. "That reminds me. I got a box in last week but haven't put them out yet. Hold up."

While he heads to the storage room, I'm happy to poke around one of the few places where I can enjoy the fun of something unknown. Inventory changes daily. I wander to a curio of clearance items and mentally work out my vision for Sofia. With centerpieces in mind, I grab a small brass owl and a box set of silver votives. Reading glasses? I hadn't thought of these, but I find two pairs of old specs.

As I pivot, it's clear I should've put the glasses on because not only did I miss Jada returning from the clothing racks, but I also totally missed her climbing right onto Neil's elevated window-display ledge. Not just ogling—she's *in* the blue velvet chair, knees poking toward the sidewalk. And I'm only marginally surprised.

I plunk my finds on the counter and march up. "Um?"

"I had to try it out." She gestures with one hand and fronts a brazen look that could defy the universe. "There's no sign saying I can't be up here."

Is this the logic she applies to everything?

"A perfect fit," Neil says behind me, unfazed that my sister is in his window doing an impression of the latest vintage find on Sunset. "I'd grab it while you can. That one won't last."

We watch Jada contort herself out of the cramped space without so much as a thread brushing against the delicate tea set. Neil gapes at me and I shrug, suspecting years of yoga at play.

She hops down effortlessly, even on platform wedge sandals. "I can't take the chair, but as long as we're both here, I'll come in and enjoy it. We'll say goodbye when it's time."

I suppose that attitude fits as well as Lulú's vintage overalls. This is how Jada is with every new city. With a new friend, too, or a sporty red car, or a blue velvet chair. Her entire life is rented by the day.

A few minutes later we leave Marlow with Jada's corduroy vest and my white shopping bag filled with three old paperbacks and the center-piece sale items. Neil is also going to pull all specs and reading glasses, and anything library*ish* that comes his way over the next couple weeks.

Neil's also the reason we're walking the opposite way from the flower shop toward Echo Park Lake. Yes, Jada has been, but only briefly after the non-memorial. No, she didn't realize how close of a walk it is. Yes, it's such a perfect LA afternoon, and why shouldn't Clary take her down there?

So here we are. *Thanks, Neil.* He couldn't have known I've just learned this girl even exists. Or about the drama she's brought, or that I've only been referring to her as sister because it's easy. But the truth is, I don't know how to make room for Jada Morrison, or what that even looks like. Where is she supposed to *go* in a life that's been working perfectly fine?

I told Jada it was okay for her to spend the summer in LA. But now I'm living that reality. I've learned just how differently my sister and I do life. We've shared some brutal words, and I've held back hundreds more because of that niggly trust factor. But also, we've hung out. Unlike Emilio and me, we've shared some space without arguing, even though we don't always agree. She's working on my street. We've been *shopping*—something Mamita and Tía Roxanne and I do. This is usually how people build relationships, and, God, this is so strange.

Meanwhile my blond visitor is happily bouncing down Logan Street toward the park. Carefree and taking everything in. Listening and absorbing the vibe. And like the blue chair, she is here today, and I am here today. If *I* listen to mi barrio, it tells me to cross the street with open eyes. To look both ways. More than Señor Montes's safe word, I have an entire safe zone. I follow the kinds of cues that keep me from hurting. Right now, that means I can try *being* close to this new sister without getting too close.

Jada gestures to the bag. "What are you doing with those paperbacks?"

I give her a thirty-second recap of the upcoming quinces. "I'm going to tear out pages and make book-page roses for Sofia's bouquet and for the boutonnieres and corsages. And hopefully more for the centerpieces."

"Sounds like tons of work. Maybe I could help."

I can be close. "Yeah. Sure."

As we enter the park, rewarded with a wide view of the glittering lake, Jada gawks at one of Echo Park's biggest tourist attractions: the swan pedal boats. "So cute!" she says, turning to me. "Do you ever rent them?"

Now, at the height of summer, dozens of white swan boats track leisurely through the water. "Not since I was a kid. They were my favorite, but I haven't been in years."

"Why not? From what I've picked up about Lourdes, this would be just her thing."

"Lourdes goes with her sister, not me," I mutter.

"Do you get queasy or something? I dated a guy in Antigua that couldn't even handle a raft without getting seasick." When my brows hike, she adds, "Let's just say my attraction falls on whomever I'm attracted to."

"Got it, and nope. Iron stomach here." I gesture toward the path. "Let's move on—"

"Clary, you obviously like them. Life is about taking time for fun."

"I'm waiting, okay?" It tumbles out. I didn't want to reveal my reason for being swan-less in Los Angeles, but I've already learned enough about Jada to know this girl does not quit. She just gets things. "I have an idea in my head about how I want it to be. And I'll wait for that."

Jada's mouth slinks upward, catlike. "Is it boy-related?"

Big sigh. "The swans are kind of fairy-tale romantic to me. I've always wanted to go with someone special. I know it sounds ridiculous, but I've built it up in my mind forever. The first guy I dated lasted, like, two weeks, and we never made it down here. And, well, dude number two thought the boats were childish. Not his scene."

"Got it. Holding out for what you want is not ridiculous. It's a form of self-care."

I've never thought of it that way. "Okay."

"But if you like the boats, go on the boats. Don't wait for some guy to grant your wish."

I don't wait for *guys*. It's more that I hold out for moments. Still . . . "Noted."

Finally, she drops the subject, and we stroll along the outer edge of the dual forked path separated by ribbons of grass. Sky-high royal palm trees mark the way toward the playground and the little grove hosting the José Martí bust. Not only were native Cubans transplanted here, but so was Cuba's national tree.

Jada shields her eyes with one hand, gesturing toward the access road circling the park. "Isn't that Emilio?"

Well. We've found the boy everyone thought I was looking for, and the one Jada introduced herself to this morning. The fact that Emilio hasn't asked (read: pestered) me about her is as much a testament to the current state of our being as any billboard. Apparently, we're all here now, with a kid zooming away from him on a bike.

"Yes, Tony! You got it, man!" Emilio calls from about ten yards away, pumping his raised fist. One of his road bikes rests at his side. "Circle back and show your mom."

Tony curves around on the sidewalk, wobbling a bit as he glides back to Emilio. A brunette in purple scrubs trots over, sidling up to the bikes.

"We should say hi." Jada strides toward the group at the perimeter. All I can do is follow, making her the new tour guide. I never signed up for this tour.

Emilio gives a chin lift at our approach, then another at Tony's mom.

"Thank you so much for everything," she says, holding the bike helmet out to Emilio. "You're sure I can't pay you?"

He holds out his palms in refusal. "That's a gift, and so are the lessons. Call it my local kid special." He turns to the boy, who looks about eight. "Be safe out there, bro."

Tony smacks Emilio's palm for a high five. Mom and son head out, and my chest squeezes around this entire scene. Emilio teaches kids how to ride bicycles. Strange that I didn't know this. Mamita might even call it un-Cuban. What doesn't travel along the usual Echo Park information channels is subsidized by the chisme club, of which Mamita is a card-carrying member. I wonder if *she* knows.

I snap back to the park and find Jada showing Emilio pictures of her summer car.

"Wow—nice. Dom came through," Emilio says.

"Thanks again for the ride earlier," Jada says. Her phone rings before she's even stowed it. She holds up one finger and steps away.

Which leaves Emilio and me sharing a single patch of concrete, the awkwardness-aftermath of the hospital wedging between us. I break first but pick an easier subject than Jada. "I didn't know you gave lessons. That's really decent of you."

He leans a bit on his bike. "One less reason to be irritated at me?"

"Don't worry. Your inability to accept one simple compliment takes care of that."

"Do-over," he says, which is weird because we never start over. We unravel. "Yeah, I've been giving lessons since freshman year to neighborhood kids." He hikes up the sleeves of his gray Henley. "My man Tony doesn't have a bike—his mom borrowed that one." Emilio breaks into an unexpected grin. "Which is why I can't wait to drop off the brand-new Crimson Fuji he's getting next week."

I can't help but match his smile. "For real? How?"

"You know those racing teams we work with? Papi and I got them to sponsor our local program. We give good-quality bikes to kids who can't afford them."

"That's . . . well, it's the best." I shift my weight on my Chucks. A quick check on Jada shows she's gesturing widely, lips moving over the phone at warp speed.

"And all this time you thought I didn't give a shit about our community."

I gasp. "That's not what I said. Ever." Or, at least, not entirely. I knew our do-over was too good to be true, but I realize he's just walked himself into a dead end. "Okay, then explain this, Wheels." I lean in because I still keep secrets. "You were planning on bailing. What about Tony and any other kids you're teaching?"

Not even a flinch. "Didn't take on any more, and today was always gonna be his last lesson."

Hmmph. "His new bike. Next week?"

"Delivered by Dominic. But I'll do it now."

Hmmph.

"Looking like the jerk poster boy seems to come easily around you. But I'd never let down those kids." His thumb grazes over his handlebar, back and forth.

Oh, but he would let down his family for a plane ticket and the clarity of being alone in this great, wide universe. I open my mouth to call him on this. His stare stops me short, but it's not locked over my face or the length of my body. Following it, I reach the cluster of royal palms, their deep-green fronds waving freely. So high, it seems they could touch the small puffs of clouds moving with the breeze.

Jada appears, breaking into my thought before it becomes a trance. "Hey, Emilio, when was the last time you went on the swan boats?"

What?

"Eh—probably like six years ago."

She reaches us. "You don't think they're childish? Maybe too far out of your scene?"

This is not happening.

"Heck no." He chuckles. "They're classic."

Jada beams. "Excellent. Because I feel like playing tourist, and all of us should go."

I want to scream. I just told her why I've been saving my swan-self. But it's not like I can say that *now*. The sheer intensity of the shade Emilio would throw—no flowers could ever grow there. I settle for lobbing my strongest glare her way. "Maybe another time. Plus, they're kind of expensive."

Jada waves her hand. "My treat, and it's such a gorgeous day. How about it?"

Who knew it would be up to Emilio to get us out of this scheme? Because, of course, he'll decline and maybe even politely. I'm totally certain of that.

"Sure, I'm game," Emilio says, and locks his bike onto the rack near the park entrance.

Por Dios, I officially know nothing.

Twelve

*I*t's tragic enough that we're in the swan line, but Jada's been entertaining Emilio with traveling stories. Entirely unsurprising, he's been firing endless rounds of questions. (Favorite city? Best airline deals? Worst food ever?) Emilio Avalos is salivating over Jada's globe-trotter life more than he has over any cinnamon roll.

While they're occupied, I snap a picture and fire it off to Lourdes. Situation. Me, Jada, EMILIO

She replies with a stream of emojis. Then, NOOOO, but your dream swan boat experience?

This friend of mine gets my entire world. RIP the experience, culprit: Jada playing tourist

It's okay, amor. You can replay the experience. But damn she is a force

I tap a red angry-face emoji into the screen and click off. At least it's almost our time to ride. We reach the last portion of the dock, and an attendant scans our tickets and hands over three life vests.

Jada rests hers against the railing, then holds up her phone. "I'll be right back. I just need to return this call. Same friend in Arizona—she's going through a mega breakup." Before I can fully process, she snakes out of line and under a bushy tree.

Emilio shrugs into his orange vest. "So, your sister. Um, wow, for starters." When I thrust out a hand in concession, he goes on. "It makes me wonder how many other people have secret siblings. Probably not as uncommon or shocking as you'd think."

"Not shocking? Speak for yourself."

He nods once, and for a flickering moment I sense that he might actually understand a little of what I'm going through. But time rushes on, and we sway into that motionless, wordless zone we know too well. Where the journey from thought to speech is near impossible.

Ten seconds pass, and Emilio gestures absently. "Jada's nothing like my older sister. And I'm not even talking about her lifestyle. Just the way she deals. Esmé is more about worrying I'm working too much and not eating enough, which, I mean—please." He snuffs a laugh. "And trying to sleuth my dating situation. But I guess that comes from her being eight years older."

"I'm sure you keep her busy." I fasten my last buckle and grab my Marlow bag from the dock.

"What's that supposed to mean?"

My cheeks heat to flaming. "I, um." He doesn't usually clap back with such obviously fake vulnerability. Luckily a surge in the line bails me out.

We step forward until only one couple remains in front of us. I turn to motion Jada back over, but the space under the tree is empty. "Do you see her anywhere?"

Emilio gets out of line, stretching up and around. He returns, shaking his head.

Keeping track of a child is easier. I send her a text. HELLO boat. Now

I wait, and wait, double-checking the service bars, but receive no reply. "I can't believe she just left." After this being her idea and a direct violation of my wishes, she ditches us? The irony is enough to send me off this dock and into the lake.

We're up; the attendant leads one of the large swan boats in front of us.

Emilio's holding the tickets and a scrunched nose. "Maybe her friend needed more help?"

The dock attendant waves his clipboard. "Folks, I got a crowd here. You boating or not?"

Are we? Jada already paid thirty bucks for our tickets. Apparently, my frugal self is louder than the one who's protesting that her swan-perfect experience turned into a what-the-swan *something* with her biggest neighborhood irritant. "Should we just ride?" *Jada, you will pay for this.*

Emilio gives a flat shrug. "Yeah, we've already waited forever. What the hell?"

This—this might come close. The swan in front of us is downright huge, with a canopy. "It's only the two of us now. Can we switch to a smaller boat?"

The attendant scoffs. "You talk like they aren't all rented. It's big mama swan or no swan."

"Big mama swan is absolutely perfect," Emilio says, giving a firm rap to the frame. "It's obvious you saved the finest swan for us. Much gratitude."

Where did *this* Emilio beam in from? My wonder doubles when he steps onto the boat with enviable smoothness and reaches for my hand to help me into my seat. His palm is strong and calloused from work and gripping handlebars. "Thanks," I say, and toss my Marlow shopping bag behind us.

After a grand push-off, this should be as easy as I remember. Physics all but promises our pedaling should create movement, but once again we prove we're best at the opposite of how things are supposed to be. We're more cartoon duck going nowhere than elegant, gliding swan.

"Wait, no," Emilio says. "You're going too slow."

"Or you're trying to go too fast."

Emilio huffs. I huff. Both of us have stopped pedaling, and the boat bobs around with the small current created by other swans that are actually traveling. There's a big spray waterfall feature in the center of the lake, and we're drifting perilously close. The watery date of my dreams would never go like this.

Finally, a text comes in from Jada. I am SO sorry. Christie was a mess. I wandered over by the Martí statue and the lotus flower beds while on the call. So cool. I saw you two out there. Walking back to the VW and going home. Have fun!

All my insides are grumbling. I don't even reply.

We coast around for another minute before Emilio chuckles. "We can't be this bad, Thorn."

I sneak a peek at him. "Little kids are out-swanning us."

"Okay, do-over," he says on a thick sigh. "It's not the pedaling. It's about rhythm."

"That's the problem." Since Sunday school.

"Pretend you're here alone. Just pedal the way it feels natural. Even close your eyes. Like I'd let us crash."

Closing my eyes violates every preemptive maneuver I've used with this boy. But if we do crash, it's on him, and I can stow the dig for later. So I lower my eyelids and move my feet, discovering my own perfect rhythm. Clary Ann Delgado speed.

Soon the resistance lessens. I'm gliding with afternoon sunlight and a water-tipped breeze flowing in, warm and summery. I inch my eyes open; Emilio's feet are pedaling in perfect time with mine. He caught my pace.

"See? Now we're the best swan out here." He exhales a long stream of air. "Man, I forgot how much of a stress reliever this whole lake is. Different from riding around the access road."

I can't help but think of his dad. "Mami Ynez said your papi isn't adjusting well to being at home."

"He calls the shop constantly, 'Pero just to check in, okay?'" Emilio imitates. "We're not taking any more custom orders for a bit, and hopefully he'll be back soon to advise Dom and me on finishing up the three already in progress." Fernando Avalos is known for his bespoke, top-quality racing bikes and usually runs a wait list. One of the dreams Emilio was escaping was mastering this trade to carry on his father's craft.

"I hate thinking of what could happen if . . ." He trails off, angling away. "Even a less severe form of MS might mean the end of our custom program."

"Which maybe you don't want to carry on." We turn into a panoramic view of downtown LA, its skyline gray and heavy with steel and glass.

"Maybe not," Emilio says. "I feel like I lost my chance to find out for sure. Guilt aside, I'd still do anything to be on that plane." He hooks a crooked glance my way. "Listening to Jada go on about her travels—I'd like to take that life out for a test-drive." Emilio's steering our boat with the little lever between us. His hand tightens on the black knob. "That's wild that she just shows up in LA after all these years."

My foot slips, and I lose our pedaling rhythm for a beat. I didn't even consider that Emilio and Jada spent at least a half hour together going to get her car. She promised not to give *Vanessa* any details. But what did she say to Emilio beyond a basic introduction?

"Thorn?"

I turn, and his eyes are wide and deep and green. They almost look kind. "Did Jada tell you why she came now?" As soon as the words race out, I realize I should've just kept quiet. I'm better than this with him.

"Whoa, what nerve did I hit?"

"What did she *say*?" I press.

His face tilts as if he's searching through the ages. It was four hours ago. "Uh, mostly that she only just found out about you and wanted to meet her half sister."

I exhale, nodding. "Okay."

"Then why do you have on your not-okay face?"

I flinch. He knows my faces? I try harder to look happy. Centered. Straightening my features. Pedaling mama swan like a pro.

"Now you have on your telenovela face."

I cast a long look. "That is not a thing."

"Is so, and you've done it before. It's when there's something huge going on but you try to push it away and act all stoic and strong. Classic novela. All you're missing are the stilettos, but those aren't good for swan boats."

A strangled noise leaks from my mouth. *Why is he right?* And here I thought Jada was tiptoeing too far into my energy field. Emilio Avalos is downright trespassing. "Listen, there's a lot of drama in our past, between Jada and me—our family. But this new . . . thing blows it all up."

"I figured. But don't forget the other night I told you the biggest secret I've ever kept."

My tone sharpens. "Which means I have to tell you a secret, too?"

"Do-over." When I relax into my seat, he says, "You didn't think twice when you promised your silence. And yeah, I only told you because you were there, but I'll admit now that it totally helped talking about my trip with someone who . . ."

I motion him onward. "This should be good, Wheels."

He shakes his head. "*Firstly*, with someone who knows me well enough that I didn't have to explain everything I was feeling."

"Lourdes is my someone, and she knows what's going on."

"Naturally, you told her. But she's like your other half, so she doesn't count." He holds up two fingers. "Hence the second part. It's also telling someone who isn't so *close*-close that they can't give an unbiased outside opinion, but only if you want one."

I cross my arms. "You're saying that if I tell you what's going on and ask you not to comment, you actually won't?" Which is new, which he knows.

"I actually will not." Emilio holds up one palm. "Las fichas."

Our old safe word. It's impossible to pedal away the significance.

We've reached a smaller section of the lake, like a balloon-shaped inlet. Without saying anything, we both stop pedaling and just drift inside the quiet and still. "There's also my own code," he says at length. "Same as you promised me. If you want to tell me because I happen to be here, too, it might help, and it won't leave this lake."

I have to believe him—we don't abuse codes. Plus, history tells me that sharing my secret won't really disrupt anything, because Emilio and I will always be one avenue apart. We'll never merge. But today it's like he's saying there are times when we cross paths in Echo Park. Just for a moment. Sometimes it's to argue about parking. And other times, it's a longer stop, in a white boat where the rest of the city can't hear us. "Family stuff sucks, Emilio."

He swallows hard, nodding. "Family stuff sucks, Clary."

After a deep breath, I say, "It's about Vanessa."

"Your mother?"

"Mami Elena is my mother."

"I knew that—I know." His head shakes. "Sorry, for real, okay? I'm already blowing your swan safe space. If it helps, I already feel Montes and his heavenly side-eye."

I snort, waving him off. "Nah, it's my deal. I've never called Vanessa . . . that. Never will. And it's always been fine to let her exist in some other dimension because, *believe me*, I can't even remember not being perfectly fine inside my family. But then Jada swoops in."

Emilio cracks a smile. "Swoops. That fits."

"Yeah. So she moved into Ivonne's place and got a job at your shop and"—I pause, scrambling for courage—"and brought a message I didn't want to hear." This is how I start, treading inch by inch until I'm baring my entire soul to the unlikeliest set of ears. It happens in a place I'd saved for a different boy—one who doesn't always dream of fleeing. One who stays. Today, though, unless Emilio's fine with a murky lake escape route, he's here to listen. And as he listens, I talk, more and looser about Barcelona and Vanessa's thievery after my birth. About closure, and my family's huge omission, and one simple phone call that will change everything.

"So that's what's up," I say in closing, sinking into my seat. I could be the newest mural model for a piece entitled *Oversharing Cubanita on Echo Park Lake*.

Emilio, on the other hand, stayed unusually quiet throughout my tale, reacting to the stickier parts with widened eyes or long fingers scratching underneath his chin. Some words were enough to part the hinge of his mouth, and for others he averted his gaze just slightly toward the pointy orange swan beak at the helm.

"Holy. Shit." This is all he finally says, with his arms held out in a helpless gesture.

And I do something that surprises myself. I laugh.

No, I do, and then I outright *decay*, cackling louder and louder because of that initial break and burst. Because even though stories like mine usually bring out tears, mine are the other kind, where you can't believe one weekend switched your life into a living telenovela.

Everything with Emilio turns out opposite.

What I've got is contagious in this boat. "Why. Are we laughing?" he chokes out.

My hand splays over my chest, and I shake my head back and forth until I'm twisted and wrung out clean. My face burns hot and sweaty. "God, I don't know, and I don't care."

"What are you gonna do?"

The soft words get me a different way, throwing off the meter of my pulse. I breathe myself back for a few moments. "Are we talking about what's best for my family? Or my nonexistent college fund? What's best for our shop if we have a bad month and can't bounce back fast enough? Those things?"

"Nah. All the other things."

"No clue what's gonna happen with Jada and me. She just got here, and I'm—we're not used to each other yet. Not even close. As for her message, I already have a mother and more than a roof over my head. I don't want anything now that Vanessa didn't want to give a ten-day-old newborn."

"Damn." He scrubs his face.

"Right." Without speaking, we start pedaling again. The motion helps. "My dad gets that. But he also said I should rise up and take what I'm due from Vanessa."

"That's how the world usually works," Emilio says. "Or at least I think it does. I'd know more if I could see more."

That strikes something inside me. "Backpacking around, I bet you'd come across a thousand people who could take that money, and it would mean the difference in their survival. That's the other voice I hear." I face him. "Like, who the hell am I to be so proud and entitled?"

He leans in, opening his mouth to speak, but catches himself.

"What?"

"The code. I'm not sure you want my outside opinion. You need to say so."

He actually asked, which makes me even more curious. I know Emilio's traps; I try to get out while I can. But today I told him my secret and all the parts that go with it. I'm already *in*, too deep inside this shallow lake. I motion him on.

He makes a play like he's cracking his knuckles. "On the one hand, why the fuck do you have to give someone closure who's never come close to earning it? Like, Vanessa plain doesn't get to ask for anything after what she did. She's holding the money she *stole* and using it as leverage. It's manipulative and super narcissistic."

My eyes spring wide. "It *is*. And now she doesn't have Señor Montes telling her I'm okay to ease her conscience. So she has to try another way."

"Totally." He exhales. "But see, here's the other side. I know your family. They're good people, Thorn."

"The best," I say. It comes out scraped. "But they hid Jada from me all those years. It's . . . unsettling."

"Sure, but that's part of my next point. They made a hard choice with your sister—that must've been super unsettling for them, too. And they've sacrificed for you. Maybe you can do the same."

I poke out my hand because he just ruined it. "So I *owe* them? God, is that how love works to you?" I knew I was right about this. About him.

"That is not what I'm saying!"

I whip around, my breathing labored.

He points forcefully. "You twisted it."

"What did you expect me to think? And don't you dare say 'do-over' on this." Our pedaling hastens. We're the fastest swan around.

"Not a chance, because I wasn't wrong." Even a handful of virtual eye daggers don't stop him. "Clary. For chrissake, you don't owe them. Mami Elena made you her daughter because of love, not obligation. But it was probably extremely hard. As was keeping someone important hidden if it meant protecting you. All I'm saying is you don't love them any less. You'd protect them. And you'd do really hard things for them, too."

Abu and Mamita. Papi and Echo Park and our flower shop corner on Sunset. I would like to say that I'd do *anything* for them. I put that dedication and drive into Señor Montes's historical distinction work. It's in my hands when I make a bouquet, and in my every desire to leave a lasting mark on this world. I do my best with what I've been given. "You aren't wrong."

"Which isn't the same as being right, because you'd never admit that."

"Never." My lips ghost into a flat smile. "I could pick up the phone and do one hard thing for less than five minutes, not because Vanessa deserves it. But because the love I have for my family is bigger than my un-need of her."

"Yeah, that's pretty much what I meant, even if I pissed you off more than helped."

I roll my eyes over a quick laugh. "My dad said take some time to work everything out, which I still need. But you didn't *not* help."

He points a playful finger. "That's totally the same as helped."

I give a shrug. "I didn't solve anything, but I'm getting used to saying the words out loud more."

"Yeah, same. With my situation."

Multiple sclerosis. Labels. Obligation. Identity. Those are his words, and I probably didn't change anything around them, either. But I heard them. "Thanks. For pretending you know nothing after we dock."

"About what?" He winks, and I'm not sure I've ever seen that in all the years we've had. "Hey, what happens in swan boats—well, you know. Also, Jada's convertible is awesome, but two wheels are better than four for working stuff out. So get on your bike—that's my next unsolicited suggestion."

I nod quickly.

"Huh." One eyelid wings low. "Why am I just now realizing I've never seen you on a bike? Like, even when we were little?"

And here we go.

"I'm, uh, not a fan. I prefer walking." This sounded so much better in my head.

"Really? Maybe you don't have the right set of wheels. Your sister gets an employee discount, and I could help fit you into something way better."

I grab my Marlow bag and pretend to be extra busy checking to see that all my purchases made it in. "Oh, that's, um, cool. I'll think about it."

"Why are you giving me your changing-the-subject face?"

Damn his FBI facial recognition skills. I was not going to admit this. But I already know what's going to happen. Emilio is going to talk to Jada, and Jada is going to turn into *Jada 5000*, which means an array of bicycles in rainbow colors are going to show up on my front lawn, and I will have to get on one. She'll want to video it, and the whole deal will not end well. "I don't know how, okay? I can't ride a bike. I never learned."

"I . . . oh." He bobs his head in thought. And that's all? Well. He's showing more grace at my revelation, at my hot-coal cheeks and curled-under lips, than I expected. Still, I am mortificada.

"I didn't know," he adds.

I grumble, still mortified. Still pissed at myself for having no way out of this trap. "No one outside my family knows. And before you ask, it's a long story, but I hit my daily storytelling limit five minutes ago."

"I could teach you."

"I don't think so." I hold up my arms in a victory pose, the best at being the worst at bike riding. "No one was ever able to teach me."

"Tell me one thing. If you absolutely knew you could learn, would you want to?"

I shrug, nodding because it's true.

"Then let me try. I have a way of teaching that I'd bet tons of money on—" He stops, wincing. "Too soon?"

Ten thousand dollars too soon. I relent with a laugh.

"Give my method one shot. Next week."

"And you want what in return?" There's always a catch with this Cuban.

"If and when this works, I'll wear the internal bragging rights like a golden shield. Again, las fichas. No one will know."

"Okay, um, I guess." We're almost to the dock. "But this means you've got another secret on me. We're no longer even."

A crooked, infuriating grin. "What's new about that?"

Thirteen

*T*wo days after I send my completed packet to the Office of Historic Preservation, Papi turns onto Ivonne's street to drop me off. A box of crafting materials rests on the back seat. Jada offered to help, and after spending the last couple nights cutting and assembling dozens of book-page petals into roses, I've adjusted my "I can do everything myself" attitude. Help—help is good.

Lourdes, however, is not good with me. It's fine. She's just miffed she's been banned from our Sunday afternoon rose assembly party. I want Lulú to walk into the Westin Pasadena ballroom for Sofia's fiesta de quince and be totally surprised. She wants this, too; she just doesn't know it yet.

In Ivonne's driveway, Papi halts midgoodbye. "Wait," he says, turning down TLC from the radio. "Diggin' on You" fades away. "Listen."

We roll down our windows. Music floods, and even though Ivonne's double bass notes are muffled, they strike a warm chord inside my chest. But there's more—a shuffling drumbeat underneath the syrupy bend of strings. The curtains on the front window are open, revealing a tousle of wavy blond hair. "Jada's jamming with her," I say.

Papi cranes his neck. "I figured someone was. Even Ivonne's not that magical."

Damn. I cast a sideways *look* at my father, which he ignores. "Help me bring in that supply box? Super heavy." It isn't. But Papi has no choice but to comply because I'm already bolting from his SUV and trotting up the front walk.

I catch a couple swear-jar words as he grabs my crafting stuff and follows. I inch inside the door, spying Ivonne playing near the fireplace and lifting her chin to welcome Papi and me. Jada winks from her seat atop a raspy cajón, tapping the box drum with the kind of rhythmic skill I should be surprised about. *Should . . .* but it's Jada.

The duo carries on, their jazzy tune resonating through the walls. A bottle of wine and two lipstick-stained glasses wink from the sideboard. These two are obviously getting along.

When the final notes land, Jada and Ivonne bow toward us and our enthusiastic clapping.

"'Caravan,'" Papi says. "A classic."

"You recognized 'Caravan' just from the bass line, Rob?" Jada asks.

He gives a shrug. "I've been to enough Puro Sabor gigs."

Ivonne smiles, and if she's going for demure, she fails. It's dazzling. "Someone's been paying attention."

Roberto Delgado turns another shade of Papi. He exhales roughly. "I'm off to watch the Dodgers lose to the Mets."

He locks eyes with Ivonne, keeping them there and adding a little wave before backing out the front door. I need to work fast. As Jada's most recent victim at the lake, I know what's coming. I go in for the save before *Jada Antics Part Two: Ivonne Edition* starts up. I grab the box, rattling its contents. "Well, we have a billion paper flowers to make, sooo . . ."

Jada drains her glass. "Let's do it." She turns to Ivonne. "Happy gig. I'll get over to watch your band soon. And thanks for the jam sesh. Oh, and the vino."

Ivonne pumps an open fist and grabs her huge black instrument case. "You've got some real chops." She steps up and plants a noisy kiss on my head. "Have fun, cariño."

A few moments later Jada and I exit out the back with a borrowed card table and extra chair, and—

Lourdes. She's parked by Jada's door wearing her new Lululemon belt bag and a sheepish grin. I'd totally missed Blue Ivy out front.

"What happened to 'Stay far away because I want you to be surprised'?" I ask.

"This happened," Lourdes says. She produces a foil-wrapped platter and lifts the corner. "Mami made extra."

"Oh my God, empanadas? *Clary*," Jada says. She unlocks the door and throws on a ridiculous puppy-dog expression. Apparently, it's two against one, and Jada is *weak*.

"Fine," I relent. "But this craft is the only thing you're seeing from Sofia's party decor. ¿Entiendes?"

"Claro," my conniving friend says. "I don't care about spoilers. I didn't want to miss the girl party."

My heart cracks, just a hairline. "Get in, you nerd."

"Finally." She fakes a dramatic shiver. "It was getting chilly out here, and I don't have my missing denim shirt."

"Neither do I!" I call out before stepping inside behind her. I haven't been here in almost a week. My sister hung a couple batik shawls over the bed and sofa as makeshift artwork. Fitting the theme, she turns on music with a sultry techno vibe. She's probably seen the group live.

Jada sets up the card table, and I show Lourdes a finished book-paper rose.

She handles it carefully, mouth falling into a pout. "This is the cutest thing I've ever seen. And it looks like tons of work. You're so lucky I'm here."

"Oh, I'm the luckiest."

I plug in my glue gun and lay out samples of the three sizes of book-page roses I'll need for bouquets, corsages, and arrangements. The materials are simple: scissors, floral wire, pliers, and plenty of glue-gun sticks. Plus the thrift-store novels for petals.

"Each rose takes a bunch of petals in these sizes." I show my assistants some precut templates, then demo one rose. My hands have long since memorized the steps from YouTube; I cut, twist, and shape the wire for a stem, then gather petals, layering and gluing them in place. After some quick plumping, I present a medium-size finished book-page flower. "There. Perfect for a bookworm quinceañera."

"Geez, how are you so fast?" Lulú remarks.

Years following Mamita and Papi around stems and shears have made me more than fast.

Jada grabs the sample, turning it. "I'm scared mine won't come out half as good."

When Lourdes agrees, I change plans and conduct an assembly line. I relegate Lulú to carefully tearing out book pages and put Jada on petal-cutting duty. We groove to the music and chat about trips and LA must-sees. Surprisingly, conversation hums along, considering the last words Jada and I said here. Those matters aren't resolved—not even close. But the space we fill in this shoebox casita seems bigger than last time. I guess there's room for crafts and laughter and fashion talk, too.

Another plus: my pile of completed flowers grows miraculously with their help. I'd never be able to make all these on my own so quickly.

After a solid hour, it's time to break for empanadas. I toss two chicken-filled onto a paper plate and join Lourdes at the dining table, away from our card-table assembly piles.

There's plenty of room for Jada, but like beans in my kitchen and snacks last week, she leans herself into a keyboard slash mark as she eats a beef empanada . . . middle first? Where on earth was she influenced into thinking this is acceptable? Wonder of all, Emilio might even agree with me.

Poof—he's right there in my head, which is inconvenient because I've barely forgiven Jada for her swan-lake escape. Friday afternoon, after fumbling through an awkward goodbye to Emilio and walking back to catch a ride home with Mamita, Jada had obviously been waiting for my rage-text. I'd sensed it.

Because when I sent: What in every hell was that?

She replied not ten seconds later with: Promise Clary I didn't ditch you on purpose

But she had to know that I would fire back saying: I TRUSTED YOU with my swan dream and you crushed THE DREAM

Because she played her ace domino tile, typing: I'll bet you a Marlow shopping spree it wasn't all terrible, and that you'd be lying if you said you left the lake without one good thing

To which I realized that even miles away, Jada Morrison has way too much reach into my energy force field, despite my skepticism. She wasn't wrong. Even though Emilio and I ended up bickering (again), he did help. He did give me one good thing. While I talked, Emilio did his best impression of an empty space as white as clouds, escaping as much as humanly possible while still filling the swan seat. He's even better at leaving than I thought.

Lourdes's outburst of laughter snaps me back. She's holding up the last of the old paperbacks I bought from Neil. *"Mink and Marauders?* Are you serious?"

Jada leans over to check out the cover. "Impressive. The way that girl is draped over that rock," she notes. "And that marauder shouldn't be running around in the woods with no shirt. That's dangerous."

"It was cheap!" I say, exasperated. "I am on a budget, and fifty cents was a good deal for something we're gonna cut up anyway."

Lourdes giggles. "I'm down with a good romance novel, but this is . . . not." She thumbs through the book, amusing herself. "'Rhiannon let out a shuddering breath against Rangor's heaving pecs.'" She looks up, already halfway gone. "Not just pecs, heaving ones."

I rise to throw my paper plate in the trash. "No one will notice the words. Again, cutting up."

"I dunno, girl. I don't think there's enough cutting and taping to mask this. 'Rangor pinched tighter, luminous beads of salted moisture whispering across his forehead like the lost gems they had been searching—'"

"Lulú." I wave my arms. "Make it stop."

"Wait," Jada says through shaking laughter. "We need to know what Rangor's pinching."

"We *don't*, though." I snatch away the book and toss it into my crossbody bag. "We'll have enough pages from the other two mystery novels."

"No, I have to show this to Fia. I won't say what it was for." Before I can protest, Lourdes is wrist-deep into my bag. Yet instead of the book, she pulls out a vendor sample pack of the tiny cards we send with arrangements. "Seriously? You carry these around?" She noses deeper. "Jesus, how many napkins do you have in there, and what mother-hen mujer got to you?"

"Excuse me, but people spill things," I note. "And I forgot I'd tossed in the card samples with the rest of my shop mail to take home." I riffle through the stack. "Besides, they're cute. Like the napkins, you never know when you're going to need a greeting card. And no one needs to write a *Mink and Marauders*-length novel to send the perfect message."

Lulú grabs one with yellow daisies. "God, the transcript of my dating life this year could fit on one of these." She pulls another with a pink tulip. "Even better, let's make up card dedications to your old boyfriends. From you, obviously." She brightens. "*Something bootiful from your friendly neighborhood ghost. Regards, Clary.*"

She didn't. "Lourdes."

But my girl doesn't quit. "And for dude número dos, let's do: *Sure was sweet while it lasted. Best, Clary.*" She turns to Jada. "Catch the running theme here?"

Jada pushes over some freshly cut petals. "This sounds like a story I might need to hear."

Ugh, Lourdes. Why does my friend live for outing me like this? I turn to Jada. "If I tell you now, will you promise to never bring it up again?"

"Promise."

It's not enough. I punctuate with my features, hoping for once that her intuitive skills are fired high. "Will you never use it as part of a larger scheme or diabolical plan?" What I am really asking is that she never bring up my past "loves" in front of Emilio. He's never paid attention to my brief dating history, and he is not on any need-to-know list. He already knows too much.

"*Promise*-promise," she says.

I send one last warning look. "Okay. Guy number one, I met as part of a friend's quinces court. We hung out a few times after the party, but, I dunno, his texts started to feel different. I didn't think he was into me anymore, so I broke it off and saved him the trouble."

"And . . . *buh-bye*." Lourdes rips up the daisy card for effect.

"Sure, yeah. And guy number two—Jake. He was a guest at a wedding I was working. We clicked over cake and met up later at Beverly Center with friends, then started dating. Things seemed to be going pretty well."

"Except for the fact that he despised the swan boats," Jada says.

Lourdes points at me with the tulip card. "But he could've been convinced."

"I never got that far. I found out his old girlfriend came back from New York. They'd only broken up because she moved. And

I mean, what was I supposed to do? Stick around and wait for him to bail?"

"Yeah, but I've been saying this for a year," Lourdes notes. "You were so sure he wasn't going to pick you that you didn't give him a chance. What if he realized he liked you more?"

And what if he didn't? "I didn't want to wait around to find out. That would've been worse."

Jada moves to speak, but Lourdes's phone buzzes, saving me from the commentary.

"It's Fia," Lourdes says. "I need to get her early from a sleepover. Big drama. I want to stay and help more, but—"

I wave her off as she types her response. "Nah, you better hurry. Nothing worse than an awkward sleepover."

After Lourdes says goodbye to Jada, I walk her out to the edge of the patio. I leave her with a tight squeeze, even though she played devil's prime advocate with her little card quips and callouts. She's a boulder in my world, and that means something.

When I return to the casita, Jada's at the counter again, munching on an empanada while studying her phone.

"I like Lourdes a lot," she says, and motions toward the last crispy turnover. "Eat that so I won't."

I grab it—this one is full of melty cheese. "I like her, too. When she's not harassing me, I like her more." After swallowing a hearty bite, I ask, "Why do you always eat standing up?"

Jada springs off the counter as if she's suddenly self-conscious. "You want the truth, or what I tell people?"

149

"Truth. I mean, the other day you said it was a habit you picked up from your stepmom. Was that part true?"

"Yeah, but it goes way deeper, and not in any good way. Stop me if what I say is in any way triggering." When I nod, feeling the heat of unsaid things, she continues. "My father had a raging temper and a lightning-fast reaction time—with his hands or fists, I mean. My stepmom learned real fast that even the smallest thing could turn him into an instant volcano. He punched or slapped. He pushed first before asking questions."

"God" is all I can say about that kind of life.

Jada nods. "Yeah—exactly. Before I go on, remember what I said last time. The fact that you had a great childhood, and I didn't, has nothing to do with you and me. We can both acknowledge where we came from. Cool. But it wasn't your fault, and it wasn't mine."

Instinctively, I step closer. Maybe I wasn't ready for these kinds of words last week. But tonight I find I can see around them—to her, a girl just a few years older than me. I lean in slightly, ready to listen. "No, it wasn't. Can you tell me the rest?"

After an exhale she says, "Yeah. If my dad was raging, it was best to leave the house and let him cool down. My stepmom would come back after an hour, and he'd be on the couch with a beer like nothing had happened." Jada angles her chin. "And, see, mealtimes always gave them time to bicker, which gave him opportunity to strike. One day she couldn't leave the table fast enough. Another she hooked her shoe on the chair leg and fell."

"So that was the end of sitting to eat?"

"It was. The counter was right next to the kitchen door. He'd curl his lip wrong, and she'd just bolt. If I was there, she'd swoop me up and we'd . . . escape."

"But you said you left that house when you were six."

"Yeah, but I kept standing because that was just how I ate. It was all I knew." Jada raps her fingers on the tile. "Now I still do it because sometimes our bodies carry on some things even after we've had therapy."

The world she calls home opens wide inside my mind. And I simply . . . see. "Is this why you keep moving? Why you never stay for long in one place?"

"Motion and an escape plan meant safety." Her hands cross over her heart. "So when I had to run from my mother because one of her boyfriends tried to violate me and she believed *him*, I knew what to do."

Too many horrors stack up behind my eyes. And for a moment I do more than acknowledge her childhood. I grieve it—the way it looks, dull and marred against the beautiful, bright life I've had. "I'm so sorry. I can't even imagine."

Jada nods once. "Good, Clary. *Good*. That's how it should be." She pauses inside her revelation for a few beats. "The situation with her old boyfriend was what she tried to fix between us recently. I accepted her apology, but we don't have a relationship. We do speak sometimes, though."

About me. About the money. "So she won't show up here?"

"Not here or anywhere I go. She and I made peace, but we're not . . . family. I find that a different way."

"On the move?" I ask.

"I grew to love the variety and the diversity of moving around more than four solid walls. And, yeah, if I traced it all back, my step-mom and that counter was where it all began." She gathers our greasy napkins. "You said you ran from guys before they could ditch you. If you even suspected there might be hurt, you were going to control it, huh?"

I give a flat shrug. "It's not like I *wanted* to bail and cut them off. It's not the way I'm built. I'm loyal to people who love me. And places."

I've always prided myself on staying. On sticking. But now, as Jada returns to our petals, another side of me takes shape. Maybe there's a big piece of my heart that's been hovering at some inside counter, too, ready to tell the rest of me to run before that first blow comes.

Fourteen

*T*he next Tuesday, we're working at La Rosa Blanca with Angela Alvarez crooning "Quiéreme Mucho," even though top-fan Abu is out on delivery. Stacks of orders are still not enough *busy* to keep the bee-buzz anxiety out of my stomach. Today I'm taking an extended lunch break. Today Emilio is going to teach me how to ride a bike.

Instead of my impending doom, I focus on my current arrangement. It's getting there but needs something more. I head to the floral cooler, zeroing in on bundles of craspedia blooms: one-inch puff balls in soft yellow with a cute Seussian look. Perfect. Instead of choosing from our website samples, the client wanted something custom, and yellow—*all* yellow. My container of choice is white glazed pottery, and inside I'm building a tousled dome with buttery Brighton roses, marigolds, and delicate ranunculus. The craspedia adds a touch of playfulness.

"Qué lindo el amarillo," Mamita says on her way in from the showroom. With back-to-back consults, I've barely seen her all morning.

I grin, placing final blooms.

"It is a good one for summer," my dad says from his workspace. He's crafting a gigantic lobby arrangement for the Hilton in purples and deep greens. "Maybe add it to the site."

"Good idea. I'll call it Lemon Drop." The vibe coming off my work is little-girl-Clary and the sour candies Papi and I would get at the corner market.

Mamita grooves to the tune and takes a swig of jasmine green tea from her tumbler. "Ynez hates yellow. Can you imagine? Hating the color that Dios chose to give the sun?"

"Beyond kids' drawings, would we actually call the sun yellow?"

She ignores me. "Last year when we did the wedding for her friend's niece, you made that tulip bouquet. In pale yellow con los stephanotis."

I barely remember this wedding and its tulip bouquet but still say, "Sure. Yep. Was super pretty." I set a completed Lemon Drop on the delivery rack.

"Ynez texted everyone on the social committee *during the ceremony* about how the color was so tacky." Mamita pulls her phone from her apron, waving it. "Texting during a wedding—that is what is tacky."

I'm grateful a message comes through on my own phone, but one glance at the sender is enough to unleash a flutter through my chest.

Emilio: It's time, Thorn. Out back

Me: You're early

Emilio: By 5 mins

Me: I have to clean up

Emilio: Like we have time for Cuban-level cleaning?

More like he can't wait to see me fail. I start tossing floral scraps like a beast.

"Clarita, what do you want from the Thai place?" From Mamita on the Postmates app.

I'm wiping and storing and scrubbing. "Nothing. I'm going out during lunch today."

Abu trails in from the loading bay, noting, "Why is Emilio's truck in the driveway?"

Right before Papi asks, "Why are you cleaning like you're on some game show with a ticking clock?"

The room capsizes.

"Espérate, you're going out to lunch with Emilio?" Mamita says, whirling around. I now have six eyeballs trained my way. "Is he taking you to a restaurant?"

"Emilio *Avalos*? Really?" Papi says.

Abu scrunches his face. "In all these years I can't remember when—"

"Can we just *not*?" I grab my crossbody bag from my cubby. "I know you'd appreciate a Google Slides presentation, but I really do need to go." I suck in all the air I can get. "Yes, I'm hanging with Emilio for my break. No, I'm not *going out* with him; he's helping me with something. And I'll be late, but I'll stay extra tonight if we're behind. Okay?" I glare at each of their slack-jawed faces. "*Okay?*"

Mamita hooks one hand on her hip. "Why are you so flustered, mija?"

Ay carajo. I spin on my Chucks and beeline to the back, calling "Love you" as I head out the rear door.

I march up to the blue Toyota pickup Emilio shares with his dad. Inside the bed there's a rack holding one of his bikes and another smaller model. *For me.*

These two words make everything too real. I can't do this. And I can't believe I agreed to let Emilio see me at my weakest; he's going to have enough fodder to tease me forever.

The window rolls down. "Hop in, Thorn. Time for fun."

"Um, turns out we're really busy today and I—"

"Clary." He's leaning out the window with his hair tied back. Gray tee. A curious sunburn. "As *you* said, if I can teach you, then my method is truly foolproof, so call it research. Plus, you promised you'd give me one go."

Great. He knows my deal with keeping promises enough to use it as leverage. I stomp around to the passenger side. "Happy now?" I say as I slam the door and click in.

His smile bends askew. It's all I get as he eases away, then turns left on Sunset during a Red Sea parting–level break in traffic. Imagine Dragons is on the radio, and as we approach the next light, I suspect where we're heading.

"If we're going to the park, you might as well turn back."

"Sorry, no turning back. And no park. I have a way better place." He lobs a quick glance my way. "Trust me?"

"Um, *no*?" Is he kidding?

His laugh floods the cab. "Good. 'Cause you hate surprises, but I love them, and you're gonna get on a bike today and surprise yourself."

He knows I hate surprises? I ditch this thought as quickly as it comes because we're passing Marlow, and I can't help but notice what's not in the window. I pull up Jada's message stream on my phone and send, I think Neil sold the blue velvet chair 😱

She writes back, Yeah, I went by earlier. Not meant to be. Another message comes through right behind it. I'm at ABW now and I saw you and Emilio in his truck. We can talk about it later

I roll my eyes into the screen, click off without answering, and switch to catching up on whatever's happening on my socials.

After a few minutes and an update on Lourdes's search for a quinces dress, I realize we've been on the freeway, and we're getting off in Glendale. Glendale? Even in LA traffic, Glendale is a short hop from Echo Park. But . . . what is he doing? "You gonna fill me in anytime, Wheels?"

"Ahh, it's back from cyberville and breathing."

"Yeah, but not breathing for long," I barely get out, then cringe because I'd forgotten it's useless to whisper around Emilio and his acute hear—

"Holy shit!" he says, bulldozing over my thought. "Owl Bar's coming."

"Huh?"

We're at a stoplight on North Brand, and he's nodding toward a billboard. There's a giant brown owl logo and a picture of a food truck with a big burger drawn on the side. *Coming soon, LA* is printed in big block letters underneath. "I'll translate."

Somebody has to when we talk.

"So, the state food map." He points one more time to the billboard before accelerating. "The green chile cheeseburger is the top New Mexico foodie pick. And Owl Bar is the *home* of that burger. That truck means I can finally try one without leaving our own state. It's the best."

"How do you know? You haven't had one."

Emilio turns onto a residential street, slowing. "I have a good imagination. Europe backpacking, green chile cheeseburgers, some other notable *things*—I don't have to have tried them to know they'd be great."

What things? What notable things? Danger—it has to be a trap. "Oh, wait, how's your dad?" I deflect, because I really do want to know.

He taps a staccato rhythm on the steering wheel. "Good about detailing every blink and headache on his symptom tracker, but still terrible about being stuck at home." He glances at the digital clock on the dash. "He's with a neurologist right now and could get clearance to come back to the shop for light duty next week. We'll see."

"Any more of those weird tingles?"

"Nothing like the day he fell." He crosses the fingers of one hand while using the other to turn into an empty space along the curb. "Your destination is on the right."

I glance, wrinkling my nose. "A school?"

"This elementary school has a huge parking lot. No speed bumps and it's empty for summer." He hops out of the cab.

By the time I get enough courage to exit the truck, Emilio has his bike out. He's removing my ride—a white model with no branding. "Here," he says, motioning for me to hold it steady while he grabs a duffel. "Good that you actually followed my suggestion to wear long sleeves."

"Self-preservation," I say, trying to get used to the weight of the frame.

We wheel the bikes a short distance around the brick schoolhouse to the lot. Like he said, the space extends for yards, long and straight. My entire system protests; I'm glad I haven't eaten yet. I'm aware of every shallow breath, and my palms glaze with sweat.

Emilio's placed his bike on a kickstand, and he's pulling a few tools from the duffel. He holds out a helmet. "We have some demo models. I thought this one would suit you. Safety first."

When I fumble with the clasp, he helps adjust it. The sensation of his hand under my chin is both calloused and moth-wing gentle. "This is how a helmet should fit. Snug, but with room for two fingers under the strap."

I test it out and only now notice what's missing. "Where are the training wheels?"

"In some shipping warehouse where they belong."

"I can't just start off on two wheels! I'm going to come home, and you're gonna have to explain to an entire Cuban family that you broke their daughter!"

"I don't think so. Plus, that helmet's top rated."

Well, that's reassuring.

He approaches the white bike, crouches low, and begins removing the pedals. He's actually taking them *Off. The. Bike.*

"What the hell, Wheels?" I don't know much about bikes, but I know that pedals are the only way to make them move. And he's just fiddling about. Unfazed.

He straightens and comes around, directly in front of me. "Breathe, yeah? It's okay."

I'm shaking, and I hate that he's seeing me fall apart, piece by piece.

But the truth is, I've always thought I should learn, and no one from the neighborhood is around to see me. It's the only reason I haven't run.

"Hey," he says softly. "I told you I have a special way of teaching, and it doesn't involve training wheels. We sell them at the shop because people still want them, but they're the worst way to learn. Biking is mostly about balance. The first thing you're going to learn is how to balance."

"So no pedaling?"

"No pedaling. They do more harm than good until you can balance. I know you don't trust me." One shoulder pops up. "But you can believe me."

At my tiniest, most reluctant nod, he leads me to the bike. He takes a few minutes to show me all the parts and then does another thing I didn't see coming. He lowers the caramel-colored seat way down before I hop on.

"To answer your next question, yes, this is also right," he says. "I know it's weird with your feet touching the ground, but that's the point for now. You'll ruin your knees if you keep the seat low once you're a pedaling pro."

"Wasn't what I was gonna ask." He lets out a low grunting noise, which I interpret as a call to continue. But one can never be sure. "Did you bring elbow pads? Wrist gear? That is what I was gonna ask."

"You won't need them for my method. I'm not in the habit of wrapping students in Bubble Wrap, either." He throws a goofy, exaggerated smile. "Only friends."

"Clearly, we're not friends," I say over a laugh. "Wait, are we?"

"Hell if I know, Thorn." Emilio thrusts up his hands. "Look, before this . . . declines, we need to start the lesson. Hang there for a minute."

He moves onto his own bike—a sleek matte black model that probably cost a few paychecks. "Watch." He lifts his feet purposely away from the pedals and glides a short distance. "Now it's your turn."

He wheels back over to the starting point. "Release the brake and glide. You can put your feet down at any time."

I do none of these things. I cannot move.

"Another promise: it's not gonna ride itself."

"Haha. Just give me a sec." I'm one more surprise away from total panic, and I need a distraction. "Um, your food map. What's Florida?"

"Okaaay. Key lime pie."

"New York?"

"Buffalo wings."

We go through a few more states until my mind quiets, just enough. I take a breath. Release the brake. And—I glide about two feet before I have to smack my feet on the ground. "I told you I suck at this."

"Nah, that's exactly right. You just have to give your body time to figure it out. Come back and go again."

I do. Again, and again, until everything I'm made of is tight and achy. My lower back kills. I already sense calluses forming on my hands from death-gripping the handles. My record is about five feet.

"Okay, that's enough for today," he says, and leads me off the bike. "See? Not even one fall."

"We're stopping?" I tell him, brows furrowed. I still can't ride a bike. Not even close. "You said to give you one lesson. That's false advertising."

He clicks his tongue. "If you recall, what I asked was for you to give me one chance at my method. I didn't say it would only take one lesson. Have you ever been able to balance for five feet on a bike before? Small steps."

This whole deal still feels sneaky and underhanded. I whip off the helmet, amped to throw it at him, but I settle for a melodramatic toss.

"Fine for now, but you're keeping that," he says. "And the bike is going home with you, too. You need to practice on your own before our next lesson."

"Which is, what? Me lying on the grass envisioning myself actually riding?"

"Pedals, Thorn. When you can consistently go ten feet with only the brake to stop you, let me know. Then we add back the pedals and learn how to steer and turn without dying."

"Way to keep your standards low."

"Only for bike lessons." He reaches for the duffel. "Never for food."

My eyes go wide as Emilio produces a smaller, insulated bag. He unveils two white sub-sandwich bags with a familiar logo. And two chilled water bottles.

"Mineo's?" He brought me lunch? "Thanks," I say as he hands over my sandwich. I peek inside to find my favorite turkey-and-avocado on a wheat roll.

"There's no mayo, even though it's not a real sandwich without it. And Italian dressing, which makes everything a total mess."

He's wrong, but I'm still stunned by these small gestures. "I thought you meant the Señor Cluck's drive-through or something on the way back."

"Couldn't take the risk of you needing a three-hour lunch break to make the five-foot glide mark," he quips. "So it's for my benefit, really. You think I'm a jerk *now*? Try an unfed me."

"You're not a jerk." I don't know when his status officially changed in my mind, but here we are. Above Emilio's escapist feet, and underneath the cocky, annoying, argumentative rest of him, he's thoughtful. He teaches kids and gives them bikes. He's good at keeping secrets. And he brought me a sandwich without a trace of mayo.

"*You're. Not. A. Jerk,*" he repeats in slo-mo. "Can I wear that on a platinum crown?"

"You've already got the gold one from homecoming."

"Yeah. That." He smiles, but it has a short reach. The rest of him is clouded soft and gray, like his shirt.

We leave the bikes on the lot and sink onto a nearby bench. Thankfully, Emilio brought antibacterial wipes to sanitize our hands. Before I reach into my purse for napkins, he hands over a huge pile from his bag and keeps two for himself. "I know the rules."

I'm slack-jawed over my bestowed wad of Mineo's printed napkins.

"Italian sub with extra peperoncini and extra mayo?" I ask as he tears into his sandwich. "Which is disgusting."

"Bingo, and it's not disgusting." Another bite. "You never did say how your napkin fascination started," he notes after a few seconds.

I swallow a hunk of avocado. "Believe it or not, it actually has to do with bikes. Call it the origin story of why you're here today."

"So it's swan-boat confessions part two?"

Except today my white swan has a caramel-colored seat and two wheels. "Like I said, my dad and Abu tried to teach me how to ride. When I was seven, I got the prettiest pink bike with blossoms all over it for Christmas."

Emilio smiles. "For a flower-shop daughter. Let me guess, handlebar streamers?"

I nod. "It did have training wheels, and now I get why you said they don't work. Even with someone holding the seat, I felt, I dunno, unstable. I was afraid."

"Of falling."

"So much. Even at seven, I was all up in my head. Like all I could see was some impending crash." I roll down my sandwich wrapper. "I feared it so much, I couldn't let go and just ride."

"Totally common. But what about the napkins?"

"Mamita said she'd take me out next. We went up to Elysian Park, and I got on the bike with trainers. I started off, and I was doing it, but then something went wrong, and I fell and scraped my arm up pretty badly. That was the hard end of bikes for me." I look up, my jaw twisted. "The only thing Mamita had in her purse was this big wad of napkins. She always saved them from everywhere. But that day, all I remember was her using them to stop the blood."

Emilio's stopped eating. "So you carry them, too, for others."

"That's what I tell everyone, and it's true that you never know when you're gonna need one. But there's another thing." I savor a tiny bite and swallow. "They remind me that my true mother didn't give birth to me, but she's always had what I needed."

And when you're seven—or even seventeen—you can't tell the difference between a first aid kit and a wad of burger-joint napkins from a handbag. Especially if you close your eyes. You just know you're not bleeding anymore.

Fifteen

*W*ork for florists starts before the sun. Abu usually handles morning wholesale market hauls for whatever we'll need for the next few days. But that's only the beginning. It's what you do with flowers before arranging them that keeps them beautiful for as long as something that's technically dying can hope to last.

My family works inside a tightly honed preservation system. Fueled by caffeine, our feet pass hours on rubber mats well before the first customers arrive. We live under waterproof aprons. The prep zone is a damp space—ripe and green and mossy, ringed with a hint of sweetness.

When the market haul or out-of-state shipments arrive, we remove low-growing foliage and trim ends so stems can drink. Part-time workers like Lourdes help a ton. She spends her non-delivery time sanitizing tools and buckets and making sure the floral cooler is sparkling clean to prevent contamination.

From a chemist's lab of potions and additives, we spray and feed flowers to prevent bacteria growth and control their bloom rate.

We remove pollen from lilies and delicately mist and hang lilies of the valley upside down before use. Daffodils are straight-up bullies. They secrete a stem-clogging sap that harms other blooms and must quarantine for at least six hours before we can pair them with other varieties.

When I was first learning to arrange blooms, Mamita would always say that flowers are like friends. You have to find out how they live best. Discover what keeps them going and give them just enough of it. And don't treat a peony like a rose and expect it to be the best peony.

Both peonies and roses are on my prep table this afternoon, along with more flowers ready for an engagement photo shoot at Griffith Park. Jada perches at my side with her own stock, cashing in on my promise to teach her how to make a hand-tied bridal bouquet.

"First rule of mixed bouquets," I say, "is picking one bloom to be the showcase." I choose a fat, pink peony. "Like this one."

"Kind of like Ivonne onstage," Jada says, and mirrors the way I pinch the bloom between my thumb and forefinger. "The front person."

"Exactly," I say, fighting a yawn. "The second rule is always work leftward." I pick up a white rose and cross it at a left angle until the height matches the peony, then wait for her to follow. "Now a quarter turn right each time, but keep placing the flowers leftward to get that nice round shape the bride wants. Her ceremony bouquet will be similar but larger and a little more free-form."

"Cool. I actually don't suck at this," Jada says after she's caught the rhythm.

Our bouquets take shape as we place more of the large blooms, plus lacy pink Limonium and some short white phlox shoots. I add my last peony, noting a hint of pride at being able to teach something to someone who's only a few calendar years older, but eons wiser in life experience. Someone who can teach yoga, and mix serums from essential oils, and thrive in a hundred different cities.

My lesson continues as I show her how to blend in different fillers and greenery, keeping the same angles. When we get the right size and look, it's time to secure the bouquets with a sturdy knot of twine.

Jada snips the twine ends and follows my lead in trimming the bouquet to the right stem length. "Now that we're alone," she says, "you can tell me about yesterday and Emilio."

The spool of floral tape for our next step becomes a Slinky in my hands, and I feel like I'm back in kindergarten learning basic cutting skills. I crane my neck—sure enough, my abuelos are in the office, and Papi's off somewhere. "Like riding in a truck with a guy is headline news? He was helping me with something." I start over with a fresh length and do marginally better. "No big deal. It meant absolutely nothing."

She snips a long portion of the green fibrous tape from her own roll. "You're making a big deal out of trying to convince me that something wasn't a big deal, which leads me to believe it was a big deal. Besides, I can just tell."

Oh, not this again. "So my energy is giving off lying vibes? Some kind of untruthful aura?"

Jada follows my motions in wrapping the secured stems tightly. "Not your energy. All your outside parts."

Did she graduate from Emilio-entrapment school? And of course

I'm thinking about him again. To be fair, he did leave me with home-work. I've been yawning all day because just after Abu left for the flower market, I threw on sweats and dragged out the white loaner bike and helmet from under their tarp in the garage. For ten minutes (that's all he said it would take per day), I practiced his technique out front and may have noticed that gliding was becoming easier.

But explaining Emilio is still wobbly in my mind, not unlike Jada and me. If I'm not careful, both could be crashes waiting to happen.

"I've been working around him at the bike shop," Jada says. "Maybe I haven't earned the right to ask, but I can't help but wonder why you two have never been a thing. And this is me just observing and not creeping on him at all. But he seems like a quality guy besides being pretty cute."

I pull a spool of matte white ribbon from our supply wall. "Just because he's hot, that automatically means we need to be a thing? Is this you playing flower-shop Barbie and bike-shop Ken and smashing our faces together?"

She laughs heartily as a smile curves across her face. "So you do think he's cute. And even hot."

I feel it. I'm turning pink from the inside out. "Lots of girls think he's *hot*. Have you met his local fan club? The ones strolling in for *stuff* for their little siblings?"

Jada swipes off the band securing her long waves and redoes her ponytail. "There are . . . visitors. He does the small-talk thing, but I don't see him closing any deals."

I cut the right length of ribbon. I know it by heart. "That's just it. He never closes anything. He 'goes out with' girls. Briefly. That's not my jam at all. My swan-boat love story doesn't come with an automatic expiration date."

"I know, Clary. He doesn't strike me as a player, though. And believe me, I've met the world's share of those."

I stop and rest the thick white ribbon because I do believe her. And I could say a few relevant things about Emilio Avalos: His biggest dream is to leave Echo Park and be left alone. He doesn't do commitment. Instead, I say something I think this blond traveler will understand most. "He's a flight risk."

She takes a step closer, our tainted family history morphing between us like a hologram. "So am I. There's a secret club of us, you know? We have merch."

This time it's a laugh I'm fighting. "No offense, but don't you think I've had enough of that in my life?" I don't even have to name the person at the holy end of all this, and that's one good thing about talking to Jada. She gets that part.

I clear my throat. "I want something that feels like what my abuelos have. Easy and steady. Emilio is not . . . easy. Sometimes talking to him is like talking to a brick wall dipped in plutonium and steel. And kryptonite."

"Well well well, if that bicycle boy doesn't have you all wired and wound."

Carajo. My blood surges, and I can't name the *why*. "I'm sorry, but he's practically memorized ways to irritate me. To, I dunno, win. It's a game." We're just a game. I grab the ribbon and nod for her to watch me place, wrap, and knot, over and over up the length of the gathered stems.

She tries, getting the angle wrong at first, then adjusting. "What about the other times?"

"Huh?"

"You said *sometimes* talking to him is like that. Your word, girl."

My lip drops. *Did I?* Images of a white boat and a white bike pop into my head. It's true—he'd listened those times, and even though we'd bickered and grumbled and poked, he never judged me or made me feel small. Not once. But . . . "There's not enough *always* in our *sometimes*."

Jada rustles my shoulder, her mouth rounded into a pout of solidarity. She grabs her newly created peony bouquet, holding it like a bride ready for a long white aisle. Her face is all playfulness and sunshine as she begins prancing around the work zone. Twirling in a burgundy mini skirt, layered and bouncy. "Don't mind me. This might be the only time I get to do this."

What she has—it catches. And instead of cleaning up, or reaching for my to-do list, I let myself into a little of that warm and welcome light. Why not? I sat on a bike this morning. What's one more "thing I never do"? With the sister I never had.

The shop is empty, so I pump up the tunes, flooding the zone with Bill Withers and "Lovely Day," a Papi perennial favorite.

I glance down at my own flowers, ready for a bride and her dream photo shoot. I've made hundreds of bouquets since Mamita said I was ready to be an official team member. But I've never held one like this, bridal march ready—elbows bent, the top notched between your belly and your boobs.

I prance and pretend, following Jada around tables and buckets.

She giggles and that catches, too, the ridiculousness of us. We don't even notice Lourdes's return from her delivery run.

Cracking up, Lulú grabs some of the blooms that didn't make it into our bouquets and bunches them all together. She juts in front of us and joins the line with her long, long hair. It's always been my compass rose, and now her locks hang loose behind her ears, trailing like a dress-up veil. Today her hair says I was right to laugh, to take a few moments to loosen myself from worries and wounds. From neighborhood dreams and destruction. From choices that still seem impossible.

Jada leads us into the showroom, and we strut, dodging furniture and mock reception tables. Weaving around and through and around again. When the song fades out, we flop onto the twin velvet settees.

"I don't know what that was, but can we do it again?" Lourdes says.

"Absolutely," I say, still a little hazed.

"Tell me everything else you designed for Sofia's quinces."

"Nice try, Boricua."

My friend groans and springs up toward the back. She returns thirty seconds later with two containers filled with a bit of water. "The window of life is passing, because science," she says, and takes both bouquets, hydrating them.

I bump her side, then track Jada's stare. She's reading the wall. Painted in black script on opposing sides of the showroom is the text of the José Martí poem that inspired our business name, "Cultivo una rosa blanca." One side reads in its native Spanish, the other in the English translation.

Jada half turns from the Spanish side. "Can you read it for me?"

I nod, suspecting she means in my Cuban-grown tongue, with the way we bend words, lazily, leaving off a few syllables.

> *Cultivo una rosa blanca*
> *En julio como en enero,*
> *Para el amigo sincero*
> *Que me da su mano franca.*
> *Y para el cruel que me arranca*
> *El corazón con que vivo,*
> *Cardo ni ortiga cultivo,*
> *Cultivo una rosa blanca.*

"Beautiful," Jada says, then glances at the other wall, reading silently.

> *I cultivate a white rose*
> *In July as in January*
> *For the sincere friend*
> *Who gives me his hand frankly.*
> *And for the cruel person who tears out*
> *The heart with which I live,*
> *I cultivate neither nettles nor thorns,*
> *I cultivate a white rose.*

My sister comes from this part of me—the white, English wall. The white, English-speaking side that's buried in a root somewhere but was left to wither seventeen years ago. That happens to girls like market flowers.

But I've grown well, taking my Cuban half and stretching it over my other half to cover all the ghostly parts. *I'm Cuban*, I say, because that's the part I know. Today, though, there's a little bud, a sprig on the other side. It's scheming and fidgety, but genuine. Even though it's another flight risk, even though it will leave in weeks, it's good. Not cruel.

Jada will go, but I think it's okay to keep this small part of her—and maybe of Morrisons and Holts, too. So far, it's the only kindness I've found there.

"Earth to Planet Clary," Lourdes says.

I flinch, then hunt for one of our tablets, but they get moved around all the time. "I need to check on the work order to see what part of Griffith they're using for pictures."

Lourdes and Jada grab the flowers and follow me into the rear. They pack the photo-shoot bouquet in one of the prepped white boxes that contains a fixed plastic container to hold a bit of water. Thick tissue paper goes all around the blooms for bracing.

At my computer near the cubbies, I pull up the engagement-shoot order for Lourdes. "The couple's starting at the observatory, so that's easy for drop-off. It's supposed to be there at four."

"Got it," Lulú chimes. The bouquet is all packed and makes a pretty presentation for the bride-to-be.

Every time I log on, I check for file updates on my historic preservation submission, even though getting news so soon is probably a long shot. A quick glance tells me two things: I was right—no update—and no one has cleared out old emails from our shop mailbox in way too long. As I scan through, my eyes halt on an unexpected header from a newer message: Autotrader.com. I blink and look again, reading that it's not some ad, but an admin message with a confirmation number. I expand the email, reading and absorbing and internalizing what the information means beyond the words and photos.

"Clary?" Jada abandons her cleanup at the prep table and sidles over.

I shift the screen and point. "It's Rose Two. My family put Rose Two up for sale this morning."

Sixteen

*T*here are so many questions, I can't get them out fast enough after I call Abu from the office. Rocco followed him out, and I instinctively reach for my little pup, drawing him into my arms and leaning into his warmth and softness.

Why do we have to sell the van?

Does Papi know?

Why didn't you: tell me, warn me, forecast me because you know I hate surprises?

We're gathered around my work counter, laptop open. Abu raises his arms, his face wilted. "Mijita, do not take this further than it is supposed to go."

Rocco's had enough of me. He squirms, and I set him down. "What am I supposed to think? I just opened our email and—boom! You haven't kept enough secrets?"

He exhales, features withering. "No, it's not like that. Óyeme, we have been auditing our expenditures with help from a financial expert. And this is one way to cut back. We can save a lot of money if we downsize our delivery fleet. Little things add up. Gas, insurance, maintenance, not to mention the funds from the sale are good for saving for unforeseen expenses."

"But what will we do for multiple-event days or big hauls?"

"We will reorganize and plan. Your Papi has his SUV. That plus the other two vans are enough."

I picture our rear lot with the fleet of delivery vehicles parked side by side and named by Lourdes. When Rose Two goes, it will seem weird and off-balance. The idea of three seems so much more complete. Three is the number of how-it's-always-been.

And I know, I know, it's only one small part of La Rosa Blanca. I'm probably the only teen around here who's stressing over a cargo van. But more than a vehicle driving off our lot for good, it feels like another constant slipping away. An old travel agency, a colorful beach-and-bird mural, a white van—this neighborhood has gotten too used to losing things.

I look up, but I can't really voice my next ask. Lourdes and Jada are hovering nearby, and it would embarrass Abu. *You said we were okay, for now. Has that changed? Are we in trouble?*

Abu steps away. "Profits have been down slightly," he says as if he's read my mind. "This is a preventative measure."

Preventative. Like the kind of drug that prevents a heart attack?

I tuck Rocco into his dog bed and catch Abu out of earshot of the others. "I didn't know you were meeting with any financial person. I work here, too, and I'm part of this family."

"You are the best of this family. Pero we—your papi and Mamita and I—know this is not a normal summer for you. Part of that is our fault."

The sister-shaped truth rings loud and clear before he kisses my forehead and shuts himself inside the office. I trudge over to Lourdes and Jada at the sparkling clean work counter.

"So, the white elephant in the room," Lourdes starts. "I'm gonna miss it—best sound system of the fleet. Comfy seats, too. Gotta love that lumbar support." She jiggles her trap muscles. "Rose Three—er, Two now—and I aren't anywhere near bestie level, but we have come to an understanding. So don't worry, I'm not gonna quit over this or anything."

"Small favor," I deadpan.

"I'm sensing we need to literally clear some air around here." Jada removes her apron, resting it on the counter. "Let's all drive up to Griffith Park for the delivery." She nods toward the entrance. "It's so warm out, and you haven't been in my ride with the top down."

So many colliding thoughts have hit me in the last five minutes, I need a few more to process. "Um." This is all I get out before I grab our cleaned shears and stripping tools and slot them into their homes. I also stow my apron on a hook and look around at a dozen undone tasks.

I come back with "How about you two go? There's prep, and what if a bunch of new orders come in?"

"You're so annoyingly predictable," Lourdes says, waving her phone. "Which is why I already ran it by your abuelo, and he said your dad's due back soon and he doesn't want to see us for at least two hours. Grab your janitor kit, carnation queen."

Oh, Abu. "You're a cheat, you know that, Lulú?"

Jada whips her bouquet from the vase and swings on a crossbody bag. "It's my favorite thing about Clary's favorite person." Her brows narrow as she tugs at Lulú's commanding mane. "Good thing I threw a straw hat in the trunk because I don't want to be responsible for what a convertible will do to *this*."

Jada was right about what I needed—a shotgun seat on a hot day at the tail end of June. My sis drives her red VW like a bullet, as much as she can in loose pockets of the traffic debacle that is Los Angeles. But I don't care, which is new. I feel . . . safe. And that brings another something new—an inch of trust between us.

Forget telenovelas, I'm living a reality show. We've got vintage Mint Condition blaring from the old radio. Lulú's in the back, hatted up, singing "Breakin' My Heart" off-key. The photo-shoot bouquet's secured in the trunk, but I'm minding its twin, the scent of blooms and all the *life* coming off the streets of Silver Lake and Loz Feliz heady and predictably polluted. But I find I don't care about that, either.

Jada nudges the flowers at a stoplight, laughing. "You're so vintage Julia Roberts right now. Runaway bride!"

At green, she peels out, and I offer up her peony bouquet to the wind—something I'd never do with a delivery item—and wonder if this sense of reckless freedom comes from the same place as Emilio's wanderlust.

Oh.

As these thoughts swirl, they leave me in a different place than the last time I'd thought about his secret backpacking trip. I love my home, so much. Enough to fight for it. But I don't want to be home right now, or even in mi barrio. I want to be in Jada's red summer car, winding up the road to Griffith Park.

Lulú and I navigate. The elevation changes and the urban planes of the city drop away as we trek through Los Feliz and reach the mouth of the park. Spanning more than four thousand acres at the eastern ridge of the Santa Monica Mountains, Griffith Park is one of the largest in the country. The Los Angeles Zoo is here, plus an outdoor theater. The recreation zone offers skyscraper-weary locals and tourists killer hiking and equestrian trails, sports courts, and the most popular feature: the Hollywood Sign.

We follow Observatory Road up to where our bride and groom are supposedly waiting with their photographer. Jada takes in her first view of Griffith Observatory towering over the southern slope of Mount Hollywood.

I've been on field trips to the observatory, absorbing facts about the planetarium and its Art Deco–style walls in warm white. Three domes command the entire structure—the largest crowning the center—crafted from greenish-brown copper panels. *A three-boob roof,* we used to joke, pissing off our teachers. The grounds are symmetrical and neatly trimmed.

But the parking situation is always the opposite of neat. Jada slows next to the endless row of cars along the hill. Right when I'm about to suggest she keep circling the loop so I can run the bouquet over to our clients, a blue Mercedes inches out from a prime spot.

Lourdes's head appears between the front seats. "Okay, you're magical. That does not happen here. Ever."

Jada swings into the spot. "I simply expressed a wish to this place that we would like a small plot of land, and would it be so kind as to provide one?"

She manifested a parking space?

"I need to try that with a combo from Señor Cluck's during AP Stats next year," Lourdes says.

My friend and I hop out as Jada secures the convertible top. I send a quick text message to the bride while Lulú carefully pries the bouquet box from the trunk.

"The lady's name is Mei, and they're all waiting on the front steps. She's wearing a pink slip dress," I read from the quick response.

"Easy. I'll run this over," Lourdes says, and trots up to the entrance plaza.

With the car secured, Jada joins me for a walk up to the Hollywood Sign lookout.

"A perfect view," she muses. "The sign still looks so small even from here."

I nudge my chin forward. "It's a long hike away. All the trails are laid out like a spiderweb through the mountains. And you're almost guaranteed to step in horse shit somewhere."

"Just like London and Hyde Park," Jada notes as we reach the railing.

Lourdes comes up behind us, and we part so she's in the middle. "All good. Mei had a little *moment* when she saw the bouquet and said she can't wait for her real one."

I grin. That's why I do what I do. "I hope she sends us some photos for our portfolio."

As for grabbing picture-perfect shots, this is the best place around. Jada's itchy to explore, and we decide to stroll a bit onto the observatory trail that splits off from the entrance plaza. Our footwear isn't ideal, but we manage through the mostly flat terrain. The Los Angeles Basin spreads around us under a skirt of smog and yellowy haze. And the trails cut through masses of green and brown chaparral and native plants with scraggly edges.

"I've been poking around LA in the car and stuff." Jada points. "Down there it seems so jam-packed—not in a Manhattan kind of way, but there's so much going on, you sometimes don't see what's right in front of you."

I get what she means. And from so high up, everything is massive and tiny all at once. Proportions change, messing with your head.

"Look at that disaster." Lourdes finds the inchworm drag of the 101 freeway during pre-rush hour. "Why do we even bother driving here?"

Jada laughs, sweeping her gaze like a living panoramic camera. "I needed this," she says. "I like getting a true sense of a place when I visit. When I was down with that stomach bug, I spent hours reading everything I could about Echo Park on blogs, and even checked out the website run by a local historical society. It was eye-opening for sure—and weird what's not on it."

I crinkle my nose. "There's a historical society?" Teens usually have a thousand better things to do besides combing the internet for historical facts about their neighborhood, but I'm surprised Señor Montes never mentioned it. Strange that the website never came up when I was researching all the murals freshman year.

"What's weird about it?" Lourdes asks.

Jada's face scrunches up. "There's tons of info about the lake and the annual Lotus Festival, which is how I found the site in the first place. Pages about the silent-movie studios that used to run out of Elysian Heights. And the historic Victorian homes and bungalows in Angelino Heights."

Emilio's neighborhood. He lives in one of those bungalows.

Jada sobers. "Here's the strange part. They only casually mention that people from all over the world have settled here. That's it. Not one article or photo about the huge settlement of Cuban immigrants, like your family. Nothing about your stake in 1960s history or roots in the Sunset commercial district. The anti-communist rallies and protest marches and backroom meetings—zip."

My mouth drops a bit. That's why the site never pinged during my mural research. There *is* no documentation. Our Cuban experience in Echo Park isn't worth a single line?

"Wow, she's right," Lourdes says, studying her phone. "I found the page and was just scanning. They do mention Latinos making up 69 percent of the population. We are the majority. But the Cubans and your history are . . ."

Left out. Forgotten. On this site, we're nameless. Sin nombres.

"That needs to change," Jada says. "You did your part when you submitted the preservation application."

Lourdes twists her hair into a loose braid. "Now we hope the board agrees."

I nod, with as much hope as I can manage, because Jada's words have taken me to another place. A slight detour. "Our flower shop is trying to keep the past alive. But today I learned we have to give up one more part of us. It's small, but ours." I pivot, tracking the landscape I know so well until I find where Echo Park sits. "How many other small things will we lose?"

Before they add up to everything.

"All this is happening around me, and I could literally fix a huge part of it. Beyond saving the Varadero mural."

Jada edges closer, and I find it's more than okay that our shoulders are close enough to touch. The scent of lavender drifts off her skin. "A ten-grand fix?"

I nod, my lips pinched tight.

"Your heart and your head are starting to disagree?" Lourdes says, strong on my other side. "About the call and stuff?"

"Put the words out there," Jada says. "Name it."

Since the memorial, the truth has hovered so close to spilling over, it doesn't take much effort. Only a small, quiet breath. "My heart says making that call, giving in, is like slashing through everything we've built inside my family. All the moving on Papi did. All the love and mothering Mamita does."

"And your head?" Jada asks.

"There's guilt over having the chance to make a difference in something else we've built. And actually—God, imagine—giving that same family some fucking security." I look up but find my eyes dry and touched by the wind. "Today with the van, that became even more real, and shutting down the opportunity makes me feel like a jerk. Like, I should just suck it up and do what I have to do."

"But?" Lourdes probes.

"But should I have to sacrifice one part of myself just to keep something else together?"

When I release these words to the mountains, they ricochet with a different kind of echo than the one I know best. They come back changed, making me think of two walls filled with poems. And just like I've always stretched my Cuban side over those untended white parts, maybe my head could do the same, covering all the rest of me. Guarding that soft, red center of me that knows a five-minute call could protect so much I love on the outside.

Seventeen

*R*ose Two sells in three days. As a result, I've been dragging a ton of restless energy onto two wheels instead of four. My renewed agency kicked up after Jada dropped me off from Griffith Park. A few hours after Papi grilled steaks, I hit the street for a bike practice session when most of my neighbors were tucked in. And the next morning, I went out again when Abu left for the flower market.

After three days of this routine, back and forth for a few minutes each time, I release the brake on an early Saturday morning with a major wedding ahead of me. Something clicks. Once I start, I keep going and going, gliding seamlessly along the pocked asphalt.

I test my luck for the next few minutes, finding I can keep up that long stretch with every run. I'm so pumped, I stow the bike and helmet and text Emilio.

Me: Bike, 20 feet each time!

As soon as the message lifts off, I cringe. I just texted Emilio Avalos before the birds are up.

Me: I was so excited I didn't realize it's like 7

Me: Ignore this until later

Emilio: And yet you keep texting to tell me it's too early to text

Mortificada. That's what I am. Clearly, a few of my brain cells drove away with Rose Two. Do I respond? Ignore him like plenty of other times? When another message pops in, I'm afraid to look.

Of course, I look.

Emilio: Just messing, Thorn. I've been up for two hours like usual. Garage workout then a long ride before the city wakes up and gets in my way

Me: Seriously? This is your typical Saturday?

Emilio: Admit it, you had me pegged for an 11 am slacker

I hate it hate it hate it when he's right.

Me: So, about my 20 feet . . .

Emilio: Yeah, that's aces. Tomorrow, ready for pedals?

Me: But that's July 4. Not that I have plans

Did I just tip off Emilio about my pathetic social life? I'm not usually this solo, but Lourdes is going to Newport Beach with her family, and Jada's tagging along with Ivonne to some ritzy gig in Bel Air. My family typically uses the holiday to simply not work. That's celebration enough for the Delgados.

Emilio: No, that's actually perfect—you'll see. Long sleeves again

Right. In case I fall.

As I log off, my mind snags on another kind of thorn. What did he mean by *you'll see*?

The next morning, after managing to leave the house and slip into Emilio's truck without any Cuban commentary, two things stand out. Emilio's black shorts and dark green tee suggest that he's not down with any patriotic kitsch. And secondly, we're heading in the wrong direction.

"Did Glendale move since last time?"

He lobs an exasperated glare. "We have a stop to make first. Did you happen to notice the shiny red bike in the bed rack when I loaded in your loaner? A *small* Crimson Fuji?"

I hadn't. "Oh! The gift for that kid you were helping. Tony?"

"Yup. Señor Antonio lives just a couple minutes from here, and I thought you might like to see his reaction."

I smile easily. "Sure. I like these kinds of surprises."

His eyes stay forward, but there's the tiniest, wiliest crinkle to his mouth. "Hmm. Noted." His tone is colored a shade I don't know. Great.

Emilio turns onto a narrow street, traveling a few blocks before pulling the truck over. "Get ready to witness one of my favorite things about being alive." He rushes out to unload the gifted bike, and I move slowly from the cab, caught in a trail of hazy warmth. An unexpected trill flutters inside my belly. Either the yogurt I downed earlier was off, or my body doesn't know what to make of Emilio in benefactor mode.

He motions for me to follow down the block as he tows the sharp new wheels. "Be *vewy, vewy* quiet," he says in admirable Elmer Fudd–speak.

We're walking . . . and walking. "Why are we whispering, and why did you park so far away?"

"Because this is not a normal bike delivery. This is a secret delivery from the bike fairy, or elf—whatever. Pick your mythical creature." Before I can respond, he lures me into someone's front yard. I'm behind a tall hedge, which backs a wide liquidambar tree on the parking strip. "Wait here and stay hidden."

I can't even argue with him, which is *catastrophic*. Forced to obey, I watch as Emilio darts across the street and shuffles up the walkway of a duplex. He positions the bike on the porch, rings the doorbell, then bolts on feet as fast as wheels.

I make room for his incoming form. He's barely panting, but still whirring with pent-up anticipation and a childlike glee I do not hate. "Should be any second now. Tony's mom's clinic is closed today, hence our holiday surprise."

He inches closer until we're pressed into the corner of the leafy hedge, shoulder to shoulder, hip to hip. He's both warm and bright with the scent of dryer sheets and coconut Sun Bum mixed with the acidic tartness of hair gel. We have never huddled. Huddling is not a move on our game board.

I study the scruff hazing over his lower jaw; it's shadowed with a hundred different shades of brown and blond. Just like his hair. While Lourdes's hair is my signpost, Emilio's is a master's canvas.

"Look." He points, angling us into a sight line between the foliage.

The woman from the other day is standing in her doorway, hands smacked over her mouth. She turns, yelling into the house. Seconds later Tony is there, jumping and screaming. They read an attached tag, and Tony's mom quakes with emotion. She darts forward over the sidewalk, scanning the block from end to end and casting her arms out in disbelief.

Surely now we'll pop out and greet them? But Emilio only edges closer, making sure we stay hidden.

"You're not going up? No 'Surprise, you're on bike cam'?"

"Shh, I'm an anonymous elf," he whispers. "This is the best part. I hide to make sure no one swipes the bike. I mean, look at that thing. Cherry." He glances down, and we could bump noses. "The note says that someone magical knows how incredible Tony is, and that he worked so hard in the second grade."

My mouth hangs open, and I pray my minty toothpaste is working. Emilio gave a kid a sweet new bike and doesn't want a word of credit or acknowledgment?

"I mean, his mom will probably figure it out," he adds. "But I'll deny it if she comes to the bike shop. Dom, too."

Sometimes people lie. I remember Lourdes musing about this the other day. But some lies create another kind of truth—secret and innocent—and we need those, too. Emilio has never cared about leaving the kind of legacy I'm still wishing and waiting for. But today I learn he's leaving one anyway. In these two-wheeled gifts, he might never be known, but he'll always be remembered. *I* will remember.

For years, I've made actual lists of ways my life would be easier without Emilio's daily opposition. But if I make another list of things that will change when he finally leaves, the items come out nearly identical. He won't be around to challenge me in the middle of the street. I won't have him here to grumble and glare over, to play a smarter word like a dotted ficha—the double nine with the most points of all.

I won't have *this*. And when that notion rubs instead of relieves, I don't have an explanation. Yes, maybe there's a realm where he and I make sense. But like website history and storefronts, that space feels like just another thing that's been erased from Echo Park.

The shift of his body rustles me back to the present. I blink, exhaling roughly as the surprised duo wheels the bike into the house. Seconds later, Emilio says, "Go time!" and we shoot down the block toward a blue getaway ride, parked far enough out of sight to keep secrets.

And sure, I'm having fun and we're laughing and not bickering. It won't last—with us, it never does. But for a few moments, we're flying.

Emilio says this will feel a little like flying, too. At the school lot, he's raised the leather seat and attached the pedals. I'm sure my stomach's already left the runway.

"Here's how this is gonna work," Emilio says, approaching. "You pretend nothing else is here and you're still at home. Just glide and wait for my cue."

At his signal, I try to block out the world and find my balance. My body remembers what to do; it's nice to trust it for once.

"That's what I'm talking about, Thorn! Ha!" he yells, trotting just behind me. "Don't think too much, just lower your feet and pedal."

I do, meeting the notched surface with my sneakers, my fingers death-gripping the handlebars. And I, Clary Ann Delgado, am pedaling.

"Yes, you're doing it!"

I *am* doing it and wearing a smile that won't budge.

He calls for me to halt and repeat the motion of start, pedal, brake about a million times. But still, I can now say that I am able to ride a bike.

"Now for the next part," he says. "There's one cardinal rule about steering and cornering. Your bike won't follow you turning the handlebars. That's the easiest way to crash."

"Wait, what?" We were doing so well, and now he's speaking nonsense?

"Look where you want to go. That's it."

"Just look? I don't know about you, but my eyes do not have steering parts."

"Carajo," he tells the clear blue sky. "Your body and the bike will naturally follow your eyesight."

"How does that even begin to make sense?"

"It's science. Do we need to call Lourdes and have her explain? Can you please, *please* trust me here? The expert who runs a bike shop?"

I, in fact, cannot. But we do not need to call Lourdes.

And to show him *something*—what, I really can't say—I simply take off before his signal, aiming to turn around at the far side of the lot this time.

"Okay, sure! Do it your way!" I hear behind me.

Look where you want to go—fine, Emilio. Look where you want to go. And that is toward the bushes and not the trees on the side. I zero in on the bushes and find the bike angles the right way. Ha! Okay, well, I guess that did work.

But the turn is coming. I have to turn this bike.

"Focus on where you want to end up!" he calls behind me.

And, fine. I see where I want to turn and the direction I should go. But my focus snaps, and the turn becomes an impossible arc into nowhere good, and I begin to stress.

And get totally flustered.

And panic.

"Brake, Clary!"

I forget how to brake. What is braking? I wiggle and zigzag, sweat streaming from all over, and—

I fall in a mass of bike and dusty black asphalt and pain.

Emilio zooms over on his bike and works to untangle the frame away from my limbs. While he moves the white menace off to the side and flips the kickstand, I attempt to get up myself. Okay, so I fell. I've spent too many years trying not to lose to this guy to let one measly school parking lot take all my dignity.

I make a solid effort to lift my torso and drag my left leg up to stand, but I'm too slow, achy and lumbering. Emilio's already back. He crouches next to me, but I can't look at him. Won't. I fold myself up like a flower in reverse.

"Hey. It happens. Deep breaths, it's okay." He reaches for my left arm, cradling it gently as that tough bit of pride I'd held on to unravels into scraps. Worse, I'm bleeding. I'm wearing a long-sleeved surf tee, but I must've pushed up some of the fabric at some point. I'd felt the slide and scrape of my skin when I went down.

"Yeah," I deadpan. "Look where you're going. I did and then I . . ."

"Started overthinking."

"It's kind of what I do."

"I know. But before, you were doing really well. Don't beat yourself up."

I shrug helplessly. "The bike already did enough of that." I'm the proud wearer of an oozing five-inch gash of angry pink, pebbly debris, and peeling skin under my elbow. I slowly look up, but I don't meet judgment or teasing. Quiet concern tips the ends of all his features.

"I don't have any napkins," he says.

My body betrays me again as I let out a short laugh. I remember I'm napkinless, too. I only brought my janitor keys with a card holder hooked onto the ring. Never again will I be so unprepared. I puff my cheeks and exhale. "Well, cleaning this up should be fun. My family is home, and *that* third degree is gonna hurt worse than whatever's going on here."

"You can't sneak in?"

Brown eyes to green. "Not like you. And Mamita will smell blood from down the block. Make me spend the rest of the day in bed."

"God, do I know." He motions for me to try to rise, bracing me easily. "How's that? Okay?"

I nod.

"Wiggle your ankles and stuff."

I do. "A little stiff but everything's working." But he doesn't let me go. He's still supporting my arm as we take a few steps.

"Come on, Thorn. Back to the truck, and I'll load everything up."

After closing my eyes on the ride home to block out the last half hour of my life, I realize we're on the wrong side of Sunset. "This is your neighborhood," I muse, blinking myself back.

Emilio turns onto his street and casts a long look. "Grand prize to

Clary Delgado. Hey, so Mami's first aid cabinet is stocked. More out of habit these days. Having a kid who lived on two wheels, you know."

And then I get it. "Oh no, you thought I was serious about Mamita. It's fine. You can just drive me home, and I'll take care of this."

"That was you joking?" he says, and swings into his driveway, clearly the opposite of driving me home. "Next time, I'm gonna need a heads-up. But look, we're here and that tissue isn't doing shit and is probably making things worse."

I lift a corner of the tissue I found in his center console and wince as the thin layer rips, leaving white particles stuck to the seeping wound. Relenting, I nod and realize I'm about to see the inside of his house for the first time.

With historical preservation on my mind, I'm walking up a stone walkway to a two-story Craftsman-style house that's worthy of a brass Historical Landmark plaque. There's deep green wood siding with ivory trim and a pointy double-gabled roof. A glossy black door with a lion-head door knocker. He ushers me through; warm is the first feeling I get. Not the stifling too-warm of an inland LA summer, but the shadowy coziness of polished walnut floors and exposed beams. The furniture is charcoal velvet and almost-matching antiques, accented by Persian rugs. Although I've never been inside, I know the story of this place. Emilio's abuelos got it for a steal in the seventies and restored it over the years, but they had to move when his abuelo's MS progressed and stairs became an issue. To keep the beautiful house in the family, they traded with Emilio's parents for their one-story home in neighboring Silver Lake. His abuelita still lives there today.

"This is nice." I do a little spin. "Like, really nice."

"Thanks. It's home." He leads me down a hallway into a bathroom with white and black honeycomb tiles and the coolest claw-foot tub. He pulls a large plastic caddy from a cabinet.

"You weren't kidding." I scan the first aid items and pick up the large jar of Vicks VapoRub, a Cuban family staple. "If you try and put *el veeks* on my arm, I swear."

He snorts. "As someone who was smeared with *vaporú* in too many places growing up, I would never." He grabs the container. "Instead, we'll just put some behind your ears, and its powers will heal up that arm in a couple hours."

Hours. Time—it hits me. I'm already wincing from trying to peel off the tissue from the wound, but I remember what's happening next weekend. "Sofia's quinces ball," I say on a grumble.

"Yeah, my suit's back from the cleaners, and I'll make sure Papi can go for at least some of the party. What about it?" Seeing the mess of tissue particles and road rash that is my arm, Emilio readies a warm, soapy washcloth.

"Thanks," I say, and begin to dab through the stinging pain. "My dress is sleeveless. Look at me—horror movie ready." I already feel bruises blooming on my left thigh.

Emilio squeezes Neosporin onto a cotton ball. "Too bad it's not Halloween themed. You'd win first prize."

I grab the cotton, glaring. "Are you sure, Wheels? With you sweeping all categories of the scary mask contest—"

My comeback is cut short when Emilio's mom pokes her head into the bathroom. "Clary?" She steps inside. "What's all this?"

Emilio dashes out his hand. "Some pavement struck back, is all."

She hooks one arm onto the waistband of her faded jeans. "Did my son have anything to do with this, chica?" she asks with amusement.

Emilio says "not even" right when I eke out "sort of," which earns a top-level glare from the boy currently covering my wound with a nifty gauze wrap from their kit.

I may have gone too far. "I mean, not directly, of course. More . . . indirectly."

Emilio caps the ointment. "Really."

"At any rate, you need some lemonade before you leave. Fresh squeezed," she says, and scoots out.

"So now I suppose you're gonna blame the end of your biking run on me, too?" Emilio asks.

"Who says I'm quitting?" This comes out before I really comprehend the reach of my words. More than not wanting to give up in front of him, I don't want to give up in front of myself.

He wraps the unused gauze and returns it to the caddy. "I was just . . . I mean, the fall. After that story you told me, I thought you'd call it done."

"I'm not seven." I carefully roll my sleeve down over the covered wound. "Unless you won't let me use the loaner bike anymore."

"What kind of shit teacher-slash-bike elf would I be then?" he says as we enter the living room. His mom hands me a cool glass while Emilio puts the supplies away. She rests his drink on top of an oak sideboard.

I sip the best lemonade I've ever had. "Did you add lavender and mint?"

"From our garden. Leave it to our neighborhood florist to pick those out." She pivots before exiting. "You're welcome here anytime.

That is, if certain members of this household don't pose too much risk for accidental bodily harm."

I laugh easily, but she's not all the way wrong about her son, and risk, and other parts that bleed in secret when they fall too hard.

Sobered, I wander with my drink to a large photo collage. Emilio and his older sister, Esmé, grace the wall at various stages of growing up. A few senior portraits are mixed in with a set from Esmé's Florida wedding last year. Remembering my Christmas morning excitement from earlier with the bike, I find Emilio's in an old photo in front of a brightly lit tree bursting with gifts. Little Emilio is lying on the rug with a nativity scene. I crack up because next to the usual players, he's lined up two Ninja Turtle action figures, a Hot Wheels racer, and . . .

"Are those LEGO Star Wars minifigures by the manger?" I ask when he returns.

"Who can say for sure who was really there?" He takes a long pull from his glass, and all I can think of is this same boy running from Sunday school into the great wide open. Because he wanted to.

A series of rhythmic clunks sound from the staircase, and Emilio hands me his drink, bolting over, a curse rolling out under his breath.

"We have a visitor," Fernando Avalos says with three more steps to carefully navigate. He's managing a walking cast with one crutch.

Emilio supports his other side. "What happened to not going downstairs without calling Mami or me to help?"

"You're right here, no? And I heard there's lemonade."

Emilio's eyes roll heavenward as he leads his father closer. I haven't seen Emilio's dad in person since his fall. He's wearing a loose athletic set and a well-loved Dodgers cap.

"Um, happy Fourth of July," I say, and instantly want to hide myself and my cheesy greeting underneath the floorboards. *Happy Fourth?*

"A ti también. And thank you for bringing such lovely flowers all the way to the hospital." He smiles warmly. "With no card, I thought they were from my sister, but Emilio knew right away."

"Oh. Well," I manage, but edit myself before I reach *Level Ridiculous*. I was already stuck on what to say about his pending health situation. I'm not even sure if he knows that I know. And if he does know, is it rude not to ask?

I settle for "I hope everything's healing and that you'll be back to work soon."

"Tomorrow, for a half day. Dominic and this guy miss my griping, but I hear your sister has organized the entire storeroom so well, the boys . . ." He trails off, laughing. "Ellos no pueden encontrar nada. I can't wait to meet this woman."

I can only nod; *organized* and *Jada* aren't two words that typically hang out together in my head.

"Stay with your friend, mijo." Señor Avalos sets off toward the kitchen. "I'll get my own lemonade. I'm not dead yet."

The air leaves my lungs. All I can do is stare at my sneakers, finding new scuffs from my parking-lot tumble.

"Papi doesn't believe in the idea of 'too soon,'" Emilio says.

"I'm sorry," I whisper. "All the uncertainty and waiting must get to him."

"To all of us."

Eighteen

*T*ime races toward the next Friday evening, where I use the swanky bathroom at the Westin Pasadena to get ready for Sofia's much-anticipated fiesta de fifteen. My family and I have been setting up for two hours, after the countless more we've spent crafting anything and everything with flowers and props. It's finally time to see my vision come together, and I'm the final piece that needs decorating.

While I primp, the marquee scene from two days ago winds through my head, when I'd come home from a Griffith Park hike with Lourdes and found Mamita and Jada in my living room.

As I'd chugged down a cool drink from Mamita, Jada had grabbed a fancy black garment bag from the couch. "I found this in a second-hand shop in Bel Air."

I smiled easily. "Must be good if you brought it all the way over here for a fashion show."

"Nope, not for me." She stepped forward. "The shop owner was putting this dress on a mannequin when I stopped in. And I nearly passed out because it seemed like your size, and I thought you'd like to wear it to Sofia's ball."

Gurgles zipped around my stomach. Jada picked out a dress for me?

"Let us see this masterpiece." Mamita grabbed one edge of the bag while Jada pulled down the zipper.

"Oh my God" was all I could say. More artwork than dress, the underlayer was a midnight-blue column with black satin ribbons forming a caged halter neck. But the top layer took my breath away. I was almost afraid to touch the black lace appliqué flowers covering the entire look and extending slightly beneath the deep-blue slip. I zeroed in on another detail. *How? How did she know?* A set of black chiffon sleeves fell, not from the shoulder, but from the bust, leaving the top bare except for the halter straps. This dress had long sleeves.

My closet held the black mini with a tiered skirt that I'd worn to homecoming and probably three other events. But my arm. I'd been planning to toss on a wrap to hide it even though that's not my style at all. Jada brought me something that would cover all my wounds.

"The flowers—qué lindos," Mamita crooned, examining the flawless stitching highlighting each lacy bloom. She frowned when she reached for the tag. "I know this designer, and none of their dresses are less than four hundred dollars."

Everything deflated.

"That's why I love shopping secondhand," Jada said. "It's barely worn, and I got it for seventy-five percent off."

"Still, that's a lot for me right now," I said.

"Clary, it's a gift," Jada said softly. "We've missed a lot—everything, actually. I never got to yell at you for raiding my closet or rescue you from an awkward sleepover. We didn't get to sneak out for midnight Taco Bell or whine about math class." Her shoulder sprang up. "Can I do something now?"

Something . . . sisterly.

I'm sure I waited too long before nodding. And when I accepted the hanger, I braced myself for a pinch of unease and uncertainty. It didn't come. Instead, I was caught inside the stream of rituals Jada had just brought up, and how they didn't seem foreign or ghostly at all. How I was able to picture them, scene by scene, even though they'd never happened.

It was then that I did something I'd never done. In a move that felt just as right as the luxurious fabric, I swung my arms around Jada's neck. "Thank you," I whispered.

"You're so welcome, girlie," she said as she tightened her grip, holding me . . . like Mamita does. Like Tía Roxanne and my father do. Like family.

And now, with my hair pinned halfway up with some loose curls trailing, and my best attempt at makeup applied, the feeling wafts in again. It remains as the dress slips on like a special skin.

Tonight, I add strappy black heels and a swipe of berry-red lipstick. I check my phone; Sofia and the Colón family should be getting out of their private mass at any moment. I scroll up for one more look at Lourdes's enthusiastic text picture. When the family arrived at the church, my handcrafted corsages, along with Fia's larger bouquet and boutonnieres, were waiting. Book-paper flowers nestle into clusters of white roses, blue hyacinths, and dusty millers in different sizes and combinations.

I gather my belongings and swing out into the hallway, almost bumping into Abu from the adjacent bathroom.

"Ay, qué bella," he says, and kisses my cheek.

I pull back, giving my handsome abuelo a wolf whistle at the sight of him in a closely cut charcoal suit. "Okay, guapo, you go."

"It's not too much?" he asks, doing a silly step that's half flourish, half salsa dance move. "I worry about, how you say, my fit being too distracting on the dance floor."

I shake my head and plant a sloppy kiss on his cheek.

He grabs my duffel. "I'll take this to the car so you can get to the ballroom."

Abu's off seconds before my dad emerges in a navy suit and silvery blue tie. "Delgado boys came to play tonight," I tell him.

He strikes a pose and eyes my look. "To quote Lourdes, *wooooow*." I laugh as he offers me his bent arm. "Shall we, señorita?" We set off toward the party venue. "It seems like yesterday that we were walking like this to your quinces."

Just like tonight's celebration, I'd planned every inch of my own ball: el jardín de Clary. Two years ago my family transformed my quinces ballroom into as much enchanted garden as they could create within four walls. My blush organza gown was set with appliqué petals that gathered tight on the bodice then trickled down the skirt. I'd designed a cabbage-rose bouquet for myself, but when I came out of my bedroom as a dressed quinceañera, my dad revealed a secret.

"I hope it's okay, this surprise. I wanted you to have something just from me," he said that night, looking like a movie star in his black tux. He brought out a beautiful pomander ball studded with cherry blossoms in a gradient of pinks and whites. Each had a pearl center. With pride, he showed me the pomander's looped handle, cut from wide iridescent pink ribbon. CLARY was embroidered along the edge. When I was born, I was supposed to have been christened Adriana, honoring a distant tía in Cuba. But when Papi returned to the hospital after a food run, he found another name filled into my birth certificate. Not a family tribute, but a purple flower. He didn't contest it. He'd gone along with the only stamp Vanessa Holt would ever leave upon his baby girl. And every day since, he's never let go, or left, or done anything but try to love and guide me the best way he's known how.

Sometimes people lie.

Those three words open as wide as a lifetime. They're in little things—as small as a floral message card—like the way Emilio denies his bicycle-elf gifts. And they're in the bigger, heavier choices we make, knowing we're doing the best we can at the time.

We're not to the ballroom yet, but I halt, realization overwhelming me. My family foundation doesn't have to be perfect to be strong and secure. At the time, my dad and abuelos did the best they could. They believed they were saving me from a part of my life I wasn't ready to live yet.

"Papi," I say, and catch the same warm smile he gave another quinceañera two years ago. "I understand why you kept Jada from me. I forgive you."

After a short walk and another long, long hug, my dad and I reach the ballroom double doors. "This is your show. I'm going in—Mamita and Abu are already at our table." With a last forehead kiss, he lets go. I let go. And get to work.

Catching up to speed, I grab a clipboard and confirm last-minute details with the hotel event coordinator. And then they arrive. Lourdes is first down the hall in a raspberry strapless minidress, her long hair wound into a flower-studded updo of twists and braids.

"What?! I can't even handle your fabulousness right now," she says with too much surprise. I'd sent photos of my dress the other day. (We never hide clothes, no matter what.)

"Stop, you're perfect." I hug my friend and wait until she snaps a cute selfie of us. "How was the service?"

"Blessedly short. But we turned into La Familia Waterworks," Lourdes says, tipping her head. Sofia floats in with their parents and two sets of tíos—the padrinos who helped sponsor the event. Sofia's escort and court follow, wearing my paper roses pinned to jackets and dotting wrist corsages.

I'm caught in a mass of hugs and kisses from Lourdes's family before I resume command mode, lining everyone up for their entrances. "Colón party of a hundred, it's go time." I flag the event coordinator. "Can you tell the band to start?"

She and Lourdes disappear into the ballroom, and I wait for the intro of Ivonne's Afro-Cuban jazz take on "Just the Way You Are" by Bruno Mars. Since Puro Sabor offered the same "family" discount Lourdes and I got, Fia gets live music at her ball, too.

After Ivonne's introduction, I open the door for the tíos, parents, and finally, the court of six wearing black tuxes and navy-blue minidresses. Sofia made a modern choice not to have the traditional number of attendants: seven damas and seven chambelanes.

Lastly, it's just the quinceañera in her baby-blue gown and her curled updo. Her escort and school friend, James, waits for my cue. "Ready to see your library?"

Sofia nods, her eyes wide and a little misted. "Thank you, Clary." She holds up her bouquet with accented flowers made from the books she loves so much. "*This* is totally me."

My heart squeezes as the song changes. Ivonne announces the birthday girl and transforms a rearranged "The Book of Love" by Gavin James. And I open the door.

Though I slip in last, the words *I should have known* are the first to pop into my head. On the stage, right behind Ivonne and next to the drummer, Jada expertly commands a percussion set. Congas at her waist and maracas in hand, she meets my disbelieving expression and shoots out a coy grin. There's a story here—fitting, as the entire ballroom is dedicated to them.

I wind through the party toward our table and slide into the empty chair next to Mamita. "Did you know about that? Her?" I ask, pointing to my sister jamming along to the last bits of the song.

"Thirty minutes ago," Mamita says, lovely in a black jumpsuit. "Rogelio had to leave town unexpectedly, and Ivonne has a percussionist right there in her casita. Entonces . . ."

Jada and good timing always seem to get along. I survey the room. With the house lights lowered, my centerpieces tell a literary fairy tale. Each table overflows with stacks of leather-bound hardbacks and silver vases bursting with white and blue hydrangeas, plus my book-page roses as accents. Vintage reading glasses and votives from Marlow create the cozy library feel.

Mamita elbows me. "I keep forgetting to tell you. Your tía is coming for the weekend. She got a good fare last minute."

My mind skips forward. "Wait, *this* weekend?"

"She lands tomorrow afternoon. We have the Loz Feliz wedding and the bridal showers to handle, so she'll just let herself in."

Tomorrow as in Saturday as in the next day. Although Papi's filled Tía Roxanne in on all things Jada, I can't begin to predict how a meeting between two of my family members who are as different as sunshine and rain might go. For the first time in my life, LA might host a hurricane.

My phone buzzes, and I shove my incoming tía aside for now.

Lourdes: I'm gonna cry! The photo area is so cute!

I crane my neck, spotting Lourdes. Instead of a photo booth, Papi and Abu built a photo stop with a faux library wall and a stone fireplace. I used sprays of fiery orange and red snapdragons for the flames.

Me: See why I didn't want to spoil?

Lourdes: No? Mami's calling me to the table. Find me later 😘

A drumroll and Ivonne's cue kick off the ceremonial portion of the event.

It's precisely then that I get my first glimpse of Emilio across the room. He's with Mami Ynez and his parents, and I'm glad to see his papi made it after all.

Emilio looks up, and I'm caught. I give a casual wave.

He waves back. The suit he mentioned last weekend is silvery gray, paler than I thought he'd choose, but somehow extra nice against his skin tone. Much product was involved in his hairdo. It's neater than ever, slicked behind his ears and likely secured by one of the leather bands he likes.

And no—I puff out a heated breath. As chief party planner, it's time to focus on my job, not Emilio's hair. I adjust my line of sight and catch myself up. The ceremonial father-daughter dance is only a few steps in, but it doesn't take long for my attention to scatter everywhere at once. I'm surveying the room to head off any possible flubs. Cross-checking the printed event schedule next to my place setting and ensuring the court members are where they're supposed to be. Then there's the living telenovela scene across my table. Papi's watching Ivonne all rapt and broody-like, as if she created music itself.

A text comes through.

Emilio: I didn't go to your quinces, Thorn

What is he doing? I do not look at Emilio, like you don't look straight into the sun. But you're fully aware it's *there*.

Me: Your whole family was invited

Emilio: I didn't know

Me: Maybe ask your abuela about the invitation, Wheels

Emilio: Nah, I can put two and two together

An excellent comeback materializes, but a situation has me jutting up from my table. Twin girls in yellow have gotten hold of the satin pillow Fia's court used to carry in her tiara. And they swiped her traditional quinceañera doll in its matching blue gown, too. Where are these kids' parents?

I rush over. "Hi, girlies, these are special for Sofia," I say, pondering how to pry the items away without causing a twin tantrum in this library. I crouch low. "Here's a secret. They're making fancy blue drinks at the bar. Hurry before more kids find out and beat you to the line."

Thankfully, they release the quinces contraband and skip away. I return the items to the cake table, double-checking the tiered masterpiece crafted to look like a tall stack of classic books. My phone buzzes, and it's the event director. Nice save. Caught that but you were faster. I'll guard the table better

I write back, Thanks. In 5, special dance

The band's slated to back the court for their choreographed salsa-dance version of "Be Our Guest" with plenty of congas. I hope Jada's ready.

Another text.

Emilio: Yellow twin menaces, check!

Which means he was watching.

Me: Getting them nice and sugared up to send back to their parents

Emilio: Devious. Were there any big drama antics at your quinces? I mean besides me not being there

Me: Your presence would've added less drama?

Emilio: We'll never know

Before I can conjure a reply, Lourdes slides over, handing me one of the blue mocktails I just sent the girls to fetch. "You need. I'm getting dizzy just watching you. I feel bad that you can't relax and enjoy the party you masterminded."

"Nope, all good. I have a vision, and it will be perfect." I sip, realizing I haven't had much to eat all day.

"Speaking of effort," Lourdes says, "Emilio put in a little tonight. He shaved, which means the apocalypse might drop any minute now."

I sputter through my next sip of the fizzy drink. "I hadn't noticed."

"Sure. Just like I haven't had Señor Cluck's in a month." At my glare she continues. "I ran into him at the bar. He mentioned that he wasn't at your quinces and asked me about it. Weird. Or is it?"

I thrust up my hand innocently. I don't like where this is going. Even though Lourdes is my best friend, I don't have the words or any desire to deconstruct *him* right now. Good thing I'm literally saved by the bell. Jada's shaking a cowbell, and the attendants and Sofia rush in for their Latin-Disney number.

Lourdes squeals with delight, arming her camera and rushing back to her parents.

As the party flows, the court clears the floor for all the guests to strut their stuff. The waitstaff serves crab-stuffed chicken breasts, but I only manage three bites before Abu and I are up again to deal with a drunk guest needing a cup of coffee and an Uber. Thankfully, Papi steps in to handle a tech issue with the slideshow because I'd definitely make that worse.

Over the next hour, I sneak in a handful of photo wall pictures with Lourdes before fielding more hijinks from the "yellow twin menaces" running off with the prop basket. Then there's a mix-up with the cake-cutting and a misplaced family heirloom knife—found. And the latest: an updo collapse from one of Sofia's damas that I fixed with Mamita's bobby-pin stash and a travel-sized hairspray from her Cuban mami purse of wonders.

When I return, everything's running oddly smoothly. But getting a chance to finally breathe only makes me crave some peace and a little fresh air. I know where to find both.

My dad suggested this venue to the Colóns because of the large courtyard adjacent to the ballroom. I head toward the paned double doors but slow as I pass the dance floor. Dance-dodger Emilio is doing the opposite of sitting out "The Girl from Ipanema." In his arms is a mysterious girl about our age in a red dress and sky-high stilettos.

Now *this* is nothing new for Emilio. I shouldn't even look twice.

I am definitely looking twice.

Maybe it's like trash TV and fender benders. You can't *not* pay attention. I also can't find Lourdes, so I send her a text before I move on. Who's the girl in red dancing with Emilio?

Outside, a long water feature runs the length of the elevated patio, with a colorful lit-up spray in the middle. A few guests are milling around. I stroll the vast space for a bit, breathing in the cooling air, then step up to the railing and the panoramic view of historic downtown Pasadena.

Footsteps sound behind me. "Her name's Mara. Since you were wondering."

Nineteen

*E*milio. Not Lourdes.

Quizzically, I turn because this makes zero sense. Emilio's supersonic hearing doesn't work across cyberspace. "What?"

He steps up. "Red-dress girl. Mara Gomez." His expression's blown wide with amusement. And I'm still a mass of confusion until he lifts his phone, shaking it.

Oh no. Please, please no.

Hastily, I reach into my chain clutch for my phone. And it's terribly clear why Lourdes never responded to my text. Of all the times I have been mortificada over this boy, this one wins the blue ribbon.

Between managing the party chaos and fielding texts from multiple people, I forgot my last messages were not from Lourdes. They were from Emilio about the fact that the cake is awesome, and he might have two pieces. And what kind of cake did I have at my quinces?

I'd ignored this. *Who's the girl in red dancing with Emilio?* That was my unintentional answer to cake flavor. I lift my head like it's made of iron.

"That wasn't meant for me, huh?" His eyes are so bright, they're still dancing. "My name in there kinda gave it away."

And that's it. I am done feeding his amusement and looking like a fool. "If you hadn't noticed, I was a little busy in there. I was simply asking who she was because I've never seen her around before." My voice comes out smooth and polished even though my heart rate's doubling every minute.

Another step closer. He pockets his phone. "Family friend of the Colóns. She lives in San Diego."

"Cool. You two looked like you were having fun."

"It was one dance. Lulú's cousin cut in after my SOS cue."

My next breath turns into a faint snort. "Wow, that's handy. Didn't even need a window to escape out of this time. I'm surprised. She's pretty."

"She is."

Well. "She's probably just here for the weekend, at most. Seems like your jam."

Emilio adjusts his shirt collar. And Lourdes was right. His skin shines clear and smooth with just a hint of sunburn. "What are you trying to say?"

"I'm simply acknowledging your type. Temporary. And a weekend *something* seems perfect for you." He glares and I add, "Name *one* girl you've dated for more than two or three days." I hold out my hands. "Not judging. Just observing."

"You think I lead girls on, then run on purpose?"

I crack a laugh, grateful to be past the text mortification. "Sometimes there's a bike."

He swears under his breath. "Have you ever considered that you might only have half the information?"

"One girl, Wheels. You still haven't answered me."

"Fine. You're both right and wrong. At first, I kept stuff casual because that felt best. Group dates, hanging out. But all senior year, I was planning on leaving for Europe. That's where my focus was. I made it clear that I wasn't down for anything long-term when I asked someone out. I don't hook up with people, then bail like it's some game, if that's the word on the street."

All through his speech, I was waiting for him to not make sense. That didn't happen. "Okay. I *might* see how some of the rumors, or labels you mentioned, aren't true and how much that must suck. Especially when the hallway the Monday after prom nearly exploded over some tea that you and Carlie Anderson were kissing on the dance floor, almost setting off the fire sprinklers."

He flinches, then shrugs. "Not a false rumor. I kissed Carlie. But that was it. Literally just a kiss—a good one, too."

"But you still—"

"We still *nothing*. She's cool, that's it. I don't ever want to go out with her again, and she doesn't want that, either, but the kiss was still good." When my face crinkles, he says, "Come on, you must have at least one memorable kiss in your past, even if the relationship wasn't."

"I . . . maybe? I mean, I've been kissed before," I mutter, realizing I set this trap all by myself. In trying to deflect from a single text message, I have officially moved into discussing kissing with Emilio Avalos.

"You make it sound like dental work. 'Sure, I've kissed a dude. I've had a root canal.'"

I exhale roughly. "It wasn't novocaine and a drill. I'm just saying they were decent. Not exactly *memorable*. I don't have a dance-floor fire-alarm kiss in my past."

"That's—" He stops as if he's pressed pause on the entire world.

"That's what? Pathetic? Sad?"

"*Not* kissing someone is never pathetic. Kissing someone because you want to and then not getting the full effect is a shitty outcome. You deserve a good, memorable kiss." Fingers drum against one pant leg. "I mean, I . . ."

"You what?"

He laughs, lifting up and down on his shoes. "Forget it. Terrible idea."

In equal parts, I want to hear this terrible idea *and* run back into the ballroom. "Well, now you have to tell me." So that's how my mind plays it. Great.

He shoves his hands into his pockets. "For the record, you asked me to tell you, and I wasn't—"

"Wheels!"

"Fine. It was a knee-jerk idea. Don't even know where it came from." He makes a sound constructed from about 80 percent nerves, and this is also new for us. Emilio has never appeared nervous around me. "I was gonna say that I could give it a go. I could kiss you."

Time is obliterated. I'm standing on acres of clouds.

And then I'm laughing.

And then he's laughing.

When we both stop, wringing ourselves out clean, a distant truth remains between us. Soft and hesitant. "Holy shit, you were serious."

"For a second. But it's a bad idea."

I nod. "The worst."

Our eyes lock for a single beat.

He quickly turns toward the historic building across the street. This hotel prides itself on postcard views of the 1920s-era Pasadena City Hall building. Now, well past dark, the massive Italian-style structure is brilliantly lit, glowing warm and yellow from every angle. Emilio tracks the span of the towering central dome before turning back. "Did we just agree on something? Without arguing?"

"I think so. But to be fair, we agree on *some* things."

"Right, but usually just the big stuff. Like cancer and animal cruelty can fuck off—that level. But little day-to-day things, not so much."

"Yeah. Next to never. So if we both immediately agree, then we . . ."

His jaw wrenches sideways. "Then something got knocked off-center. Clearly, we can't trust either of our responses, and we're missing something. And we *could* put things back to normal by, you know, doing something shockingly opposite to our reality."

My stomach heats, anxiety flooding in deep. I grasp the railing. "To be clear, because we rarely are, you actually want to kiss me? You said *just* a kiss like . . ."

"I wouldn't have mentioned it otherwise. And yeah, just a kiss. Then you can say you know what a good one is like. A memorable one. I would hope I can do better than those other dudes."

"Cocky much?"

"I didn't mean it that way, promise," he says. "If afterward you still find you're stuck in unmemorable land, then I'll concede that I'm really not that good at it."

"Have you ever made this proposition before? You kiss many other friends on the fly?"

"We're not friends," he says, his mouth quirking suspiciously. "But we keep each other's secrets. You told me about your birth mother. And let me help you figure out those pesky two wheels."

I deflate. "You taught me how to ride a bike, so now you're moving on to other skills I'm lacking, like kissing? Seriously?"

Big cringe. "My offer isn't about *teaching* anything. It's the double-nine domino. Equal on both sides."

My shoulder pops up. "I had to ask."

"That's fair." He steps forward; he's wearing the same cologne as on our bike-riding days. "But we need boundaries. It's one kiss, not a promise ring. I'd never want you to feel awkward or hurt tomorrow."

Somehow, I rise above the earthquake inside my chest. "What about *me* worrying about the state of *your* being tomorrow?"

His grin. Instant and brighter than the glowing Renaissance dome in the distance. "Touché. And one more thing." He reaches out a hand. I take it. "Las fichas."

A word that's decades old for an act that's entirely new between us. "I understand and thank you. But parts of this don't feel safe."

"Maybe the best parts." He reaches out his other hand, and we get used to the sensation of fingers locked tight. "This okay?"

It's my last chance to back out, but I'm frozen in place, mind and heart racing. Por Dios, this goes against everything I've ever wanted: Real, lasting feelings. Security. But if I'm honest with myself, that same wanting part also craves a single leap into a different sort of place. Somewhere foreign and fleeting and nowhere close to home. Work-weary, trapped under the reckless buzz of a summer of impossible choices, I strip this one of all its thorns and surprise myself. "All good."

Emilio licks his lips, closing all remaining space and—"Oof." Of course, we start out comically out of sync.

"I'm pretty sure that's not it, Wheels."

"Swan boat part two." His forehead tips against mine, awkward giggles bubbling between us.

I squeeze his hands. "I think you're supposed to move the other—"

His mouth is on mine—the right way—hands wrenched free and cupping my face as gently as this summer night.

The kind of gentle that lies like people do.

A billowy thought comes, saying I shouldn't sink too much into these next few seconds. I could hold myself up better, bracing all of me. (I do this with tulips, but not on a balcony with a flight-risk boy.) And I should *know* better. But I can't remember what I'm supposed to be guarding. I forget what part of myself wouldn't lean into his silver-gray suit. Into woody spice and honed muscle and a wild, thundering heart. I can't remember.

I am erased. Sin nombre.

The blankness stretches long into my limbs as he shifts. I'm fully in his arms now. Deeper, closer, his mouth vanilla-sweet from the bookish cake I ordered. His lips hum with a crackling-fire warmth, so unhurried they're almost lazy.

Seconds tick before he breaks away, staying gentle. He's a little too winded for his level of fitness, and when my eyes open, I catch the movement of his throat working through a swallow.

"I hope," he starts, sliding his hands down my sheer black sleeves and clasping mine again. "I hope that was enough to be memorable."

As in all our other signature games and squabbles, I want him to lose, and to be so pitifully wrong. But he's not wrong. And I can only say, "That wasn't *not* memorable."

He smiles, my hands still trapped inside his. Silence carries over the balcony, and there's only the sound of the sprinkling fountain for too long.

"Is it weird yet?" he asks.

I decide it doesn't have to be. I know what our kiss was and what it wasn't. "We're already weird, so not really."

"Noted. And same."

"Now what?" I ask softly.

He glances toward the ballroom. "Did you get any cake yet?" When I shake my head, he frowns. "Did you get to dance?"

"Too much running around."

"We could dance."

"You hate dancing. Which is why I was surprised to see you out there."

"Clary," he says in exasperation. "We. Could. Dance."

I stare at my black heels, inches away from his polished oxfords. "Yeah, okay."

We have a couple false starts, righting ourselves and gearing up for our return to the party. We settle on walking in with a respectable distance between us. I'm glad to find the band on a break—their canned hits queued up. Even recorded, the music fills the ballroom with sound that feels like color.

The dance floor's fit to burst, but we find a spare corner, and I immediately try to locate my people. Emilio draws me in, and I loop my arms around his neck. Lourdes and other friends are showing off their best moves in a circle with Fia and James; I don't think they've seen us yet. Moving compass points, I smile across Emilio's shoulder— Papi's dancing with Ivonne, so closely it feels like the universe is intruding. Finally.

Abu and Mamita shuffle across the floor like ballroom champions. "They're making everyone else look like amateurs," Emilio says. "Your abuelos."

I glance up, half existing in our post-kiss realm. "They practice in the kitchen. Always in sync."

"Speaking of, we're not that bad out here," he notes with a playful curl through the words. "I'm shocked my toes are still intact."

"Song's not over yet." The tune is Ivonne's sultry take on "Sway."

If Emilio suggested dancing on purpose as a way to ease us back into reality, it was the right call. I'm always prepared for this boy to turn and walk away. But if he had, I'd be lying if I said it wouldn't have bruised a little.

"Your dress is really pretty," he says as Ivonne croons from the sound system. *Sway me now.* His arms cinch behind me, shortening the gap between us. I know it's because there's not a lot of real estate on this dance floor. But we're so close, there's barely a tiptoe between his mouth and the shell of my ear. "I didn't say it earlier because . . ."

Is he blushing or is it just the house lights accentuating his sunburn? "Right, that. And thanks. Jada came through a couple days ago." I drag my injured arm down his chest and into his view. "Hides the horror show. Covers the kindergarten finger paint on my thigh, too."

I expect a laugh. Instead, I get bashful. "I still feel bad about your fall. It's actually why I came out to the terrace. I saw you leave, and it looked like you were in pain."

I looked like I was in pain? My reaction to watching him dance with Mara had made it seem like my bike wounds were aching? I need a minute to let that settle. "It's just a little sore now and healing up fine. Cool suit," I deflect. "I like the gray."

"Thanks. My wedding go-to. And I've worn it to every quinces lately." His face goes all wry. "Except for—"

"Yeah, yeah, except for mine. Why have you brought that up, like, five thousand times tonight?"

"This was one of the best themed events I've been to, with really creative details. I noticed right away when we got here. I mean, who would've thought of a library? It just made me curious about what you planned for yourself."

"English garden. A lot of flowers—like, truckloads. You would've given me shit with your valleys-over-vases obsession. But I did what I know and love more than trying to surprise everyone."

"You're not *not* surprising, Thorn."

My mouth goes dry, and I detect a general sense of space for two seconds before I realize he's pulled back.

"Mami's giving me the time-to-go wave. I think Papi's reached his limit, and I'm their ride."

"Oh." I jerk away, maybe too quickly and entirely too anxiously when I consider how my dance with Mr. Unlikely would pique certain key people at this ball. "Totally." I smooth out my dress. "I'm glad he was able to make it for most of the party."

"Me too." We've stepped off the dance floor, but he stays in front of me, motionless. "Look." And he does—anywhere but my face. Left, right, the stage as it populates again with Ivonne and the band. "Just checking one last time that we're good. You know, on the same page and it's not awkward."

A flat smile pulls across my mouth. "We're good." *I'm almost positive.* "I'll see you on Sunset or something?"

"Or something," he says, and takes a step back. "Night, Clary."

I'm certain I make a noise of agreement. But the second he's off to round up his parents, I pull out my phone, if only to have something to hold. That will stop the jittery trembling, right? I'd purposely shut my mobile down after the red-dress debacle, and when I power up again, I find a ton of messages from Lourdes. I scan, my belly dropping.

Lourdes: Hey, where you at?

Lourdes: I see you. Explain please so I don't die

Lourdes: Hellooooo, answer me. You and E and no room for El Espíritu Santo

Lourdes: I walked right in front of you on the d-floor and you didn't even notice

Lourdes: Turn on your GD phone

Lourdes: Clary!!!!!!

The mild headache I'd felt creeping on earlier jumps to full-force hammer mode. I rise up to my tiptoes, searching out my friend, even though facing Lourdes—or anyone—is number twenty on my list of top ten things I'd want to be doing.

Feeling an elbow rap against my shoulder, I turn. Jada's behind me, holding two plates of cake.

"Quick, follow me" is all she says. Right now, it's my best option.

There's a partially concealed door near the stage. I slink behind the flowy tiers of Jada's lime-green dress into a small service area. Racks of linens line the wall, and a push door leads into the kitchen.

"What are we hiding from?" I question.

"Not hiding, regrouping." She shoves the cake plate and fork into my hands. "You haven't stopped for five minutes all night. Except for, well, I'm glad you got at least one dance in."

My jaw clenches, and I prepare for the Jada version of the third degree Lulú just pulled. Only, it doesn't come. Jada simply digs into her own slice of vanilla heaven.

I take a tentative bite. "Um, wow."

"Right?" Jada says, drawing out the word. "This is seconds for me. But I've had a stage view all night, and no band member has come close to working as hard as you. I figured this secret hideaway I found during sound check wasn't my worst idea."

It wasn't, by far. Already, my blood is cooling, and the cake settles in like a miracle. Jada's happily shoving in forkfuls. How did she know, just like this dress, what would fit best around the last fifteen minutes of me?

We're in no hurry, lingering in this quiet alcove. Jada launches into a tale of the time she sat in on a street music concert in Rome. We eat the sugary wonder while my phone buzzes on repeat in my bag.

And when the plates are empty, she looks at me, a thousand knowing questions in her eyes.

Mine try to say that I'm fine. No, I am. This is just how it always is with me—sometimes I need a little time to recalibrate when a lot of *new* and *novel* and downright *extraterrestrial* rushes into my life. (Misdirected texts and kissing your irritating neighbor and dancing with him, too.) Surprises? Talk about telenovela-level bombshells.

"Here's my next idea," Jada says. "The event's winding down, and you look partied out. The VW is in the back lot." She pulls the key from her beaded bag. "You run through the kitchen and out the service door. You wait while I tell everyone that you're beat and your blood sugar's all wonky, so I'm taking you home."

"You mean, I just leave?"

"You just leave. I've got this."

The door is five feet away, but this is not who I am—I don't run and avoid. I stay and fix and deal. But I remember what Jada said one time about self-care. Tonight, mine changes shape until I'm craving a fraction of the freedom Emilio must feel at an exit sign. There's one on this wall. My imagination soars, reaching to borrow a shaving of bike rubber. To steal a shred of his plane ticket to a place where nobody knows his name.

I don't even know the name of the girl who acts like I don't, who snatches the key from Jada's hand. And escapes.

Twenty

To: clary@larosablancaflorals.com
From: mark.sonder@parks.ca.gov

Office of Historic Preservation
File: Echo Park Commercial District
Case Number: 982728
Status: Denied*

*The district submitted for consideration for the National
Register of Historic Places was not found to have adequate
cultural or other historical impact, according to the
guidelines outlined by the Office of Historic Preservation.

I learned about the rule of three when we discussed it in my
English class. Some people claim that bad luck comes in threes,
but my class looked at other sources that were totally contradictory—
written by glass-half-full types, saying that it's actually good news

that arrives in a three-crested wave. Now, as I'm crafting a suite of bouquets for a backyard wedding (blushing Akito roses, white stock flowers, hydrangeas, eucalyptuses), I'm convinced those opposing "rule of three" opinions are both correct because life is just that bizarre.

I'm living out the evidence.

It started last night with Mamita's (good) news about Tía Roxanne flying in today. And I wouldn't have thought anything of the timing, beyond the short notice, until I got into Jada's getaway car and logged on to Mail before shutting down my phone for the night.

The unread message at the top of my inbox became happening number two. And this time the news was more than bad. It was devastating.

Being so consumed with Sofia's event all day, I hadn't even thought about checking my email. It, *IT* had arrived Friday morning—the rejection of Señor Montes's final wish. A *DENIED* stamp over our hard work and heritage. Over my chance to save the Varadero Beach mural from demolition.

Looking back twelve hours, I was more shocked than I should've been. After all, the local historical society hasn't included one sentence about the Cuban experience on its site. We were left out well before they could erase us.

To the thousands of settlers who launched a bloodline of people and businesses on this street, the email says they're not significant enough. There's not enough lasting merit to note, with pride and appreciation and a brass plaque, that we were ever here.

And we *were* here. Estuvimos aquí.

Some of us still are.

So, yes, this news comes with a sting that outlasts the shock. And it hurts personally, as a Cuban who wants to matter and make a difference as a human.

Lo siento, Señor Montes. I'm so sorry I failed.

Only Jada knows about the email; I couldn't disguise my face when I read it through. Purposely, I haven't told my family yet. We woke up this morning to heavy floral prep. And I fear talking about Echo Park and Señor Montes's dream will only funnel into talking about Vanessa and Señor Montes's money. It's too connected, and just for a little longer, I want to disconnect.

I'm alone at the shop, too. My abuelos and dad are handling two high-profile shower events, so the outdoor, intimate backyard affair at a Los Feliz estate is all mine to manage, along with one of our weekend event temps. Now I'm finishing my last bouquet—the bride's. I hand-knot the stems with vintage lace, wondering what sort of news is coming next.

My phone, purposely on silent, vibrates. I rest the bouquet and check without swiping in, screening messages, which I never do. In the passing hours, I've replied to both Roxanne and Jada.

I can't wait to see you too, safe flight

Yeah, all good, and thanks for the rescue

I answered my dad's text about the wedding venue, too. Yup, I have the address, and I'm driving Rose One home after

But Lourdes's thumbs have been incessant since last night. Instead of inspiring communication, her messages make me want to crawl down the long, spongy tunnel of a tulip stem. Hiding. I'm purposely ignoring my best friend for the first time ever. I did send a few words:

I just need a minute and big wedding day. Current situation is more TS "Shake It Off" than "Style"

Sometimes Taylor Swift hits do the best explaining. Lulú speaks Swiftie. I think it's working because her messages stopped an hour ago.

But now the name flashing across my screen sends an icy-hot trail down my body. And in the sharpest twist of irony, Emilio isn't the most unsafe person to talk to right now.

Emilio: Happy Saturday. Friendly neighborhood check-in

Me: Thanks but since when do you check in? And since when are you friendly?

Emilio: Guess I'm not that memorable after all

My organs no longer reside in their correct positions.

Emilio: ...

Emilio: Thorn? You alive? Maybe I am that memorable

Me: YES, CARAJO, I AM FINE JFC

Emilio: There she is. All good. See you later, then

Me: Wait, are you fine?

Me: How did YOU sleep?

Me: Later, Wheels

As LA merges into late afternoon, the scene awaiting me when I pull Rose One into our driveway doesn't help with the unease filtered over my entire life. Parked along the curb with Papi's SUV are Blue Ivy and Jada's Cabriolet. The answer to this puzzle is likely buried somewhere in my list of unread messages.

I can't ignore the scene behind the front door any longer. As soon as I exit the minivan, the smell hits me, then downright assaults.

Garlic and cumin. Citrus and savory pork grease and heat. It's lechón asado with mojo. Mamita doesn't make this.

Roxanne. Tía Roxanne—who loves cooking, unlike her mother—makes this dish. She's here.

I pull my janitor keys and let myself in, the delicious aroma intensifying. Before I can walk three steps forward, I'm lovingly attacked by a schnauzer *and* a micro-size Chihuahua. Roxanne rarely travels without Ginger, and my entrance has inspired barking at some kind of unholy pitch.

"Okay, little monsters. Calm down." I pet and scratch and appease.

"Ginger!" Tía Roxanne calls, her voice hailing from the patio. "¡Cállate ya!"

Ginger pretends to never have heard her mommy, leaping and nipping through my every move. I tuck into the kitchen, finding not one, but both sections of our double oven lit with roasting goodness inside. (Why two pork shoulders?) There's a huge pot of simmering frijoles that Mamita had to have soaked late last night. No people are here, but the sound of a hair dryer whirs from the hallway bathroom. Mamita? Lourdes? But why would my friend be getting ready at my house?

Instead of investigating, I let it go. Channel one of Jada's meditative mantras to attempt to clear my mind. It's a job.

"Clarita! I need me some baby girl!" Roxanne calls from outside.

After one last inhale-exhale, I edge through the cracked-open door and instantly receive a few answers. My tía is cutting hair—everyone's hair—which usually happens during her visits. Papi's up now, sitting in a draped dining room chair wearing a plastic cape. Abu's sporting a fresh trim and drinking a Fresca.

"Ay, my beauty." Roxanne rests her razor on the patio table and swallows me into a hug ripe with the scent of Cuban cooking and tangy styling products. She's in her customary all black (skinny cropped pants and a sleeveless mock turtleneck), her own bleached hair molded into a pixie fade.

"You've been busy," I say, jerking a thumb backward to the kitchen. "Didn't you just land?"

My tía laughs and points to her carry-on suitcase still resting by the back door. "Yeah, but I'm always in New York mode. Gotta keep moving. Mamita picked up the roasts and ingredients for me, and I put them in as soon as I got here. I wanted to throw a little fiesta."

"All her friends are in town," Papi says from the chair. "Un milagro."

"Mm-hmm." Roxanne tugs on my locks, still bearing leftover kinks from my quinces hairdo. "Tomorrow, these are mine. Your papi is my last victim because we need to set up." She cranes her neck toward the house. "Mamita went over to Porto's for a bunch of papas rellenas and croquetas. And we'll do an ensalada de aguacate y tomate."

Abu plunks his soda on the table. "And I need to go pick up all the drinks."

"Use my SUV," Papi says. "Since I'm being held captive against my will."

Abu salutes, then disappears into the house.

"Porto's catering and two roasts?" I ask. "How big is this party?"

Roxanne shrugs and returns to Papi's trim. "We'll see. Besides my high school friends, I asked some of the neighbors and a few of your friends. Mamita and Jada took care of that when you weren't texting back."

I swallow a lump. "Oh right. Sorry. I was handling the garden wedding. Super busy," I add, now seeing why Lulú is here. Somewhere . . .

My best friend slots herself one step backward in my mind because Jada has been sitting at the patio table this whole time. She's relaxed in the padded chair, posture loose and easy. I'm slightly thankful I wasn't the one who had to handle introductions between my tía and sister. The fact that Jada's still here either means things have gone well, or Jada doesn't give a shit.

Finding out which is true should be fun. Ginger hops up into Jada's lap, happily, so that's a good sign.

I plop down in a spare chair and grab a Fresca.

Jada leans close, a palette of concern coloring her features. "The email from last night—you okay?"

I give a flat shrug; there's no good answer. I'm okay in the broad scope of life. But I'm back to the starting point in a race I didn't know I needed to run until last month. And now I must finish. I have to find another way to honor what the state of California has deemed unworthy of attention. And to preserve all that's left. Cuban Echo Park is worth remembering, and one email hasn't changed that.

"So. Worlds have collided" is all I say, louder, hoping to decipher the mood around here.

Jada grins. "They have. You missed the volcanic eruption when I got here."

"Eruption might be pushing it. Okay, maybe a small benign volcano. *But*," Roxanne says, cleaning up Papi's sideburns, "not just any half sister gets to waltz into my niece's life without me having some words about it."

"Hermana. Seriously?" Papi says, weary. "Must you be so predictably . . . you?"

"*You* stay quiet. And keep still," Roxanne tells her little brother. "Or I'll turn your precious look so lopsided, no mujer will go out with you."

Papi glares but obeys.

Jada snorts with mirth, petting a blissed-out Ginger. "No worries. I'm just glad Clary has such a loving team to look out for her. I can handle a little third degree."

Roxanne points with her scissors. "That earned her some points right away. Plus, she was in the dark for years, too," my tía says. "I could say a lot of things about her mother, but I will not." One hand on her hip. "As if Vanessa's moves years ago weren't enough, now she–*hmmph*. Good thing she was halfway across the globe when I found out."

"Which I agreed with," Jada notes, and sips her drink.

"Which brought us to a nice understanding," Roxanne says.

"But not before there might have been a bit of a shouting match when we were making the beans," Jada supplies.

My mouth drops. "¡Tía!"

Papi shakes his head, eyes to the sky.

Roxanne whips the cape off my dad's shoulders, shaking out the hair. "She is still here, no? I'm not that scary."

I rise, smacking a kiss on my aunt's cheek. "Yes, you are. But I love it. Now be nice."

"PffIt," Roxanne says, then puts on a clownish smile that I only catch the end of when Lourdes appears in the doorway.

I swear my eyes are just being cruel. I cut away and try again, but the view stays the same. Lourdes let Tía Roxanne chop feet from her hair—her gold-star trademark. My compass and weather vane. A wonder of our world.

"Would you look at her?" Roxanne says. "For years I've been dying to have my way with this fine mane. Do you like it, mijita?"

Lourdes's gaze rolls a flurry of icy silence between us. One I probably deserve. Where she used to cocoon behind the *Do Not Disturb* sign of her pulled-forward locks, now her face does all the warning. She turns to my tía, wearing the biggest smile ever. "It was so easy to dry, and the layers are so pretty, and it just moves. I love it."

She loves it. And soon (just give me a few seconds-minutes-hours) I will love it, too. But I'm not past the shock stage yet.

"Óiganme todos, some help here!" Mamita calls from inside, back from the bakery.

Everyone scrambles.

Papi's already swept all the hair off the patio. He drags the chair back inside.

"Time to get this place party-ready," Roxanne says, clapping her hands. She faces me. "I'm bunking in the casita. Can you two take up my bags?"

"Uh, sure." The dogs follow my tía inside, and I lift Roxanne's suitcase. I lock eyes with Lourdes a half second before she grabs a smaller tote and Ginger's travel crate, following up the casita stairway in the worst, most awkward silence of our small century.

Papi's door is unlocked. I flip on the light and set the suitcase by the pullout love seat.

Lourdes halts across the room, which isn't far but still feels like a hundred miles away. "Well?" she asks sharply and flicks the ends of her new shoulder-length layered style.

"You look amazing," I say, because it's true. "But you haven't gotten more than a trim in ten years." I'm still shook. Long hair is Lourdes, and Lourdes is long hair.

"I've been thinking about it for a while now, but not seriously. Then I saw this documentary on Locks of Love, and I figured I can always grow it back if I want. Roxanne cut a ponytail big enough for a donation."

I imagine the chopped-off section. More than hair, it feels like a piece of our history trimmed away. "Donating is awesome. I just figured you would've told me."

Lourdes glares. "Told you?" She whips her cell from her pocket. "You mean on this nifty little gadget? Where your friends type *letters* and then *magic words* travel right to your little gadget? Forget my new hair, you're the stranger around here."

My gut absorbs the force, the bruising truth. I stare at my sneakers, at the dusting of pollen and smudges of mossy green I can never entirely clean. "I know. Sorry I've been MIA. The quinces was . . . busy. And then we had so many jobs today. I got behind."

"Nice try, mentirosa."

"What?"

"You're la princesa de multitasking. Like that time we finished that group project for US History on Zoom while you made twelve bridesmaid bouquets for two weddings."

I cringe. Sometimes I forget Lourdes's memory is yards longer than her hair used to be.

"You're hiding something under all these excuses. You did a complete one-eighty at the fiesta."

I thrust my arms up, the word *fiesta* rushing to the front of my mind. Yes, there's another root to this problem, but I won't dig it up. It's unformed, unnamed, and I have no idea what it will grow into. But . . . "Didn't you see me running laps around the ballroom? Handling drunk relatives and menacing twins and all the mishaps? The whole night was my responsibility."

Lourdes angles away. "I thought you *wanted* to plan and manage everything."

Tears well in the corners of my eyes. "Of course I wanted it. And I loved the job. But then you started texting me five thousand times, and I got overwhelmed. It felt like our whole neighborhood was watching my every move. I couldn't handle all the party stuff plus . . . that, too."

My friend steps closer. "I get that, but even the next day you couldn't answer one simple question about Emilio. Come on, Clary. What I saw didn't make sense."

"Because none of it makes sense to me, either! I just needed a few minutes to figure it out; I still do. And the last thing I needed was you doing the same thing as always."

Her face crunches up. "What are you talking about?"

"You live for calling me out! And you dissect and analyze me and all my failed love stories like I'm one of your lab experiments. You bring back every choice I've ever made and, por Dios, I love you. So much. But sometimes *that* feels like too much."

"You mean acting too much like a friend?"

My head weighs down with fuzz and heat and confusion. "I tried to tell you."

"No, you tried to ghost me and still won't admit why. Jada had to tell me you were leaving last night." She backs away toward the door. "You want to be alone? Cool. But I am not leaving because that would only create more questions from your family. A good *friend* thinks of that."

God, I feel like a worm. A small and silent destroyer. "Lourdes, I know. I just hit a wall."

She flings open the door. "See, that's it. I'm never on the wrong side of your wall. I go where you go. Or at least I thought I did."

Twenty-One

*O*n the party side of my bedroom door, laughter, Celia Cruz, and the stir of bodies test the span of our walls. Back here, there's the rustle of my own mind over how Lourdes and I got, well, here.

If I'm being honest, last night's big evasion felt like the best remedy at the time. I'd sucked in pure, unfiltered relief in the passenger seat of Jada's convertible (top down, tunes pumped). I'd thrilled at the power of an iPhone off button. I'd run with both, savoring a few licks of frozen-cold freedom. Not freedom from anyone or anything—not really. I ran from *me*.

Activist-me who's suffered major failure on the historical preservation project. Birth child–me who has to simply-not-simply pick up a phone to gain some security. And friend-me who couldn't discuss Emilio, because opening my mouth about him right after *his* was on mine felt like a thousand years too soon.

Like Jada, you can flee from a toxic family situation and never go back. Some Echo Park Cubans have left Sunset Boulevard, never to return. Emilio evades sticky situations on the regular. But when you run from yourself, you end up going home eventually.

Running works for Jada and Emilio, but not for my kind of escape. And it's time to go home.

Las fichas. I picture these words and end up with Señor Montes's photos. I still haven't done right by them; they deserve more than a pile on my desk. I shuffle through until I find my mural. Sin Nombre beams in white silk and lush grass and gifts. A clutch of purple hyacinths, a chalice. I stare long and hard, so deeply I'd swear something has changed, making the whole photo appear different from all the other times I've looked. Or maybe it's just me and the place I'm looking *from.*

All I know is that the subject's eyes seem to be staring back at me in a way that's just as new, calling me out. It's time to fix *LourdesAndMe.*

I rise and smooth my hair, breathing in the scent of roasted lechón. First things first, I need a better outfit that doesn't smell like my work. I move to my closet, and after the case-denial email, I'm in the mood to love on something neglected and forgotten. I slide a section of hangers and find a short periwinkle dress I haven't worn in forever. The fabric skims just right, but the spaghetti-strap top puts "the scab I do not wish to explain" front and center. Since it's too hot for a denim jacket or my trusty gray sweater, I rummage farther and yank at a thin white cotton cardigan. And my stomach plummets.

Dangling lopsided in the cleared space is THE SHIRT. Lourdes's lost denim button-down has been here all along. I hold it close and feel the phantom shape of its owner. And hope the blue chambray will make a good enough white flag.

After I emerge from bedroom purgatory, it takes two asks to learn Lourdes is out back. A domino match is already raging inside the dining room with Abu at the helm, talking shit and nursing a beer. I pass through the lively scene until I spy my friend beyond the slider. She's flopped onto the staircase leading to Papi's studio, texting like always, but alone like hardly ever. This is worse than I thought.

After a breath filled with dusk and smog, it's clear that only drastic measures are going to reach this friend. I toss the denim shirt over my face and prance over doing a wonky duck walk with my arms like goalposts. I decipher enough shadows through the fabric to not trip.

"What the ever-loving hell?" Lourdes says. "Hey—my shirt! I *knew* it."

I lock my spine. "I screwed up. I am a very bad and terrible friend. I am a thousand fields of carnations and a moldy combo from Señor Cluck's. And your hair looks so good, I've stopped missing the old you already."

Lourdes huffs. "Sit and take that ridiculous thing off before Mamita or your tía does something extra up in here."

I obey and hand over the blue denim. "I know you're pissed. But can I say some things?"

"Oh, *now* Hushy McQuiet Mouse is ready to talk."

"Fine. I deserved that."

"Ehh." Lulú shrugs. "Just had to say it so no one accuses me of going soft."

At this precise moment, I know that Lourdes and I are going to be okay. I give an innocent smile, and she rolls her eyes, and I bat my lashes, and she elbows me a little bit hard. Yup, we're fixable. "First the shirt. I remember now. It was Disney, spring break."

Her jaw wrenches sideways. "Ohh. You got cold during the parade."

I nod. "And we were so tired, and my stomach hurt from two Dole Whips, and I wore it home and hung it up on auto-mode and fell into bed."

"Then I left for Hawaii and forgot."

"Me too." One beat, two. "It's a good shirt."

"Goes with everything," she muses. "The first thing I'd save in a fire. Along with the ripped Levi's I got at Marlow, and your mangy ass. In that order."

I study my shoes. "Sorry for ignoring you and being ghosty."

She bumps my side. "Yeah, well, I didn't mean to overwhelm you. When I was showing Fia my new hair, she said I was maybe acting a little extra. And by maybe, I mean totally."

I start a laugh but it fizzles. "I feel bad that we didn't get to hang out more, and I ruined the quinces for you."

Her little calloused hand on my knee. "Not possible. It was the greatest thing you've ever done for me. I was so blissed out, I forgot that you need processing time when stuff gets nuts."

"Like this." I pull out my phone to show her the email from the Office of Historic Preservation.

She scans, her frown deepening by the word. "Oh, amiga, no. This is bullshit."

"Totally." I click the screen off. "I didn't see the email until after I went home with Jada. It's partly why I went dark today but not why I left last night."

As if I've taken up conjuring, Jada breezes out from the house and strides over with the dogs. "Hey, since you hate surprises, I need to warn you. Emilio just got here. He's chatting with Elena. I forgot to tell you that he got caught up in the invite corral when he called about a shop thing. And see, he—"

"Nooo, he actually showed up?" This from Lourdes, while my brain shuts down and two pups who double as empaths trot closer.

I grab my emotional support schnauzer, and Ginger parks herself near my feet, tongue askew. "He must really like lechón."

"Clary," Lourdes stresses, "does this have anything to do with you dancing with him?"

I exhale roughly. "No—yes, I mean. Ugh. I think he's messing with me or trying to check on me since . . ." I trail off in the face of two sets of piercing eyes and sky-high brows. "Take a seat," I tell Jada. "You'll find out anyway because you're you."

Lourdes and I make room, but Jada simply plunks down in front of us, cross-legged on the rough brick, as if it's fine if her delicate silk maxidress snags because she can just get another one. Disposable, like her homes. Like her cities. Yet as these piercing thoughts come, another one sneaks through. *You hate surprises.* Jada was thinking of me and considering the way I process. And this settles like the softest flannel.

"Emilio and I sort of kissed last night," I start, and push through Jada's too-pleased amusement and Lourdes's hyperventilation, somehow managing to explain just enough. "Again, it was a one-and-done. An experiment."

"Excuse me," Lourdes says. "But me in the lab with goggles and a Bunsen burner is an experiment." And then her face changes, smoothing out. "Ohh, no wonder you couldn't text and were barely functioning. God, I kept pressing you." She grabs my forearm. *"Clary."*

"I know. But the kiss was like a wager, and it's never ever happening again." I fiddle with Rocco's beard fur. "We all understand this, right? Why it won't?" Why it can't.

Lourdes and Jada have gone missing inside some private conversation.

"Stop right there," I demand. "Stop romanticizing and analyzing. ¡En *serio!*" They hold up their hands, conceding. "He and I agreed to let it go. There were terms and actual rules."

Lourdes juts out her chin. "Listen to yourself. Emilio. Rule-following. *Emilio.*"

"About that," Jada says tentatively. "There's something else. I'm almost positive he just came to hang with you and join the party. Not to mess with you."

I spurt out, "Why?" right when Lourdes asks, "What kind of something else?"

Jada rises, glancing briefly at the house. Guests are traipsing back and forth with heaping plates. "He showed up in your kitchen with a clary sage plant."

Which does not mean Emilio is not messing with me. Quite the opposite. Jada's mistaken, and Lourdes is halfway to life support, and me? Well, I'm off, after securing oaths from my two cohorts to stay put and let me deal with my own two-wheeled party guest situation.

I'm pulsating by the time I reach the house, failing at not attracting attention as I breeze by:

◊ Roxanne, holding an overfilled wineglass, calling me over to greet a college buddy.

◊ Ivonne and my dad all giggly and waving (but I'm currently too piqued to look twice).

◊ Mamita spouting out, "Clarita, did you know that Emilio is here?"

I hold them all off and finally reach the kitchen. Sure enough, there he is with a plate of croquetas. Some guy I don't know fist-bumps him and exits through the opposite doorway.

Emilio turns. "Oh hey." Then a flashlight smile.

I have a million places to start, but I'm broadsided by his outfit. Product-perfect hair in a style you'd call tousled. Nice jeans and a tan linen shirt. *Linen?*

"You expected me to show up in my greasy work clothes?" he notes, reading my mind and inhaling a croqueta in one go.

"It's more that you never show up here at all."

He shrugs. "Jada invited me."

This answers nothing and he knows it. I sidestep, pointing to the windowsill. And there it is, with its little terra-cotta pot and green surfboard-shaped leaves and a tag with care instructions. *Salvia sclarea.* "What's this bullshit?"

He scoffs. "It's polite to bring a gift when you're invited for dinner, Thorn."

I send a *look*.

"Valleys over vases." He gestures with his head. "There's dirt and roots, and you can repot it as it grows, or plant it out back. A compromise I don't find so unnatural. Plus, I thought Mami Elena would like the purple flowers when they come up."

And it's you. Your name. He doesn't say this part, but the thought taunts me like the third bickering force in this room.

The pallor of my skin must change because he pushes his plate of croquetas in front of me. I take one, hunger beating out overanalysis. "Thanks. I haven't eaten in hours." I grab another and curse this amazing food for cutting through all my comebacks.

Emilio piles more croquetas from the tray onto another plate. Hands it over. And it seems like both five seconds and five years have passed since we were eating Porto's sandwiches at Señor Montes's memorial.

He takes a swig of cola. "You're wondering if I really came here to make sure you're okay."

"Where'd you get that? Like I'm so fragile, you have to spy on me to make sure I don't fall into some eighteenth-century swoon?"

All his features sharpen. "Who said anything about spying? And you are *not* fragile. I should know . . . I mean . . . coño." He slams down the soda can. "Do-over."

Tired, scrambled sideways, I tip my chin and eat another croqueta.

"Is it all right with you if I stick around? It's *lechón*."

What was I supposed to say? Me kicking Emilio out would've signaled that our kiss experiment had affected me so much that I couldn't handle his mere presence at a party. To drive in my level of unaffectedness, I escorted him myself to the food table, and even shadowed him as we filled our plates with avocado and roasted pork and congrí, all slathered with Tía Roxanne's mojo magic.

I didn't nag or mention the word *pancreatitis* when he snuck meat scraps to Rocco and Ginger, who are now permanently tethered to him. (Hope he likes dog hair.) And I even let him sit with Lourdes and me while Ivonne performed an acoustic version of SWV's "Weak" on my dad's guitar (while I tried to think of running laps in PE, or roaches, or anything but feeling weak in the knees).

Now it's dark and the fiesta has lapsed into a domino tournament. Earlier, Mamita moved her puzzle and our dining room table, leaving our special domino table front and center. Pairs of game players have been going all night, but now the entire crowd packs the small space. Lulú and I pass by on our quest for drinks, but my name rises above the mayhem.

"¡Clary Ann Delgado, ven! I see you," Roxanne repeats, louder.

"She means business," Lourdes says, hooking my elbow, toting both of us back to the dining room.

"Ahhh, that's more like it," my tía calls with a slur that hints at one too many cervezas.

"What's going on?"

Roxanne throws her arms wide. "Madison and Jack had to relieve their sitter. And because it's my party, this tournament is not over until I say it is. And I choose *you* to fill in."

Team Papi and Ivonne are the last two standing. I appraise the crowd. "Seriously? What about Abu?"

Snickers ripple through the space. "El rey was eliminated a half hour ago," Papi says, eyes dancing.

"Porque Elena was not paying attention," Abu claims.

"*Me?* ¡Qué porquería!" Mamita calls, and the jumble of jeers and laughter rises to near boiling.

Roxanne full-on wolf-whistles. "Don't let me down, baby girl." She gestures to one of the two empty seats. "Pick your partner."

Sometimes when all eyes are on you, it's best to do the harder thing, which, in this case, is facing off against my dad and Ivonne. Besides, Tía came all this way. So I concede with a big hand gesture, and Lourdes scoots off to the side with Jada.

"I'll play on one condition," I say as a single memory barrels through. "Hold on."

It takes less than ten seconds for me to retrieve the cherished wooden box from my room. "We use this." I hold it up. "Señor Montes's domino set from Cuba."

The room falls into reverent sighs and murmurs. Papi is already packing up the set they've been using.

"Ay, qué bueno," Roxanne says, one hand over her heart. "This match will be in his honor."

"Which doesn't mean we're not going to destroy you," Ivonne says.

"Prepare to be obliterated, Clarita," Papi adds with way too much satisfaction. "Now, who's your partner?"

Ordinarily I'd be fangirling over Papi and Ivonne's merger, even if it's only for gameplay. But my big historical-preservation loss means I want to win more than ever. For Señor Montes and for me.

And I have one more twist of my own. I scan the room until I find my unlikely mark slanted against the wall. We lock eyes, and the note of surprise in all that glossy green is worth the jitters riding underneath my skin.

"I choose Emilio."

Twenty-Two

*T*here's plenty of trash talk in dominoes, but code words or hand signals to tip off your partner are never tolerated. In this dining room, while guests refill drinks and Ivonne opens the heirloom tile set, Emilio pulls me aside. Technically, the match hasn't started yet.

He goes in tight. "I'm game, Thorn. But why me when your best friend is right there?"

"You're the last person those two expect, and that could, um, help," I whisper.

Realization dawns. "Ahh. Nice."

"Keep cool. Everyone's staring." I step back from his Dr Pepper breath and the summer heat rolling off his skin. "For Señor Montes? Two of his barrio kids, right?" I declare, louder for the people in the back.

"Claro." Emilio nods, playing along before we even start gaming. "For el señor."

We sit across from each other. Abu's custom table has notches on each side to hold tiles upright. It's been a while since my last game, but as soon as Ivonne begins mixing the set, the *clack-clack-clack* sound stirs my memory, shooting through my fingertips.

The four of us choose ten fichas each, and Emilio, drawing the highest tile from the extra bone pile, plays first. He eyes me proudly as he places the double seven—a high-value piece. One that would add many undesired points to Papi and Ivonne's collective score at the end of this round if left behind. At this table, Emilio has to consider me even if he doesn't want to, and vice versa. It's not the usual way we've played at life dominoes, standing at the opposite corners of most things (streets, issues, goals). But Abu once told me, *You cannot play dominoes just to empty your own hand, nena. You will never win that way.* This time Emilio and I are on the same side of the block.

And, see, the best teams act intuitively. They win effortlessly. They catch hidden rhythms, studying opponents for signs and tells. And though I'd hoped our telepathy would click on because of the vie-jito we were playing for, it's not exactly working. I can't read any of Emilio's vibes. I guess my underhanded strategy was cursed from the start.

As gameplay moves counterclockwise, my teammate grumbles when I match a three-dot tile on one end of the chain instead of the six on the opposite side. *Carajo.* I wince in apology; I had a six to play.

Soon after, I mentally beg him to block a chain of fives because I'm sure Papi has a ton of them. And, of *course*, Emilio plays a double five instead, shedding a high-value tile but allowing Ivonne and Papi to win this one.

But in the next round, I score a killer draw from the bone pile. The highest-value tile thrums between my fingers, earning my team the right to go first. I flash the ivory piece to Emilio before placing it. "La caja de muertos," I mumble, if only to see if he remembers that last night, he called our little experiment a move as equal as this double-nine tile.

And something happens.

Emilio teases a smile. His spine lengthens against the chair. And when he murmurs *las fichas* like he did before he cupped my face, my stomach fizzes. It's as if he also realizes that to win this round, we need a language carried ninety miles across the sea. On a boat, or a plane, or tucked inside a balsa-wood box. That's where our secret rhythm is. The fine tools of this game are already mixed into our blood, like sugar and coffee and acres of tobacco. We only have to find them.

"Hey, bike boy," Ivonne taunts as Papi plays the nine and four. "What's with the code-word cheating crap?"

"Cheating? How?" Emilio says on a dark laugh, consulting the rapt crowd. "Tiles." He jiggles a couple from the bone pile. "What could she get from that?"

But I do get it. That there's a web of history binding Emilio and me. Tonight, he's not fighting to escape it. No magic windows or bikes wait to take him far away.

When he places an eight and four against Papi's last move, I say, "Do you think Señor Montes ever pictured the two of us on the same team?"

Emilio winks. "Not until now, Clary."

I throw in an innocent giggle as Papi almost chokes on his beer. And when I glance at Ivonne, she's frozen inside a one-way day-dream. Jada notices, too, sending me a little chortle from across the room next to a slack-jawed Lourdes (who may never come out of this night intact).

"Ivonne," Papi nudges. His partner has totally forgotten it's her move. Scrambling, she plays.

I peer at Emilio from under my lashes, sharing a wink of satisfaction that there's no way Ivonne and Papi have kept proper track of the tiles in this round. But we have. I clock Papi's early play of el unicorne—the double one and lowest piece of all—and get a huge hint at what he's keeping. Emilio holds the double seven until it counts. He smirks at me when he places it this time. "The stinking one," he says of its nickname. "Just like all our jokes."

"Sometimes we land a good one," I say.

Then, in pure domino magic, Emilio blocks a two chain from Ivonne, leaving it open for my last tile: the mariposa. I've been saving it. I seek out Abu before making my move, pausing to imagine how he flew it like a butterfly. How he taught me this game, and so much more.

With a grin, I place the double two and declare, "Domino!" Our win triggers a backdrop of cheers, and our opponents' dramatic grumbles. And to a rightfully smug Emilio, I mouth *las fichas* once again.

The only problem is that our good fortune doesn't last.

We soon learn that winning one round isn't enough for us to win the match. Sometimes you simply choose a terrible hand, and no amount of strategy can save it. That's what happens in round three. Papi and Ivonne quickly lock us out, reaching one hundred fifty points with all the collective dots Emilio and I leave on the table.

The crowd disperses, clapping over our good effort and the lively entertainment. (You're welcome, Roxanne's party.)

"Okay, fine, it wasn't total annihilation," my dad concedes as he and his partner jump up for cheek kisses and handshakes.

"There will be a rematch," Ivonne notes, and exhales deeply. "Well, it's been fun, but I have an early day tomorrow." She reaches for her tote, and I cannot be any more obvious in my daughter-dad hand signals and brow movements.

Miraculously, he clues in and steps forward. "I should walk you to your car. The streetlamps are out and all."

The *streetlamps*?

But it works because the duo sets off into the flurry of people. Emilio holds up his phone, signaling an incoming call, and disappears out the slider.

Jada and Mamita are gathering cups and bottles, and Roxanne's at the front door dealing goodbye hugs. That leaves Lourdes and me to pack up Señor Montes's dominoes. We do it slowly, careful of the fragile balsa wood. I need this set to last forever. Caught in the ritual, I ignore my phone when it buzzes from the table. Lourdes barely glances at the lock screen.

"Did Roxanne cut away your nosy parts along with your hair?" I ask. Lulú typically helps herself to my messages and plays text-to-speech for me.

"Nah." My friend slides on the box top. "It's probably Emilio telling you he's leaving."

I make a low grunt.

"But this is me not pressing you about him because you're clearly not ready to spill." She slides the resurrected chambray shirt over her tank. "And while it's totally like me to bug you for hours, I choose no bugging."

"You do?"

She scoffs like this is obvious. "I'd be mostly talking to myself. Even though there's a clary plant in your kitchen to discuss and certain terrace stuff. Not to mention you choosing him as your partner for eye-sex dominoes."

"Eye-*what* dominoes? And this is you not pressing?"

She ignores me. "I'm around when you figure it out. Love you. Me voy."

And then she does. She leaves.

I grab my phone, scanning Emilio's message for myself. Heading out to help Abuela. Lechón was killer and the game was fun. So we almost won

Me: It was, but almost doesn't count

Emilio: Look at you quoting 90s love ballads. And before you ask, Dominic digs them as much as your dad, but we will never speak of that publicly

Finding a half laugh, but no good response, I stow my phone and secure the dominoes. My family's in the kitchen dealing with dishes and packing up leftovers. Beyond the archway, the pups are curled up on Rocco's dog bed. I'm twenty feet from the much-needed solitude of my room, but Roxanne appears, ruffling my hair.

"Tomorrow, my chair?" she asks, pantomiming a few snips.

"Sure. Do your worst, Tía," I say with maybe too much frustration tearing into my tone.

Roxanne backs up. "Hey now. You're not pissed about losing to your papi and Ivonne?"

"Nah. It's just been . . . a day." After a *night*. "Not sure even one of your new hairdos is gonna be magical enough."

"Who do you think you're talking to?" she taunts, and hoists a trash bag into my hands. "You know where that goes. Along with that shit about my nonmagical haircutting."

I roll my eyes, spin on the ball of one foot, and escape into the balmy July night.

Stomping toward our side yard, I manage to open the trash can without touching the lid, dump the bag full of party scraps, and catch an absolute fright at the shape of Emilio a few feet ahead.

The noise I make clocks in at Mortificada Level Five Thousand. "God, you can't just sneak up on me like that!"

He holds out his palms. "Who's sneaking? I was already here. *You* flew around the corner with a trash heap the size of a Santa Claus bag." He exhales roughly. "Look—sorry. It's your house and everything. You all right?"

"No." I take a couple breaths. "Yes. Why did you come back?"

"I never left."

"Huh?"

"I got a call from Abuela and came out here. Her router was acting up, and she wanted me to come over. But I just walked her through shutting it down and restarting it. Which was a *joy*."

I snort. "Like you do with us."

"When have I ever installed a router here?"

"Jesus, no." I smack my forehead. "Not a router."

"You just said . . . What are you—"

"Our do-overs, dingbat. You're always calling do-overs and restarting us. You and me."

He grins. "I knew that. Was just messing with you."

I fix him with a glare.

A weighty scraping noise sounds from inside—probably Abu and Papi dragging furniture back into place. Emilio moves, waving at me to come with him. "Come on. Last thing we need is someone catching us bickering in your trash alley. Too weird." He squeezes through the rosemary hedge separating my house from the neighbors' blue bungalow.

I follow him up the walkway, and he helps himself to their top step.

"What if the Woods are home? We can't just take over their porch."

Unaffected, Emilio checks his phone and pockets it again. "Who cares? Have a seat. Plenty comfy."

Ignoring him, I creep to one of the front windows, but the blinds are wrenched closed too tightly.

"I'm sure it's fine."

I'm already at the opposite side. I climb up on my toes and peek into a wide gap.

"Thorn, I will give you one million dollars if the Woods show up and arrest us for sitting here."

I freeze. Edge back two steps into a pivot. And with extreme dignity, I lower onto the concrete beside him, tugging down my dress. "Happy now?"

He doesn't have a comeback. His body juts forward and the fabric of his shirt glows in the lamplight. "Can I ask you one more time if we're cool? I know I texted, but then we were sort of arguing in the kitchen, and I did bring a clary plant, which was kind of a smart-ass move. Which you called me out on."

"From shock. I work with flowers every day, and no one has ever brought me a clary plant."

The devil himself darts across his face. "It was for Mami Elena."

I bite my lip, and the rise of heat in the cramped and chesty part of my body is dizzying. Terrifying. "Well, Mamita thought it was pretty cute. And she'll try not to kill it."

"That's all we can really ask for in this world." He's silent for a few seconds that span an entire midnight. "Are you, though? Okay?"

Dizzying, terrifying . . . "I'm trying to be." It's a different answer than I gave last night, and this morning, and in my kitchen. And searingly honest.

"How so?"

Buck it up. "I follow the rules. Safety first."

He's closer—too close. And his features have gone softer—way too soft. And he's so unsafe, no neighborhood phrase could save me now.

This is why I blurt out, "Vermont? Food map?"

"Apple pie with cheddar cheese," he says.

"Cheese. On pie. Gonna need a minute to process that."

"I didn't make the map." He bumps my knee and licks his lip.

"Missouri," I say.

"Fried ravioli. It's like an appetizer." His pale linen brushes against my white cotton. "A must-try."

"Yeah, that sounds pretty delicious."

"I'd bet on it."

I dare to look up right when he looks over, and *we're* over, after the simplest conversation we've ever had. As quick as a traffic-light switch—green to yellow. A wink. A backfire. A blown-out candle wish.

We fuse on a throaty sigh that's full of mouths and hands. My fingers rake into his hair, twisting into the gold sandy softness. He fists into the small of my back, pressing me closer as he leans against the wide beam holding up this porch.

"Wait." I pull back; he instantly follows, blinking while I'm breathless, my mind screaming through all the words we said. "We. But."

He swipes a thumb across my cheekbone. "I know."

Dammit, he can't. He can't know. But he's there, one arm gently evading my bicycle scrape, knuckling fingers down my forearm.

Another wave of nonsense comes, where I end up in his lap, held and kissed across my cheeks, the swell of my mouth. And the small bits, too—corners and bows. Dimples. Our fingers thread, and his right hand tangles with my left, pulling them both over his heart. And somehow this is what deals my own heart a crushing blow.

Because I know this is going nowhere. And I don't blame him. I'm the one who stole one too many fairy-tale kisses from a boy who never promises an ever after. Or even any kind of long-enough. I've never misunderstood this about him.

"*Wait.* I mean it." Desperate to hide the sheen clouding my eyes, I cast my vision low. "We said never again because it's *us*, Emilio. We made rules about this because we needed them."

"So what if we did?" He forces my gaze. "I kissed you because I wanted to. And not just now. Last night, too."

I squeeze his hand. "Yeah, but you might not want to tomorrow. Or next week. And I can't risk that—not when my entire sense of family and security was shaken so hard. I'm just finding my way through that."

"I get why you'd worry after everything this summer. And your past." He draws in a thick breath as I lower back to the step. "But did I already use up my one chance with you before I knew I was asking for it?"

I rattle my head. "For years you never asked."

"That's another conversation we'll probably fuck up. Carajo." He makes a growl of frustration. "Speaking of asking, why do you think I kept prodding you about being okay after the quinces? *I'm* not okay. I can't stop thinking about it."

His words grab me by the neck. Truth does, too. "You *will*, though. You'll stop. And you'll be more than okay. Give yourself twenty minutes or a few days." Pained, I find his eyes. "I'm no different from dance-floor Carlie or red-dress Mara. Or anyone who's made you not okay for a bit before you move on."

"You think I'm comparing you to everyone? To anyone?"

"It's not about me measuring up. Or that I'm not as smart or pretty or fun as any other girls you've dated. I am all those things just fine." I stand, my chest pattering. "Look, for years you've called me Thorn. And I am really good at irritating you and maybe pricking your attention for a second. But you'll ride on—totally intact and unbothered. I *know* you will. Because thorns like me don't go deeper than that for guys like you. Not deep enough."

He drags his hands over his face. "Hold on, so that's it?"

"Don't change any rules or yourself for me. That's not fair to either of us."

"Clary!"

But I'm already running, back to my tiny house, back to my tiny room. Somehow I close myself inside, unnoticed, and I despise the tears that push through. I dash them away, more furious with myself than I've ever been at Emilio Avalos. Because it's not about the fact that I'll remember that first kiss from him, and all the ones after. It's that I'll never ever forget.

Twenty-Three

*T*wo days later Roxanne flies back to New York, and Jada's text finds me alone with a project at the dining room table.

Lourdes said you're home. Can I bring carne asada burritos?

I send her a thumbs-up, wondering if it's smart to let an energy-reading empath into the epicenter of *my* energy. It's lunchtime, though, and I could eat.

Saturday night, I consoled myself with Señor Montes's Echo Park photos after the Emilio-porch episode, simply needing my roots. And maybe it was because of my mood—my heart turned around and troubled—that a notion struck me so hard. Photos are like flowers. If not properly cared for, their edges and colors decay a little more each day. I can't let that happen to el señor's snapshots. Not when there's an email in my inbox (one I finally told my family about) that spells enough erasure on its own.

Yesterday I went to the art supply store and bought an archival scrapbook. I got acid-free tape and special pens to notate dates and anecdotes about a man who lived in a place. He was here, and I won't let that fade away.

I glance up at footsteps, startled that Jada's already through the back slider, twiddling her fingers hello. She went for simple today in cropped jeans and a plain black tee, topped with a hint of one of the essential-oil brews she calls perfume.

"Hey," I deadpan. Her scrutiny is at Level Full Force, and I brace for the inevitable. I allowed her in and all.

Yet quiet seconds pass, and she merely drops her tote and a couple take-out bags on the sideboard. I have most of the table covered with craft materials. "Elena said you decided on a scrapbook for these." She thumbs the stack of remaining photos.

"I was waiting for news from the preservation board. If someone wanted them for a library display or, I dunno, something more." I show her a few of my completed pages. "This feels kind of basic and not important enough. But they'll be safe."

"It's looking beautiful. He'd be proud." She wiggles her hand over my shoulder. "I can help? I'm extra good with those annoying tape squares. But after lunch." She heads toward the kitchen. "Unless your abuelo went on a sugar bender, there should still be a bunch of left-over IZZEs from the party."

"Blackberry, please." I push my project out of salsa-splatter range while she grabs two of the cold sodas and unpacks gigantic burritos. *Lupe's*, the wrapper reads, and I freeze. The utter domination Lupe holds over carne asada is one of those few LA food matters Emilio and I agree on. Like he said, we do jibe on the major stuff. But I can't help but wonder if he recommended this joint to Jada earlier today. Did they talk at the shop about . . . ? I stop myself, deflating my anxiety in a lingering breath.

"Lupe is the nicest lady ever," I say. "She always throws in some off-menu salsas."

Jada pops the top on her drink. "Super nice. She was up front when I ordered, and we started talking. And she did throw in extra chips and some pico de gallo." She retrieves a condiment container and two little sacks from the sideboard, tossing one over.

I swallow a hearty mouthful, unsurprised that Jada made friends with my favorite burrito slinger while waiting for her order. It's what she does.

"Lupe said business is booming, and they're going to open up in Portland, too. Her husband's hometown. And they bought this cute rental over there to get in the Airbnb game."

"Portland's supposed to have a cool food scene," I say.

"Totally. She showed me some photos, and I told her about my travels. I took down her info, just in case." Jada dips a chip. "For my next adventure."

My bite goes down sour. Of course there's a next adventure. This fact has lodged in the back of my mind since that first night in my living room. But . . . this has faded, too. I've gotten used to Jada as much as Rocco's begging and Papi's Rainbowl breakfasts. I forgot to remember that moving on is also what Jada does.

My throat burns. "Were you thinking about going to Portland before?"

Jada steps back to the slider and cracks it open. "Nope, but that's the fun part, and how I often pick places. Emilio sends me to Lupe's, and she and I happen to talk, and there's a new opportunity along with a meaningful feeling. I usually follow those."

I munch on a couple hot, greasy chips.

"I followed one over here," she adds. And there it is. I hold my tongue while she sits and spreads her burrito on the big square wrapper. Takes a long sip from her IZZE. "There was definitely an energy shift around you Saturday night."

It's useless to pretend around this person. "I already told you about the kiss at the quinces."

"Not the quinces. I was talking about the dining room heating twenty degrees over one domino game. Then you ran inside from next door carrying a small universe on your back."

I cringe. "You saw me?"

"From the side yard. Big party, lots of trash bags." She dips a chip into the bonus tub of pico de gallo. "And you hiding out in your room was fine, 'cause sometimes we need to be alone to *feel* stuff, and then the next day we . . ."

"We suck it up and try to deal," I supply.

This lands in the middle of her chin, crumpling it. "Yeah, but then you took the day off, which Lourdes said never happens unless you have a fever. And you'd typically work on something like this scrapbook after hours, not in the middle of a good beach day. I'm just connecting dots, no pun intended."

My eyelids droop. "So these burritos come with a question list," I say more than ask.

"They come with two ears and a mouth." She smirks and produces a paper wad from another bag. "And extra napkins."

My heart thumps, and she doesn't even know why. And from the familiar memory-filled pile of that, I ask, "You move on from a city when you get a certain feeling, right?"

She nods.

"I needed an extra day to go back to Sunset because I did the opposite," I admit, and use a bunch of those napkins to wipe grease off my fingers. "I stayed too long in a place that's not mine."

"What place?"

She knows, though. How could she not know?

"Emilio," I say anyway, and find there's power in saying the name somewhere else besides my head. It reminds me that Emilio runs on the same kind of temporary that Jada does. I forgot to remember not to kiss a boy like this, that of course it would be impossible for me to not be affected. I forgot that I wasn't supposed to . . . care.

It's not too late, though. I can go back to when Emilio was just an annoying boy across the street, and I didn't have a sister a mile away with a red escape convertible and timely burrito deliveries. I can go back.

"Clary."

I blink myself present, finding Jada pegging me with a thoughtful stare. "I came here for another reason besides lunch and checking on you like the nosy bitch I am. But I didn't think I should come straight out with it." I freeze midchew but she keeps going. "I promise it's nothing bad. Since you got that denial email from the state and after everything that happened at Roxanne's party, I think you deserve some good news. Something easier for once."

I remember the rule-of-three law that's proved two-thirds true since Friday night. Is Jada's good news the third big happening that's about to happen to me? "Okay," I say, and when she reaches into her tote on the sideboard, nerves bubble up in my stomach.

"Things have changed, and you deserve this." She places a check in front of me. My eyes travel over the pale green rectangle. *Cashier's Check. Clary Delgado.* And the part that turns those bubbly nerves into a raging chill: *Ten thousand dollars.*

"Señor Montes's money?" The check that's been dangling on the hands of a ticking clock through summer vacation? "But I didn't do anything. I didn't contact her like she asked."

Jada shrugs. "Vanessa's had a change of heart. I think she expected you to call immediately—weeks ago—and take the funds. And when you didn't, when I told her you actually might not accept it, well . . ." Jada runs a burgundy fingernail across the paper. "She said she's terribly sorry. She realized her ask was manipulative and selfish. She'd still like closure, but this gift comes with no conditions."

My mind reels; everything I've been stressing over bursts into fragments yet again. "I . . . Wow."

"You can live the rest of your life and never say a word to her if you want. See?" Jada rustles my arm. "I told you this got a whole lot easier."

"Right. Easier." I stare at the check.

"I know you hate surprises, but this one means *you're* in control now."

I glance from the tiny print to Jada, waiting for the *easier* and *control* to show up. It's ten big ones, made out to me with no strings. But there's still the matter of this money feeling tainted. And the other matter of these funds being a huge boost for my family. And impossibly, there's one last thing rounding out a different kind of rule of three. Jada came here to oversee this issue for Vanessa. Now, with the check in my hand, there's no real reason for her to stay. How long before she packs up and moves to Portland?

I push the trio of thoughts away and slide the check to the other end of the table. "I need a minute with the money on my own, before I tell my family."

Jada pantomimes her lips zipping shut. "It's not going anywhere. We can work on Señor Montes's photos."

Our lunch is down to salsa stains, so I clear off a clean space for the craft supplies.

In seconds Jada proves her pointy nails *are* perfect for peeling off the tiny acid-free tape squares. She preps a stack of photos for me to arrange, by decade, inside the scrapbook. History, ancestry, and going back to the treasured black-and-white era where I came from are exactly what I need to ground myself. The task is relaxing, too, like arranging flowers.

When I reach the early eighties and my most treasured of all the photos, I hold it for a bit before it gets fitted with tape. My favorite mural in full color. Sin Nombre.

"I'm sure it's hard to put that one in the book," Jada says. "You should frame your own photo. Or one of mine." She pulls her phone and scrolls through her camera app. "The light was perfect, so I took some shots of her after I left Marlow. When I found out that blue velvet chair had sold." She expands her modern-day shot of the mural, and it happens. Something—a feeling or impression. A twitch of energy and a whiff of elsewhere.

"What is it?" Jada asks at my bewilderment.

Tingles skitter, a dozen times more electrifying than when I saw the cashier's check. It's almost as if I'm guided where to look, like Jada always goes on about—I get it now. Something was different during Roxanne's party when I picked up this photo. I zoom in closer; something *is* different. Pairing Jada's new iPhone shot next to Señor Montes's classic relic allows me to see it for the first time.

The murals are not the same. The new one has been changed in one distinct way that has me kicking myself. Someone with my job should've noticed it. "Look at her left hand in both photos," I tell my sister.

She obeys, wrinkling her nose. "Oh weird. The flowers are slightly different."

I nod. "Besides my school research, I've always known this mural by the way the neighborhood talked about it. Sin Nombre with the white dress and the lush grass, and the snake choker and goblet. And the bundle of Roman hyacinths in her hand."

My working encyclopedia of flowers falls open inside my mind.

"In the original picture, those are definitely purple Roman hyacinths. I use them in arrangements all the time. They work well in bouquets because they're a little airier than the more common type."

Jada's brought both photos closer, too, and I'm not prepared for the wave of shock pulling her features. The uncertainty and eeriness drawing her eyes wide. The ways she swallows and jiggles her head back and forth. "These are . . ."

"Clary sage. All this time I never noticed that the blossoms are tinier in scale, and the leaves are smaller and scattered. Roman hyacinth blooms are a little thicker and star-shaped, and the leaves are long and skinny." I point to Jada's photo. "I was never looking at hyacinth. I mean, the purple shades are really close, and so is the general shape of the plant. Why were they changed? I don't get it."

I glance over. Jada's eyes are fogged, one hand dropped over her mouth. I wait for her to execute a series of breathing exercises as she keeps peering at the two murals.

"I know why," she finally says. "At least, I have a really strong suspicion." She grabs my arm in a steadying way. "But explaining violates a promise I made to you. That I'd never talk about Vanessa's past."

"Vanessa?" The mere mention of that name typically strikes a full-body blow. Today it's a bruise, still purpling after the news Jada dealt over lunch. "Tell me. I don't care what it is."

She nods, shutting off the iPhone. "In Barcelona, the day Vanessa told me about your dad, and Echo Park, and you, there was more. About a year before she got pregnant with you, she took a local art class taught by a well-known Cuban artist. One of the Echo Park murals had sustained heavy water damage. Because the original muralist had passed away, her teacher was hired to refurbish the mural. He chose Vanessa to assist."

My breaths come labored as I hold up the photo. "This one? Her? I'd learned that Sin Nombre had been restored at one point. But by . . . her?"

"It has to be. Vanessa never told me which mural, only that it was in the Echo Park business district." She leans closer. "Look, there's more, and it gets, well—"

"Wait, take me there. Right now." I rise and stow the check in my purse. "I need to see for myself."

"Okay. Sure." She pushes her chair back, and I grab the mural photo and hastily organize the scrapbook stuff in case my family returns. Jada works on cleaning up the trash from our lunch.

Around the rustle of paper and foil, another feeling slices through. Something that flares through a body already feeling so much. I look from the table to the take-out bags to my sister's face, then to the cherrywood surface again. We pause there without saying what we both know, stuck inside another one of those moments that lasts longer than clocks say it should.

Jada ate her lunch with me, seated at the table. Not standing against a counter or a sideboard. Not close to a door—cracked open today to let in the breeze. Propped open decades ago to let out a stepmom and daughter, saving them both. Without realizing it, she sat.

Twenty-Four

*W*e don't mention what happened at the table or voice what it could mean as Jada drives us to the Sunset business district. We don't say anything, really, keeping the radio muted as if our thoughts are loud enough.

Because it's Jada, she scores a prime spot near the insurance agency. She holds back, letting me approach the mural first. I hold Señor Montes's photo by its withering edges and stride up to the wall where Sin Nombre lives.

Today I can't unsee what's true. I can't reach the flowers, either, but I touch the coarse surface, tears pricking through. The blooms *are* clary sage, purple-blue like the ones that will sprout from the plant Emilio brought. A hundred times I've looked at them, accepting them as hyacinths because that's what all the neighborhood stories said.

"I didn't know, Clary," Jada says softly from a few paces behind. "But I felt it—something I couldn't explain. The first day you brought me here."

"She did this," I say, my voice scratched. "Vanessa."

"Yeah. I'm almost certain."

I fix my eyes on the purple blossoms. "She changed my name on my birth certificate." I dash my hand out. "She helped with this mural and changed the original design, too. Her teacher must've been okay with it. But the flowers are the only thing that's different in the restoration."

Jada draws me close. "Your name and these flowers must mean something to her."

In some way that my tiny, new body never did. But I blank out that part, like always, and focus on the colors and shapes in front of me. Clary salvia. Clary Ann Delgado.

Lourdes's shirt hung in my closet for months, and I never saw it. Purple sage sprouted where any good florist should recognize it, but I never did. Not once in front of my little-girl eyes. Not once inside the stories I made up about Sin Nombre, and all the words I plucked out of my imagination. They swarm in a hot, heady rush.

She's angry, Mamita. Her eyes look like she's mad because of bad people. She has enough juice for everyone in her cup. She wants to be important.

I wanted her to matter—to be important—before I ever knew how much I wanted to matter, too.

"Why doesn't anyone know about this?" I ask Jada. "The petals are really similar, so I get why non-flower people don't notice the change. But it doesn't make sense that no one ever talks about Vanessa working on this mural."

"There's a reason for that. But . . ." Jada trails off, and I remember there was more she hadn't said. I'm the one who stopped her at the dining room table.

"I need to know everything. Even if it's about her."

Jada clasps her hand over my forearm. "I didn't realize her story was connected to this particular mural. But Vanessa confessed something more in Barcelona, and I'm only now matching it all up." She draws my gaze upward. "The art teacher I mentioned was obsessed with her, and that's why he chose her to assist with this restoration. But he told her to keep her involvement quiet so other classmates wouldn't complain of favoritism. He also insisted they work after hours and had the area blocked off. No one saw. He told Vanessa it was to protect the artwork. Turns out he only wanted to protect himself and his, well, ulterior motives. Vanessa had an affair with him when the work was almost done."

"She cheated? On my dad? But could that mean he's not . . ." My mind reels backward, calculating and sifting through the disjointed bits of my past the best I can. Horror rushes through in every dark and dismal color. "When exactly did all this happen? What year?"

Jada shoves out both hands. "No, Clary, listen. It's okay," she says. "Your dad is your biological father. Vanessa confirmed this because I asked, too. The teacher moved away soon after the mural was done. Before Vanessa got pregnant with you."

I let out a thick exhale. "Still—my poor papi."

"I know. It was Señor Montes who found them out. Vanessa said he walked in on her and the teacher in the alley." Jada cranes her neck, pointing a short way up the block. "Which has to be right there. Back then, the second floor of this building had a couple apartments. Señor Montes was renting one."

I study the site I've only known to house office space. "I never knew he lived up there. When I was young, he lived in a little house near mine. Then he moved to Ivonne's casita."

"This mural wall backed his old place," Jada adds. "And the leak that ruined the original artwork came from his apartment. He'd known something was wrong but delayed the repair. He's the one who petitioned the Lions Club for the funds so the mural could be restored."

"So if it wasn't for him, Vanessa wouldn't have been here."

She turns to the wall again. "Right. He felt guilty about how things turned out. Vanessa was so young. He knew about her background and felt she'd been manipulated. The teacher was older and brilliant, and she got caught up in all that, and it was really toxic."

Pieces merge, fitting together like one of Mamita's puzzles. My eyes drop to the old vintage film photograph, then track upward to Sin Nombre.

She still has a story, Clarita, **Mamita** had said.

Only I didn't know that the one she's holding is part of mine. This mural was a huge part of my childhood, and it seems like forever that I've been building this good and happy life without Vanessa. It can't help but burn that this place I love has been carrying pieces of her the entire time.

My fingers clamp onto the photo, and I rattle my head impossibly. "Does my family know about all this?"

"From what Vanessa said, yeah, they have to."

Like they knew about Jada. The extra burst of shock, the needling sting after a weekend full of so many other thorns, sends me into the only arms around. They're not here to stay, but they're here right now. And I go.

After the short drive to La Rosa Blanca, the cashier's check still sits at the bottom of my purse, but I produced another kind of printed paper. Mamita only needed one quick look at the old photograph to understand why I was here on my day off. "Ay, Dios mío," she said, ushering me into the office at La Rosa Blanca.

Jada left after dropping me off, and the people who work here are scattered like wildflowers. Abu is setting up a big hotel job, and Lourdes is out on delivery. My dad went to a trade show in San Diego.

But Mamita is here now with Rocco in her lap, as if she's the one who needs the emotional support pup. She waits, with the kind of patience most Cubans don't claim as their strongest trait.

I had several versions of speeches worked out on the short drive from the mural to the flower shop. Accusations and a dozen *whys* and *how comes and how could yous*—they were armed and ready. But this time the words wouldn't stick together. Wouldn't click like the puzzle pieces Mamita loves to tinker with after a long workday. So, today, I'm not going to run. I'm going to, as Jada says, *put the words out there*. And I'm going to listen.

Since I keep staring at this old photo printed on Kodak paper, I start from there. "All this time, I thought Vanessa never left anything in Echo Park except me. Except my name. And that wasn't true."

"No, mi amor. And I promise we never wanted to hide anything about your past from you."

My breath comes out heavy. "Every week we walked by this mural when I was little. You took me there, knowing everything."

Mamita leans in. "One of the reasons we decided to wait to tell you about your sister *was* the way you reacted to that mural."

"What do you mean?"

"Querida, you ran to Sin Nombre on your own. I never took you there. You noticed her when you were two or three and pulled me to her. That first night I cried over this with Abu. And he said we should follow your lead and let you enjoy her."

"I did." My memory's so hot, it burns. "I gave her all these words and feelings, not knowing that my name was there all along. My history."

Mamita draws a troubled breath. "We could not predict how you would grow up and into this life after Vanessa left. What it might do to your heart and mind. We just didn't know."

"All I knew was that I thought of you as my only mom."

She nods, her face painted with a mix of love and anguish. "By grace, you bonded to me and to Abu and your papi instantly. And then we watched and waited. We followed *your* lead. And instead of growing up longing for Vanessa," she adds over a frown, "you grew the opposite way. You knew the basics of where you came from. But mentioning any more about her was like talking about a stranger in your eyes. And we went on with that. We let you decide and be happy."

A small world opens inside of me. "You never wanted to keep things from me. You wanted to keep me feeling safe and loved."

Mamita nods. "And maybe it was not all for the best, or the most honest way. I am not sure I would make the same choice if I had the chance. But—"

"I understand, Mamita. I get it. You did the best you could at the time," I say plainly. Understanding, forgiveness—they're right there at the edges of me, unlike they were in my living room a month ago. Sometimes people lie for a greater good, and truth is not always painted black or white. Life and love come in as many shades as flowers.

And so does confusion. "Everything I know about Vanessa is all twisted up now."

"Dímelo, niña."

"I mean, none of these revelations change the fact that she left," I start. "But she left something here. It's been so easy to believe I just came into your world, and that she was barely a part of it. If not for science, I would have believed that, too. That, like, a stork dropped me off or something. But now I've learned she left footprints here. There's another trace of her besides me."

Mamita nods, then lets out a gust. "She left a lot more than that, Clarita. Not in paint, but in problems. And the trace of her remains in all of us. Especially your papi."

"Tell me everything," I say, and reveal the parts I already know first. The art teacher and Señor Montes's apartment leak that started everything. Her cheating on my dad.

"Salvador caught them one night after the mural restoration was done," Mamita says. "They were trying to break it off. Pero, you know how that can be. They were kissing, and it was supposed to be good-bye. But Señor Montes wasn't alone. Ynez and Fernando Senior were with him, coming back from dinner."

My head drifts back and forth. Emilio's abuelos.

"Vanessa promised right then and there that she was done with her games and was going to stay faithful to your papi. She begged for their silence. At the time, Ynez was very close to the teacher's wife, Annabelle. The three of us went to the same high school. The teacher—and I will not speak his name—also begged Ynez not to tell Annabelle. He swore he would come clean on his own. A couple weeks later Ynez received a message from Annabelle saying she knew about the affair and needed some time away and didn't want to talk about it." Mamita looks up at me. "I never knew any of this until much later."

"When?"

"When Vanessa left Echo Park with her band. I found out then that Ynez had known all along about her cheating. I was her best friend, nena. And she didn't tell me—*me*—that Vanessa had betrayed my son!"

My arms cross over my stomach.

"I was heartbroken for your papi. But it was his right to know, and I thought it might actually help him find closure. Annabelle was living in Florida by then, but Ynez and I lost touch with her because of the move and Fernando Senior's worsening health. When I finally called Annabelle to talk about Vanessa, I quickly learned she was never told about the affair. The teacher had faked the message to Ynez from Annabelle's account, then deleted everything. Of course Annabelle was devastated, and she ended up leaving her husband. In my grief and anger, I called Ynez clueless for believing that ridiculous fake message."

Mamita leans in.

"That behavior—pulling away and not wanting her friends to help—was not like Annabelle at all, and Ynez should've questioned it.

I told her so! Well, Ynez got upset with *me* for calling her naive."

"You are kidding me." I push out a dark laugh. "All this drama. This is why you and Mami Ynez are all weird around each other? The feud and constant one-upping?"

Mamita nods slowly. "We've tried to talk it out, pero . . ." She gives a shrug. "The trust has never been the same between us."

"You let a shady artist and a communication fail ruin a really good friendship."

Abashed, she nods again, running her hand down Rocco's back. "It's caused so much strain. Between me and your abuelo, too. A lot of hardship."

"Seriously? You two are the perfect couple. You speak your own language and are always in sync. It's verging on disgusting." Aren't they? Hasn't this been my truth for my entire life?

Mamita rises, displacing Rocco, and draws me over to the tan love seat in the corner. "Do not confuse love and life." When I wrinkle my nose, she says, "No relationship starts out and stays como un fairy tale. If you're lucky, it's a novela. Not that I watch them so much anymore."

I side-eye her.

"Bah." She waves it off with a teasing smirk. "Abu and I have always loved each other so much. But the life part, the day-to-day part, we've had to work hard on. We had to learn to communicate, to listen and not judge. To not hold grudges. Yes, I know, like the one with Ynez. I am hearing what you don't say."

And I absorb this, letting it seep backward into my childhood. The things I've witnessed. Kitchen dancing and tandem laundry folding and stolen kisses—the peace of all that. Peace that came by fighting so hard.

And not running away.

The image of a lamplit porch creeps in. Really, it's never left. And neither has the nagging truth. Saturday night, I was the one who ran, not Emilio.

"Mi vida," Mamita says when my face shadows. "I know all of this hurts."

I sink low and stare at my shoes. For now, she thinks the torrent raging inside is all about Vanessa. But there's more. My failed historical preservation application. The check made out with tainted ink. A sister who brought me burritos and hard truth. The boy who works across the street. And if that wasn't enough, an unsettling feeling comes, swirling around everything at once. I can't name it now except by the way it feels. Like an inky shroud spanning the only world I know, dimming all the stars.

"Ojalá que . . ." Mamita trails off into a fresh sheen of tears. "In my heart, I hope you've never questioned what I did after Vanessa left. Clarita de mi corazón." Her lullaby stirs softly in my mind. "I hope you do not start now. Because seventeen years ago, I picked you up, and you were mine."

And I'm still hers, no matter the shame that pulls at our past. No matter the uncovered and unresolved parts clouding thick around me. I push through all of them and sink into Mamita's embrace, fitting as easily as I did as a child. It's a mother's hug. And for the first time, I trim her name like the end of a long, green stem. "You're mine, too. Mami."

Twenty-Five

*L*ourdes is mine even when she's bugging the life out of me. To-day, though, there's only loyalty in her ask to see my namesake mural for herself in the afternoon light of all that's new. We eat orange sherbet on the curb nearest the wall, and I summarize as much as possible in one twenty-minute break that yawns into a half hour.

There's a point where Lulú says, "Eat your ice cream. You can tell me more details and stuff later, and by that I mean Emilio stuff. You've had a day." She licks a trail around her cone. "You'll need a minute to overthink. And that's cool, unless you want to come up with some songs that fit your situation. But it's also fine if we just sit here and try to see who gets brain freeze first. Also, why did we get sherbet when mint chocolate chip was right there?"

And I want to cry, the good kind, because each and every word of her speech sounds like *I love you*.

But the next day lulls like being stuck in an LA traffic gridlock—emotionally. The cashier's check sits in my desk drawer, my conscience unsettled about how to use the funds without feeling like *I'm* using the worst part of my past. Even after a decent sleep, it's still not easier. And I'm pretty sure this isn't what control is supposed to be like.

I go to my flowers with all this, mixing colors to match my rainbow of emotions. At least there are plenty of arrangements to assemble for Lourdes, who's pulling extra shifts until Papi returns.

After a workstation cleanup, I grab a soda from the office fridge. "Where's Mamita?" I ask Abu. "Thought she was back here."

He swivels from his desk. "She is probably still outside with Ynez."

"Wait, what?"

Abu shuts his laptop screen. "When I drove in, they were in front of the bike shop."

I'm already backing away. By the time I reach the showroom, Abu's a couple yards behind. I turn and level him with an accusatory gaze.

He gives a shrug. "She *has* been out there a long time."

That settled, we dash to the picture window. And there they are. Talking. "Huh. I don't think they're yelling."

"Or pointing fingers. Or doing that hair flip they do." Which Abu demonstrates, looping a stitch into my worn heart because this ridiculous human is all mine, too.

I squeeze his side as a miracle happens. The venerable Echo Park mujeres clasp hands. It's not a hug, but they're touching and nodding into each other's personal space before Ynez backs away toward the bike shop entrance.

Abu and I turn speechless for an unknown count. "Do you think they finally worked everything out?" I ask at last.

"I am thinking I do not understand this life, pero . . ." He trails off because we have forgotten how fast Mamita can move.

"Aha!" Mamita says from the doorway. *Now* a hand hooks onto her hip.

It's not even worth trying to deny our spying. Abu flutters his caterpillar brows at her, which is a nice touch.

Mamita huffs. "Sit, you fools. I have good news."

It must be good because she dishes no more shade as we gather on the velvet love seats. "Listen, Ynez and I have not had the talk we need to have." She nods once. "But we will. Today was about Fernando."

My heart clenches. Emilio's dad.

"He went in for help after a severe headache—he and Wendy were so worried," Mamita starts. "The doctor did a follow-up MRI and found no new lesions. From these results and after reviewing Fernando's system tracker, the neurologist has ruled out multiple sclerosis."

"Gracias a Dios," Abu says as I replay the words a few times more.

"The issues he is still having point to complex migraines. Of course, this condition is painful, but it can be managed with medication. Fernando will not suffer what his father did."

Emilio must be so relieved. I swallow hard around my next thought: the tether keeping Emilio in Echo Park is cut free. *He's* free, just the way he likes it.

And maybe just the way it should be.

Whatever sort of resignation spell I'm under doesn't stop me from checking my phone at least six times in the next hour, though. I'm also wavering back and forth between two outcomes: Emilio eventually texting me himself about his father because it's huge. Or him never texting me again. Right now, and leaning toward the latter, I go in for one more look as Lourdes bounds into the shop with her limbs pulled to their tightest setting. Her new hairdo spins everywhere with frizz.

"Explain." I poke her a couple times. It's alive, at least.

She grumbles. "A water-main break on La Cienega. And a wife snooping in front of a house while I bring flowers to the dude's *girl-friend*."

"Eww."

"Exactly." Lourdes gives a big huff. "Then there's this *thing* I couldn't even deliver so I just brought it back here." She pulls a little white envelope from her pocket and slaps it onto my worktable. One word is penned on the front.

Clary.

A wave rolls through me. "Lulú. That's a floral message card." With no flowers.

Her mouth twitches with amusement as I freeze over the tiny scrap of parchment. Never let Lourdes Evangelina Maria Colón play poker. "How have you not opened it already?"

While my friend is now grinning like a monkey, I'm trembling as I reach for the envelope. Wide-eyed as I lift the flap and pull out the miniature rectangle dotted with purple flowers:

T,

You're wrong.

W

"What the actual *fuck*?" I yell into the verdant green void of my floral shop.

"Shhh, your fam!" Lourdes says. "Are you trying to surrender your entire paycheck to *el es-swear yar*?"

I flash Emilio's shitty excuse for a card in her face. "This isn't *supposed* to piss me off?"

Lourdes snatches the note. "Oh hell. Leave it to a dude to halfway follow directions. But it's still kind of adorable, no?"

"No!" But that's not entirely true, and my heart's a snare drum tapping out *MENTIROSA*. "I mean . . . Wait, you talked to him. Why did he—"

"Amiga." She braces my shoulders head-on. "He wants you to find him."

"He does not." Lulú pegs me with her *don't test me* face, and my next words come out as small as my hopes. "He does?"

"Yes, amor."

"But, Lulú. He's . . . and I'm . . ." I trail off in a rush of panic-fire-helplessness.

"Yup." Her fist pounds over her heart, and she studies me for one, two, then three painful beats. "But you caught feelings."

It's useless to deny the truth to my best friend. And finally, to myself. I nod slowly. "I wasn't supposed to." And when the heart of that truth rushes in, I have to drop into a stool, my head buried in my hands. "I've spent so many hours and brain cells counting him out that it's only made him there the most. Then, in trying to deal with him or handle him, I'm always thinking about him. I compare everyone to him, too. Like, this boy isn't annoying like Emilio. That guy would probably stick around, unlike Emilio. How un-Emilio is every other guy at school?" I raise my hand. "Ask me, I know."

"All your holding out for some future dream dude has never gotten you that person." Lourdes crumples her chin and points toward the bike shop. "Your longest and most real relationship rides on two wheels."

She's right, and I let out a low noise. "How did I let this happen? How did a flight-risk escape artist become the most constant guy in my life? And then, I'm *wrong*? It's the same one-up garbage as always."

"Is it?" She slides the card my way. "Go see for yourself." She pulls her keys, setting Blue Ivy's metal fob on the table.

It looks like a dare. I resist for about five seconds before curiosity wins over uncertainty. "Go where?"

"He said a girl who likes to know stuff should already know where to find him."

It's more a feeling that pulls me to Echo Park Lake than any kind of knowing. A sensation that if I took my hands off the wheel and closed my eyes, letting the universe drag me on some invisible string, I'd end up here. Vowing to never admit this to Jada, I save the universe the trouble and just follow.

After parking Blue Ivy, I earn a victory moment when I spy a certain road bike locked on one of the racks. Yet as I set off toward the legendary José Martí statue, the feeling dims. *Not this way, not there,* my gut whispers. The bronze bust honors our shared ancestry. But Emilio and I share another history, a newer one that's fought its way into the space between us. The start of that is where he is.

I change direction, walking the lakefront path on an overcast day. And when I'm almost to the swan-boat dock, a familiar sandy head bursts through the scene like another sun.

Emilio turns, flinching when he sees me. He starts a smile, but it freezes in some unsure place. "You came," he says, like it means something. "And in swan-perfect time."

I resist the laugh. "Yeah, and warning, if I smell like a Señor Cluck's combo meal, it's Lourdes's car's fault." I sink onto the grass, grateful to have something not-us to talk about. "I heard about your dad. It's the best news."

"Thanks—a lot." He links his fingers over bent knees. "Mami is overjoyed, and Papi still has a lot of healing to do and some changes to make. But he's going to be okay."

"It's kind of everything."

"Almost everything," he says quietly, gazing away.

Almost doesn't count strums into my head, and I produce the floral card, pinching it between my fingers.

"You want to know the deal with that."

"Of course I do. I'm *wrong*?"

He toys with a long blade of grass. "I wasn't sure you'd come if I didn't make it interesting."

The vulnerability in his tone stops me short. My brow pinches.

"I ran into Lourdes while she was getting coffee between deliveries," Emilio continues. "I figured I needed to tell my pride to back off. It was time to consult the bestie."

"About me," I say.

"About you. More specifically, how to do something meaningful."

When I go slack-jawed, he continues. "Lourdes told me about the floral cards you like, and she happened to have some in the van." He pauses on a snicker. "She told me to keep the message short and to make it personal. Oh, and to not be a total cabrón and screw it up."

I wave the little paper. "Calling me wrong is your idea of not screwing it up?"

"Yeah, as a matter of fact it is. And sometimes being wrong is actually very right. And good, I mean, not good that you—"

"Wheels."

His breath stumbles, and he reaches out a hand. It's the kind of move that stabs into my rawest places—the ones I've run from. The ones that believe doubt is easier than hope sometimes. Still, his eyes are big and hopeful enough for both of us. I grab on, and he squeezes tight.

"When I got home Saturday night, it hit me—so hard—what you said. I mean, by some miracle I heard you clearly." Emilio smiles briefly at this. "You seemed so hurt, and I realized you assumed something that's totally not true, probably on my lead."

"What something?"

He runs his thumb over mine but stares off-center just a bit. "You said you're just a thorn and could never get to me enough. That *you're* not enough to matter to me for more than five seconds, and maybe no one is. And you're wrong because that's not true. God, Clary, you could cut all the way through and drop me flat."

I shake my head, my feelings extraordinary and bewildering all the same. "How? I can't—"

"You *do* matter to me, okay?" He clenches our joined hands. "So much. And I should've told you right then, but I was all messed up in the moment. Trying to figure out when it was that I first saw you as more than the pretty and funny and super-annoying Cubana across the street. But I still don't know."

"I don't know, either. For me about you," I say to a boy who was there all along like Lourdes's shirt and purple flowers on a mural. I never saw him like *this*, and now he's all I see. "I ran because I was feeling too much, and I thought you'd never want anything real with me. I always give you shit about escaping. But I'm the one who left when you had more to say."

"I don't blame you, Thorn. I had it coming." He arcs his free hand over the deep blue lake. "But you came back. And you want to know what's real? At the quinces, I followed you out to the terrace because you looked sad and hurt. And that wasn't okay with me. And Saturday I went to your tía's party with a fucking plant simply because you'd be there. And after we played dominoes, I paced your yard for fifteen minutes, trying to work up the nerve to ask you to come with me somewhere. Anywhere." He scoots closer. "I can't stop coming back to you."

"I couldn't stop wanting you to," I admit. "I tried so hard, but it didn't work."

"Good. I applaud your failure." As I shift into a side-eye, he makes a chastising noise at himself. "I really need to read the room better."

"Well," I say through a chalky laugh, "our conversation track record is sort of the worst."

"Dismal," he admits, which I knew, but it still swipes a bit of gray across my heart. "No—*no*," he says, reading my face. "I was thinking we work on that. Maybe try to listen more and not always assume the worst?"

My pulse calms as I nod, and Abu and Mamita flash into my head. That they've had to work, too, instead of giving up and running away. "Some stuff will never change, though. We're always going to annoy each other. And argue about sandwiches."

"Always." He exhales and brings our joined hands to the edge of his cheek. "Be with me anyway? All in for real and no timetables. No escape hatches. Just be with me?"

Shivers burst across my arms—no one has ever asked me anything quite like this. And I don't wait another second to answer in the best way I know. I grab his face, my lips fitting with his on pure, good memory. A low tone strums from the back of his throat as he moves in deep—my new favorite bass line. In seconds, I'm blissfully trapped in soft cotton and sunscreen skin. Close and sheltered, nothing in the world could ever find me. Not even myself.

We stay so long, we grow roots in the lakefront grass. The sun peeks through, eavesdropping as we stretch out fully, kissing and kissing, touching and touching until all the leaving I've ever known with him dies like cut flowers and old photos. Fades with all the things we used to believe.

It's from here that I lift up and say—yes, I say, "You need to go on your backpacking trip." I trace my finger along his jaw. "I want you to."

He tips his forehead against mine. "Nothing means more than you saying that. There's a difference between going away and leaving, though."

My life knows the difference. "I . . . actually get you."

He chuckles. "Progress. But yeah, I need to go. And I'll be honest with my family this time. But things have changed on both legs of this trip." He kisses me and tugs at *my* leg for fun. "I'm not going yet. I want to spend the rest of the summer with you. Beach bike rides and concerts and hanging with our friends. Anything we want."

I grin. "Next you'll be making me a Spotify playlist."

"Like I don't already have one? It's full of nineties R & B." He bops my nose. "Also, I'll never bring you flowers for obvious reasons. I'll bring you hospital cinnamon rolls."

I laugh, but it fades into something gray and woolen. "And then you'll go."

He nods. "And you'll have an awesome senior year, doing all the things. And I'm not going off-grid with you. We'll FaceTime as often as I can." He draws a circle over my cheek. "It never felt right before, asking a girl to wait for me."

I shake my head. "I already waited for you and didn't even know it. I can wait again."

He pinches his eyes closed, nodding. "But not as long as you think. That's the other change. I'll be home in time to take you to prom, I promise."

I believe him.

Emilio draws us down over the place that grew us. Long-limbed across this historic barrio and the gentle dotted memory of the ones who kept us safe. "I'm not leaving you. I'm just going away."

"And coming back."

"And coming back."

Twenty-Six

*T*hree hours later I'm climbing the steps to Papi's casita with a cashier's check and a schnauzer.

Two hours ago I managed to stop kissing Emilio long enough to tell him about the family secrets hidden in one mural off Sunset Boulevard. Like Lourdes, he wanted to see for himself. After returning Blue Ivy, we walked to Sin Nombre, hands intertwined. And on a repainted wall and down an adjacent alley, we found the point where our histories intertwined.

It was then that Papi texted, Come home, I'm back early. Mamita told me everything

Emilio read my screen and planted a kiss on the top of my head. "He's the only one you haven't talked to yet."

I leaned into his side. "I'm ready."

"Good. My truck's at the shop—I'll take you. Then if you're up to it, I'll come get you later? The Owl Bar food truck will be in Santa Monica tonight. Remember the green chile cheeseburgers?"

"Like an actual date, Wheels?"

He stared at me like I was daft. "Do I really have to explain what's been happening here?"

"You eat burgers with friends all the time."

"We're not friends," he said, toting me along Sunset with the kind of bright-eyed affection I wasn't used to yet.

Sometimes Emilio lies, too.

Now I hold the recent memory like a rosebud. Pin it to my chest as I enter the propped-open door, apprehension buzzing when I see my dad.

Despite all that's changed, it's still him here. His ever-steady face and gym-sock feet. His sweet-father heart and arms that pull me close before we share a word.

"I'm so sorry, amor," he says into my hair. "Sorry you found out like this, and I wasn't here. I know this makes it seem like we—I—failed you even more."

"It's okay," I whisper, nodding at the flicker of surprise on my father's face. "I see the whole picture now."

Papi squeezes my shoulder as I pull back to scan the room. His suitcase rests by the bathroom door. And Rocco's already rustling through the comforter on the bed. But something on the dining table draws me over.

It's an assorted pack of tiny kid cereals in every flavor of sugar there is. I grab the attached note:

You two have a lot to talk about. This should help.
Besitos, Mamita

I spin as it hits me. "Mamita *knows*? She knows about Rainbowl?"

"Apparently. I found that when I came in." Papi grabs two

bowls and spoons. "Are we really surprised she found out?"

I retrieve the milk. "We are not. But we'd better not speak of this."

"Oh, we'll never speak of it." He sits, and I follow. We spend a few minutes opening the little boxes and creating our special mixes. Bite after bite, the comfort of our ritual settles in enough for me to pull the folded check from my jeans pocket and smooth it on the table.

Papi rests his spoon, staring. "Looks like we both have some things to share."

I start, relaying the message Jada received from Vanessa, using extra stress on words like *selfish* and *manipulative* and *closure*. "I never have to say anything to Vanessa. But I . . ."

Papi reaches out to rub my forearm. "But what?"

I've been feeling ripples and nudges since I got the check—the kind that changes everything. The kind that takes a second. Now I'm ready to give them a voice. "Maybe I should contact her after all." I hold up my hand. "I'm not sure I want a conversation. That would be a lot. But maybe there can be something. Just not today."

"Maybe there can," Papi says. "You'll know when it's the right time. Putting it out there is enough for now."

"You're starting to sound like Jada."

He laughs, but it quiets and closes into something fatherly and soft. "My turn. It's been so hard keeping the mural and all the secrets from you—Jada. You already know that, but not all the reasons behind our choices. I was so young when you came along. Life was day by day." His chin crumples. "It still is, even though I'm . . ." He scrapes his chin.

"I know. Vanessa's felt so far away for my whole life. I guess the mural hit me so hard because I found out she was in a place I've always felt was mine." I draw aimless circles in my bowl with the spoon. "Did she ever tell you about the art teacher?"

"No. I knew about her work on the mural. But I didn't realize what she'd done with the flowers or even what parts she worked on until later." His eyes fill. "But that's not the whole story. The art teacher wasn't her only affair, Clary. She cheated on me before with some random guy at a club she was gigging at. And like a goddamn—" Papi stops himself, drawing in a gust of air. "I took her back, hoping like a fool that she'd change."

"Maybe she just *couldn't* change."

"No, you're probably right. And she promised, *swore*, I was it for her. I believed her, and for a while we were good. We found out you were coming, and I got her a ring. And she said she wanted to go to art school. I thought we'd be taking out loans." He lifts the check. "I didn't know Señor Montes gave her this money, and why. She hid it. And then, like, three weeks before she went into labor, she found out her band was going abroad. And I mean everywhere. She wanted to delay school and take you—a newborn." He bends forward. "Clary, this was not some cushy tour with nice hotels or buses. This was rough and disorganized. Her band members were strung out on everything under the sun."

"Oh my God" is all I can say.

He nods. "It was never about me holding her back. I asked her to wait a year. Even six months." Papi's eyes fill with anguish. "There was no way in hell she was taking you into *that*. I never told her not to go. I asked her to wait."

"But that wasn't good enough, so she went anyway," I finish. She left anyway. And all at once the ugly part of this glaring truth rushes in. Clearer than ever. It's the part that wasn't formed all the way when I talked to Jada, or Mamita. But now, like chambray shirts and flowers and Emilio, I can't not see what's always been there. "Be honest, Papi. Please. If Señor Montes or Mami Ynez or any of them had told you about the art teacher, would you have taken her back a second time?"

My dad scrubs a hand, forehead to chin. And the words that come out are softer than moth wings. "No, mi amor. And I wouldn't have if I'd found out she'd abandoned another baby."

And if he'd known about Vanessa's truths, there would've been no second pregnancy, no second baby. No me. My body absorbs the reality I only half knew. "I wasn't supposed to be here."

He juts out his hands. "God, Clary, no—"

"This isn't about you and Abu and Mamita loving me. Only that it makes sense now. Everything I've wanted. And still want."

"What makes sense?"

"I want my life to matter," I say, my voice wobbling. "I have ever since I can remember, and that comes from *somewhere*." I look up at Papi's full-moon eyes. "I'm here because a few people kept a secret. You didn't plan to have me. So I want—I've always wanted—to be worth my place in the world. I want to leave something big that proves I was worth this bit of chance. It's one of the reasons I wanted to be the one to get the historical distinction for Echo Park."

I know I've admitted a ton, but I don't expect Papi to entirely shut himself off. Silent, motionless. But instead of prodding and tugging his hand like I did when I was little—*When will the parade start? How much longer until we're at Disney? When is the ice cream truck coming?*—I hold back, giving him space to draw his gaze far and wide beyond the walls.

Ultimately, when it seems a thousand years have passed over the roof, he rises to walk his tiny casita, back and forth, carrying all I've said. There's a point when the weight becomes too much, and he sits and buries his face. That's when my father full-on cries for the first time I can remember.

Stunned and cleaved into two, I stare like I'm watching behind protective glass. Rocco darts to my side, and the warmth, the little pup's concern, reminds me that all I have to do is go to Papi in this same way.

So I do.

He senses my form on the couch and pulls me into his side and a lifetime of emotion.

"Listen to me," he finally says, his voice like weathered bark. "Óyeme, cariño. No, you were not planned. But sometimes life gives us what we need instead of what we plan for." He grabs my shoulders. "You *are* my life, and I wouldn't change a thing about us. You are not a whim of the universe or a random ficha drawn from a pile. You are a gift. You hate surprises, but you are the best one I've ever had."

I fall into his arms, tears pouring. My heart changing and rearranging.

"You were exactly what I needed. And you've already done a million little things to change my world, and the whole world, too," he says into my ear. "You add beauty and color to people's happiest days. You create meaningful tributes for their hardest times. A kind word, a smile, the care you put into your work—that part of you never dies even when your flowers wilt. For years you pinned a single bloom on a viejito's lapel, and you brought him joy." He pulls back and swipes damp fingers across my cheeks. "You matter because you're here. Do you believe me? Please say you believe me."

Sometimes people lie, but not today. Not this man. "I—yeah. I'm going to work on that."

Papi nods roughly. "Good. Listen, I know you still have a dream and want to leave a legacy. And I think I can help."

My gaze narrows.

"I've been considering adding an event-planning component to La Rosa Blanca, for you to carry on. Not even Abu knows yet."

"Event planning? I just planned Sofia's entire quinces."

"Watching you gave me the idea. I haven't said anything because I want to research and plan before I go and risk our business and *every-thing*. I want to be prudent." His gaze shifts. "I want to do better this time."

Because of the ruins left from another time. "Papi—"

"I said I wouldn't change a thing about our past, but it still changed me. My confidence tanked when I took Vanessa back and she ended up leaving us. It's made me doubt myself and become too wary. Of my ideas, my judgment. And my heart."

His heart. I bump his side. "You do know Ivonne isn't anything like Vanessa. And I like her. A lot."

"Me too." He snuffs a laugh. "I'm going to get off my ass and ask her out for real." All through my clapping he continues. "And I'm going to involve you in setting up the event component. You and I can grow our business together. If you want?"

I don't even have to overthink. "I want. And we can cater to Latino families and the way we celebrate. But we can add modern touches to our traditions, too."

Papi nods. "Like what you did with Sofia's library theme. Talk about so many little details that came together to make something great."

A hundred ideas flood from another place besides parties and hotel ballrooms. They narrow and sharpen as I lock onto the check still resting on the table. My mind travels the streets of my barrio, skipping along from past to present. And this time, hope paints a new scene behind my eyes. "I know what I want to do with Señor Montes's money. And it finally feels right."

"I'm listening," Papi says.

"Some will go to my college fund. But for the rest, do you think our landlord would let us put a mural on the side wall of our shop?"

"Well." He flips out his hand. "I'm almost positive he would. We asked about painting a big rose years ago, but we did the poems inside instead."

I nod. "Good. I couldn't save the Varadero mural. So I want to design a new Echo Park mural, honoring all the Cubans who settled here."

Papi hinges his neck upward, smiling softly. "I think Salvador knew you would carry on what he started and find your own way. He didn't leave you his domino set on a whim. It was his final move." My father grabs my hand, clenching tightly. "And you made a good match."

Speaking of matches, it takes my family about thirty minutes to go from zero to full Emilio awareness. I blame Lourdes, who is not at my house. And Jada, who *is*.

Abu (Who made him the fashion police?) made me change twice, finally giving his approval to my black sundress and gold sandals. Papi is pretending to "fix a screw" on one of the kitchen cabinets. And Mamita is everywhere. At the window to check for Emilio's truck. In and out of the bathroom with her Le Labo perfume. And shimmer lotion.

When she chases me with her setting spray, I go off. "I love you all to the ends of the earth. But it's simply a date. One of many because, yes, Emilio and I are happening. And I know it's totally unexpected and maybe a little weird, but I'm happy. So can we all just—"

"Ay, he's here!" Mamita says out the kitchen window, her recon spot. Right next to a certain clary sage plant.

I'm expecting someone to call out, *Places, everyone!*

This is worse. It's Cuban with a side of Jada and barking schnauzer. Right as I'm considering bolting out the back slider, intercepting Emilio on the sidewalk, and shoving us both into the truck (and kissing the stuffing out of him), Papi is already swinging open the front door to . . . a chair?

Bodies make way, and I step forward. It's Emilio's blue Dunks in the doorway, then the faded black jeans I've seen a hundred times. But the top half of him is covered by a rust-colored wingback chair that's seen better times.

"Ay, put it here," Mamita says, sliding her club chair over.

Emilio sets down the threadbare velvet piece. "Er, hi, everyone." He winks at me.

"What is that thing?" I ask as Emilio shakes Papi's hand and waves to Abu.

Emilio approaches and kisses my cheek to a backdrop of sighs. I am a red, red rose. But I accept the warm and steady hand.

"Hey, you," he says. "Look, I'm just pre-date delivery guy with truck." He motions toward Jada. "She hired me for the heavy labor."

Jada?

My sister plunks herself down in the old sunken seat. "I found this beauty abandoned on the sidewalk. And I thought, with some pretty new velvet and some brass rivets, well, it could get a second chance." Her eyes are glassy when she looks up at me. "I thought you might want to work on it with me. I mean, it could take a while."

"What about Portland? You can't bring this with you."

"No, I can't. That's why I've decided to sell my father's Atlanta house. I'm going to need funds for a place here, you know, to put the chair. Maybe a little condo in Los Feliz or Silver Lake. And while I'm working on the chair, I think I'll get a permanent job so I can afford more chairs. And a bed and a dining table."

Emilio rubs my back as my eyes well, blurring everything I thought I knew about Jada Morrison. "Aww, this is the best," he whispers.

And it's more than I can make sense of. "You're not leaving? But you love to travel."

Jada approaches, her gold bangles clanging. "Yeah, well, I love you more." My knees give out, but before I can form my next thought, she says, "I'll always travel. But this is the last place I needed to escape to. And now every time I return from a trip, I'd like to come home." Jada bumps my side. "Where my sister is."

Not leaving. Going away and coming back.

I disintegrate, releasing a sob and the secret thoughts I didn't realize were wishes until now. They come out strong, but Jada's there to catch me. *She's staying.*

My new boyfriend looks on with the softest smile, and my family huddles close. Emotion rings; I feel it, hear the sniffles and muffled cries.

But this little tan house with its red wooden door is large enough for an ocean of tears and joy that could overflow a lake. It's stood through lifetimes of both and done the best it could to keep us strong. No good flowers grow out back. Instead, they grow inside from roots that bend and change. And never truly die.

Epilogue

April

Hedychium coronarium: The white ginger lily is the national flower of Cuba, where it is known as **flor de mariposa** due to its resemblance to a white butterfly in flight.

Admit it, Thorn. You're into surprises now," Emilio says.

"Fine." I clutch his hand tighter, partly because I'm blindfolded, mostly because I've barely let go of him the past five days. "I don't *not* like them."

A laugh rumbles through his chest. "Almost there," he says as he guides me along—somewhere. All I know is we're outside after driving at least twenty minutes, after he told my family and friends that the evening of April 28th was all his. Emilio didn't just keep his promise about being home to take me to prom; he beat it by a month. Five days ago he delivered himself to La Rosa Blanca straight from LAX, and that first kiss was better than anything that blooms.

Tonight he slows our steps. "Ready, birthday girl?" He peels the bandanna from my face.

"Oh my God!" I cry, because we're not twenty minutes away from my house. My boyfriend's a sneak, and we're at the Echo Park Lake swan boat dock. He moves us past the line to another section where a large swan waits with an attendant.

I squeeze Emilio so tight, he laughs.

"Thank you, thank you. How did you know I wanted to go at night like this?" When it's dark and dreamy and all the swans are lit with tiny bulbs.

Emilio steps into the boat and helps me in. "Guess."

Translation: Jada. I arrange myself and my ivory minidress. He shows me everything he pre-stocked in the back—a birthday party for two with balloons and Cuban sandwiches and bakery cupcakes. I snuggle into him as we pedal out, this time in sync enough to keep us moving forward.

We worked on that while he backpacked from London to a host of other cities. With only screens between us, we learned to listen better, navigating long talks from hostels, always with sleepy *I love you* sign-offs.

But now that he's home, we agree that we've done enough talking. We glide, content just to fill the same space.

From here, Echo Park Lake reflects our pocket of Los Angeles across its inky surface. Pedaling due west, we'd reach a ground-floor condo with potted herbs on the porch. Tapestries and a drum set and a restored green velvet chair warm the living room. A dining room table, where we sit for loud family dinners or quiet girl talks, looks on. A glass sparrow crowns the middle, wings folded in.

If we turn and pedal around the center fountain, shifting east-ward, we'll crash into the backyard casita where my "in a relation-ship" father can barely be found lately. But there was one fall day when the room needed un papi y una niña, because it was the right day. And as midnight fell silent in some far-off place, Papi dialed and listened to a voicemail message from a person he used to love, then handed over the phone, gripping my hand.

"Hello, it's Clary," I said after the beep, surprised my words were as steady as this lake at dawn. "I probably won't call again, so just this. Thank you for leaving me in a better place than you could've given me. It's the only life I've ever needed, and I don't hate you, in case you were wondering. And thanks for the amazing sister I never knew I needed. So . . . yeah—what you did will never be okay, but I am more than okay. I hope you've found everything you needed, too."

Now Emilio kisses the side of my head. We pedal again, and the swan knows where to go. Our boat creeps toward a slice of Echo Park that lives between a green velvet chair and a house with a studio over the garage. Somewhere in the middle, there's a cross street where two neighborhood kids were raised and kept safe by more than two words. A bike shop guards one half, manned by an heir and hijo. On a seven-month journey, he exchanged a few labels for a next step: we'll be college freshmen together in the fall. That's all he knows tonight. It's enough.

Keeping watch over the other half of the street is a flower shop. On its side wall, a mural that I designed and funded lives, after I commis-sioned an emerging Cuban painter to do the artwork. The idea came from the little white cards that come with floral arrangements. And it came from my father, who reminded me how great and meaningful small things can be.

The mural on my shop depicts the flor de mariposa, the national flower of Cuba. A grand perennial with long elegant fronds in the deepest green, dotted with white flowers that look like butterflies. Like Abu's mariposa domino tiles, hundreds of white ginger blossoms flutter up and outward from the main plant across a powder-blue sky. But there's more—the kind of more that took months to complete. Many of the flowers bear the names of original Cuban settlers in this part of Echo Park. (Ynez and Elena and Fernando, to name a few. And Beatriz and Margarita and Irene. Betty and Juan and Rosa and Ignacio. Salvador Ángel Montes.) Mi barrio rallied around my cause, and the local news tracked my progress in reaching those who'd moved so I could collect their stories.

As of today, no record of these Cubans and their contributions exists on any formal historical society website. I wrote it on another. Our mural directs visitors to a new section on La Rosa Blanca's website. There, an interactive version of the mariposa mural is replicated. Anyone can zoom in and click on a single white blossom, a single name, and the story of that immigrant pops up across the screen.

These flowers form the greatest bouquet I'll ever make. Here, my people are painted, not erased. Here, they are kept and not abandoned. And here, they are named, not nameless.

Our mural has a name, too, etched into an adjacent brass plaque that stands in place of the one a state government denied.

Estuvimos Aquí.

We were here. And it matters.

Author's Note

Four years ago I had the distinct honor of being hosted in Los Angeles by the esteemed Porto family, who came to Echo Park in one of the final waves of that notorious period of exile showcased in *With Love, Echo Park*. They are also the owners of the same Porto's Bakery I'm proud to showcase in this story. I drove by the site of their original shoebox-sized storefront on Sunset Boulevard and felt immensely proud of what they've accomplished. Now the Porto family owns and manages multiple wildly successful locations.

As we ate, the Porto heirs and two of their childhood friends shared stories of their journeys from Cuba to Miami and then to Echo Park. They spoke of language and cultural barriers, resourceful families huddling together, the Los Angeles workforce they joined—proudly— and the unique mark they carved into Sunset Boulevard and its surrounding streets.

As this amazing family added their seeds into my budding story, I began to learn how I wanted to tell it. Today it's true that most of the original 1960s and 1970s Cuban immigrants have moved on from

Echo Park. But as each story starts with a what-if question, mine became: What if two of those immigrant families hadn't left? What if they'd stayed on Sunset and weathered all the changes? What might their teenage children feel about Echo Park today as witnesses to gentrification and erasure?

This is how the book you just finished was born. Any liberties in geography, architectural features, businesses, and the current workings of today's Echo Park are my own. But the history of those Cubans in that place is real. And their legacy matters.

So thank you, Betty and Margarita Porto, Ivonne D., and Margarita G., for opening up your hearts and memories and sharing them with me. I will never forget you.

Acknowledgments

Somehow this book makes number five? As I'm typing this and looking back at my life since debut year, I'm filled with nothing but gratitude to God and to my family and to you, readers, who make it possible for me to keep working inside this little corner of publishing that I treasure so much. ¡Besitos!

Thank you, Natascha Morris, my faithful agent who continues to hold up every word I write, as well as all the matters that go along with them. Especially the surprises. The next margarita is on me!

Thank you, Lane and Stefanie and the entire Tobias Literary Agency team, for being the most supportive managers of my books.

Thank you to my extraordinary writing partners, Joan F. Smith and Allison L. Bitz. Nothing exists in my book world without you, and I love you both.

To my editor, Sophia Jimenez, thank you so much for your valuable insight, and for possessing one of the best eagle eyes in the business!

To the entire team at Atheneum, thank you for working so hard to make this book so beautiful, inside and out. Feather Flores,

Rebecca Vitkus, Jessie Bowman, Tatyana Rosalia, Morgan Maple, and Samantha McVeigh, I appreciate you so much.

To Emily Ritter and the entire Simon Teen social media team, thank you for the adorable memes and fun games and especially that YALLFest friendship bracelet!

To Karyn Lee and Heedayah Lockman, my cover is truly a work of art and straight out of my dreams about everything a cover for this book could look like. I adore it, and I'm so grateful.

To Gloria Garcia, thank you so much for your help with all the flowers.

To Dr. Oliu, thank you for your expertise and for making sure Fernando's health details were portrayed authentically.

To Leah Lewis-Nguyen, thank you for sharing so many of your fabulous skills in marketing, social media, and photography. You're the best assistant and an even better friend.

To my husband, thank you for driving me around Echo Park while I snapped pictures of all the beautiful Angelino Heights houses and every mural I could find. And, as always, for dealing with Draft Mode Laura. Which isn't always my best mode.

To Miranda McCauley, thank you for Blue Ivy, you incredible star. I love you.

To Lisa Wood and Ximena Avalos, thank you for making sure I got all those Spanish accent marks correct, and for your insight and creativity.

To my incredible author friends, and so many librarians, book bloggers, booksellers, and teachers, thank you for your unwavering support. You mean the world to me, and you're all part of the most beautiful bouquet I've ever received.